COWBOYS
of Crested Butte

BOOK ONE

USA TODAY BESTSELLING AUTHOR

HEATHER SLADE

A Cowboy Falls
© 2017 Heather Slade

All rights reserved. No part of this book may be used or reproduced in any manner whatsoever without written permission, except in the case of brief quotations embodied in critical articles and reviews.

This book is a work of fiction. The names, characters, places and incidents are products of the writer's imagination or have been used fictitiously and are not to be construed as real. Any resemblance to persons, living or dead, actual events, locale or organizations is entirely coincidental.

ISBN: 978-1-953626-58-5

Certain song titles and lyrics in this book are by GB Leighton
and are reproduced by permission.

All I Want is You

Your breath and your heart
The way that you're smart
The charm of your tease
When you make me say please
Your eyes and your hair
The look of your stare

You make my soul lift higher
You set my love on fire
Baby, every word I say is true
All I want is your mouth, and your lips
And your soft fingertips,
The curve of your spine
Well it's gotta be mine
The warmth of your kiss
When we're lying like this
The heat of your touch
Well it's never too much
You make my heart beat wild
Turn me into a child
Where the hell would I be without you
The soft skin on your bones
And the smile I would own
When the blood in my veins flows
With all that remains of doom.
All I want is you.

—GB Leighton

MORE FROM AUTHOR HEATHER SLADE

BUTLER RANCH
Kade's Worth
Brodie
Maddox
Naughton
Mercer
Kade
Christmas at Butler Ranch

WICKED WINEMAKERS' BALL
Coming soon:
Brix
Ridge
Press

K19 SECURITY SOLUTIONS
Razor
Gunner
Mistletoe
Mantis
Dutch
Striker
Monk
Halo
Tackle
Onyx

K19 SHADOW OPERATIONS
Code Name: Ranger
Coming soon:
Code Name: Diesel
Code Name: Wasp
Code Name: Cowboy

THE ROYAL AGENTS OF MI6
The Duke and the Assassin
The Lord and the Spy
The Commoner and the Correspondent
The Rancher and the Lady

THE INVINCIBLES
Decked
Undercover Agent
Edged
Grinded
Riled
Handled
Smoked
Bucked
Irished
Sainted
Coming soon:
Hammered
Ripped

COWBOYS OF CRESTED BUTTE
A Cowboy Falls
A Cowboy's Dance
A Cowboy's Kiss
A Cowboy Stays
A Cowboy Wins

For cute, guitar-playing, songwriting boys
and the cowgirls who can't help but love them.

Table of Contents

Chapter 1 1
Chapter 2 8
Chapter 3 18
Chapter 4 25
Chapter 5 43
Chapter 6 71
Chapter 7 87
Chapter 8 104
Chapter 9 122
Chapter 10 142
Chapter 11 151
Chapter 12 169
Chapter 13 187
Chapter 14 202
Chapter 15 213
Chapter 16 223
Chapter 17 242
Chapter 18 256
Chapter 19 276
Chapter 20 291
Chapter 21 306
Chapter 22 318

Chapter 23 336
Chapter 24 351
Chapter 25 369
Epilogue. .375
About the Author 377

1

Summer

Liv raised her arms and swayed as the warm breeze of the Colorado night danced and swirled around her.

Sitting in the sixth row of the outdoor amphitheater, she closed her eyes and sang along, as the opening band played her favorite song.

She didn't remember how she found them, or the first time she listened to their music, but this was the first time she saw them perform live.

I don't wanna play it cool
Act like meeting you
Ain't got me all jumbled up inside.
I don't want to play along,
Dance with you for just one song,
Then politely step aside.
Let's don't let go of this
No, let's don't let this go.

I don't wanna move too fast
If I let this moment pass
May never get the chance again.

Tomorrow I will either be
Tangled up in you and me
Or lost in thoughts of what could have been.

"Open your eyes," her best friend, Paige, whispered. "He's singing to you."

When Liv opened her eyes, CB, the lead singer of the band CB Rice, was looking right at her. When she smiled, he nodded and smiled too.

"Oh my God," Liv's daughter, Renie, giggled. "Look, Blythe." Renie nudged her best friend.

"How embarrassing," Blythe murmured.

"Ow! Jeez, Mom. Why'd you hit me?"

"Let Liv enjoy this moment, and don't be such a brat, Blythe."

The people behind them leaned forward. "Shh…"

Blythe turned around. "You want us to be quiet during a rock concert? Seriously?"

Paige swatted her again.

"Ow, Mom. Stop hitting me!"

"Shh…" whispered Liv, wanting to hear nothing but CB's voice singing her favorite song.

In my mind I've already let this go too far
Saying goodbye tonight
Would be just like a broken heart.
Let's don't let go of this
No, let's don't let this go.

The song ended, and Liv wished she could hit replay, like she did so often when she listened to their music. It was as though the words of every song were written just for her. She'd never forget this night, finally having the chance to see them perform live.

Since CB Rice was the opener for the opener for the headliner, their set was short. After six songs, CB thanked the bands that would come after them for inviting them on stage tonight.

"Playing Red Rocks has always been our dream," CB told the cheering audience.

Every band she'd seen at the spectacular venue nestled into the mountains outside of Denver had expressed a similar sentiment.

The natural rock formations created an open-air amphitheater with perfect acoustics. A large, tilted, disc-shaped rock formed a multi-story backdrop behind the stage, and a huge vertical rock angled outward from the right. Several more large outcrops angled outward from the left.

From the stage, rows upon rows of wooden benches led up to a vast and open view of the starry Rocky Mountain nights.

"Ready for a beer?" Paige asked.

"Sure. Why not?" Liv smiled. She'd insisted they rush to their seats when they arrived, so she didn't miss a single minute of CB Rice on stage.

"We're going to look at merch," Renie told her mother, pulling a pouting Blythe behind her.

"All the years they've been friends, you'd think Renie's personality would've rubbed off at least a little, on my daughter."

"She's fine," Liv answered.

She hummed the last song the band played, wishing again she could hear it one more time.

"You should get a t-shirt," Paige teased.

"Maybe I will."

Two beers and one of every t-shirt CB Rice was selling later, Liv and Paige returned to their seats just as the second band took the stage.

Their seats were situated just outside the roped-off area, which was designated both for VIPs and for the sound equipment. When Renie came and sat beside her, Liv leaned against her daughter.

"Having fun?" Renie asked.

"Thank you for doing this," Liv answered.

"I know how much you like Red Rocks, and with three of your favorite bands playing, it seemed like the perfect way to end our summer."

Her daughter was a pre-med major at Dartmouth, and would be returning to school next week.

"I miss you already, sweetheart."

The second band began to play, and soon everyone in the ten-thousand-person audience was on their feet, dancing and singing along.

"Look." Renie pointed to Liv's left.

She looked up at the large rock formation, expecting to see something projected on it. "What?"

"Not up there. There." Renie pointed again to the VIP area, where CB and his band were seated.

When Liv looked over, CB was looking right at her, just like he had been while onstage. Warmth traveled up her cheeks, and she looked away. A few minutes later, she looked back. His eyes still rested on her; this time he smiled and winked.

"Hey, you." Paige smiled when Liv scooted closer, putting Renie and Blythe between her and the ropes.

"Mom's hiding from CB Rice."

Paige leaned back.

"Don't look," Liv gasped.

"Why not?"

"He's been staring at her all night," Blythe groaned.

"Shh…" the people behind them whispered again, which only made Liv and Paige giggle.

When the second band's set ended, Liv sneaked a peek at the VIP area, disappointed that she didn't see any members of CB Rice.

"You were ignoring him, so he went home," Renie smirked.

Liv rolled her eyes.

Soon, the third band took the stage, and the audience went wild. Liv forgot all about CB and his band as she danced and sang along for the rest of the two-hour show.

Too soon it seemed, the band played their encore, and the audience slowly began making their way to the exits.

"Wait," Liv heard someone yell.

"Mom, stop."

When Liv turned around, CB was standing right behind her.

He smiled. "Hi."

"Uh, hi."

"What's your name?"

Liv looked around. "Me?"

CB laughed. "Yeah, you."

"Liv," she answered, and then turned back around. "And this is my friend, Paige, my daughter, Renie, and Paige's daughter, Blythe."

He bent to see around Liv. "I'm Ben Rice. Nice to meet you." He waved, and then rested his gaze back on her. "Thanks for coming to the show tonight, Liv."

"You're welcome. Um…well…nice to meet you, um…Ben." Liv pushed past Paige. "Come on, let's go."

"Nice to meet you." Paige waved and followed Liv, who was already beyond the end of the row, near the exit.

"What has gotten into you?" Paige asked when they got in the car.

"Nothing. Why?"

"You weren't very polite to him, Mom."

"What are you talking about?"

"He was flirting with you."

"Don't be ridiculous," Liv murmured and turned up the volume on the stereo.

2

December

"I have a week before I have to go back," Renie said when they finished cleaning up from the Christmas party they'd hosted the night before. "Let's go skiing."

"I'd love it. Where to?"

Renie stopped what she was doing. "You're kidding, right?"

Liv laughed. "There may come a day when you want to go somewhere else."

"No, Mom. Crested Butte is our place."

When they woke the next morning, the sun was shining, and the weather forecast was good for the rest of the weekend.

They packed their bags and skis and got on the road, making the two-hundred-mile drive to Crested Butte in a little over five hours.

"Let's go to The Goat tonight. I've always wanted to hang out there," Renie suggested after they checked into the hotel at the base of the ski area.

Liv yawned and checked the time. They'd arrived at the hotel a little after five, and she was hungry.

"Do they have food?"

Renie shrugged. "How would I know?"

Liv laughed. "Right."

Her daughter had recently turned twenty-one, so it would be the first time she'd be allowed into the bar that was a Crested Butte institution. It was located in the middle of the historic downtown district, on Elk Avenue.

"If they don't, we can always leave and eat somewhere else."

They took the shuttle from the ski area down to the main part of town, and walked a half block to The Goat.

"I look like I'm a hundred years older than anyone else in here," Liv mumbled when they walked into the bar.

"You're not, and you're gorgeous. Everyone will think you're my sister, not my mom."

They'd been there a few minutes when Liv noticed a poster promoting bands scheduled to play at the bar. CB Rice was playing the next night—what were the odds?

"What's up, Mom?"

"CB Rice is playing here tomorrow night. Remember—"

"The guy you met at Red Rocks. Yeah, his family owns this place."

"What?"

"The Rice family. His grandfather developed the ski area. They owned most of the businesses downtown at one point."

"How do you know this?"

"Haven't you ever read the history of Crested Butte in the magazines they leave in the hotel rooms? We've been coming here at least once a year since I learned to ski."

No, she hadn't read the history of Crested Butte. As a single mom, she had her hands full unloading bags and getting skis, boots, and snow clothes ready. Then she'd have to figure out where they'd go for dinner, and how she'd entertain her daughter until bedtime. Not that Renie wasn't helpful, or able to entertain herself, but most of the responsibility for everything they did fell on Liv's shoulders. It had been that way since Renie was born. By the time she fell into bed each night, Liv had no energy left to read a book, or even a magazine. It was true at home and worse when they traveled.

"By the way, I didn't *meet* him at Red Rocks; we saw him *play* at Red Rocks."

"He's the guy who introduced himself, I know he is. Look." Renie pointed to a photo behind the bar. "See, that's him."

Liv studied the picture. There was something about the man that spoke to her. She couldn't explain it, but he made her insides quiver.

"And, wow! There he is." Renie pointed behind her mom.

Liv turned to see him greet customers as he took off his red and black plaid Woolrich jacket and hung it on the coat rack inside the door. The man was gorgeous. Well over six feet tall, he had the broad shoulders of an athlete. He was muscular—not body-builder muscular, but hard-as-rock muscular. He reached up to put the wool cowboy hat that covered his shaved head on the rack with his jacket.

CB, or Ben—that was the way he'd introduced himself—turned and looked straight at her, bestowing on her his charming smile.

"Hey, sweetheart." He reached for her hand. "It's good to see you again."

Liv doubted he recognized her, and even if she looked familiar, she was sure he didn't remember from where.

"You were at the show at Red Rocks last summer. Liv, right?"

Gah. She almost swallowed her tongue. He remembered her name? She nodded. "That's right."

He turned to Renie and held out his hand. "Hi, I'm Ben. What's your name?"

"Hi, Ben. I'm Renie. We met at Red Rocks, too." She shook his hand, and then smiled at her mother.

"What can I get you to drink?" Ben motioned for the bartender, who came right over.

"I'll have another beer, thanks." Liv turned around but didn't see Renie.

"She's over there." Ben pointed to a table filled with people that looked closer to her daughter's age.

"Oh. Um…" Liv wasn't sure whether to stay at the bar and talk to Ben, or join her daughter.

"Here you go," he said, handing her the beer. "So, tell me, what brings you to Crested Butte? You don't live around here. I mean, I'd know if you did."

"Skiing," she answered between sips. "My daughter goes back to school in a few days. We thought we'd sneak a quick trip in before she did."

"I'm glad. Were you out there today?"

"No, not until tomorrow."

Ben glanced at her near-empty beer, the one he had just gotten for her. She was so nervous, she'd chugged it.

"Be mindful of the altitude, Liv. Beer goes to your head a lot quicker at nine thousand feet than it does in…"

She felt the heat spread into her cheeks. Why did this man have such an effect on her? Maybe because he was the first man who'd paid this much attention to her since Renie's father. "We're from Monument."

"Is that near Denver, or is it Colorado Springs?"

"Both. It's between the two. And we're at seven thousand feet. But you're right, I must've been more thirsty than I thought. Listen, um, I'm going to take the shuttle back to the ski area. It was really nice to see you again, Ben. And thanks for the beer."

Rather than interrupting Renie, who appeared to be having a great time, Liv made her way through the crowded bar, and out the front door, without looking back at him.

Liv half-walked, half-ran down Elk Avenue to where the ski area shuttle was parked, and jumped on.

"You're my only passenger this run, ma'am. Where are you headed?"

"The Grand, thanks."

Liv sat in the first row of the bus and buried her face in her hands. God, she'd just left her daughter in a bar. Alone. What was she thinking?

Her phone vibrated in her pocket. She pulled it out, and Renie's name lit up the screen.

"Where did you go?"

"I'm sorry. I don't feel well. It's the altitude." The driver turned around and glared at her. Maybe he thought she'd get sick in his shuttle bus. She waved her hand and mouthed, "I'm okay," which seemed to pacify him.

"What? I can't hear you. Where did you say you are?"

"I'm on the shuttle," she shouted into the phone.

"Why?"

"I'm not feeling well." The shuttle driver was going to pull over and kick her off the bus.

"Okay, I'll leave now."

"No, stay. You looked like you were enjoying yourself."

"I'll see you at the hotel in a few minutes, Mom."

Liv disconnected the call. There was no point in continuing to yell into the phone. And now that she'd ruined Renie's good time, she could rest easy that she was on her way back to the hotel and, at least, safe. She tilted her head back and closed her eyes. That was the second time she'd raced away from Ben Rice. He not only made her heart race, there was something else about him that made her want to run fast and far in the opposite direction.

It wasn't as though all men had this effect on her. Or that she hadn't dated. She'd dated plenty the last twenty years. Or maybe the last ten. And, okay, not plenty, but some. Although not much at all really. Paige had tried to fix her up a couple of times, but no one she met interested her. Not like Ben Rice did.

"Ma'am, we're here," the shuttle driver said, startling her.

"Oh. Sorry. Thank you." She pressed a five-dollar bill in the receptacle, hoping he'd consider that enough of a tip.

"Thank you, ma'am, and I hope you feel better," he said as the doors closed behind her.

"What's going on with you?" Renie asked when she opened the door and walked into their hotel room.

"I drank my beer too fast. That and the crowd in the bar—I was very overwhelmed. I'm sorry I ruined our night out together."

"It's okay. I was worried about you. If we'd stayed longer, we wouldn't have wanted to ski tomorrow. Here." Renie handed her mother a folded piece of paper.

"What's this?"

"Ben's number. He wants you to call and let him know you're okay."

Liv crumpled the paper in her pocket. Could she have handled leaving the bar in a worse way? How humiliating. He probably thought she was crazy.

Ben had recognized the petite ash blonde as soon as he saw her sitting at the bar. Liv was her name. The first time he'd seen her, after they played Red Rocks, he couldn't keep his eyes off her. She was sitting in one of the first few rows and caught his eye.

When she smiled and her bright blue eyes met his, he couldn't look away. He sang the rest of the song right to her, and the one after that, too.

After their set was over, he and the band took the underground tunnel that ran from the back of the Red Rocks stage, up to the soundboard area. They sat in the roped-off section, and Ben spent the next two hours watching her.

It was obvious she loved music—and she felt it. Not everyone did. She danced, she laughed, she smiled, she lived. That was why he remembered her name when he introduced himself at the end of the show.

"I'm Liv," she'd said, and he was ready to. He'd endured too many struggles in the last few years. He'd worked hard to keep the music and his band going, and it was about to pay off. This was the year they would take it to the next level. No more local clubs. Instead, they'd tour nationally; he felt it. They'd recorded a new album, better than any other they'd released.

When he saw her again tonight, he knew fate brought her to him for a second time. It reminded him not to lose focus, keep his eye on the prize, to keep living. *One day at a time.*

Besides how pretty she was, which she seemed unaware of, something about her made him yearn to know her better. He made her skittish, though. Maybe she was feeling the same magnetic pull he was, and that's why she ran. The draw was so strong, if he didn't know he was ready for it, it would've scared the hell out of him too.

3

March

Liv picked up her tablet and hit repeat on the song playing through the wireless speakers. She intended to set the tablet back down on the ledge in the barn, but hesitated, and scrolled through a social media feed. It took her a minute to zip through the hundred new posts, but there was nothing from the only person she hoped for. Why would there be? It was ten in the morning.

Liv had checked at least four times in as many hours. What rock star was on social media between midnight and noon? Logical, but it didn't stop her from looking. Besides, Ben would never define himself that way.

A car pulled up outside the barn as she tapped the screen to check another social media site, also for the fourth time that morning.

"Aren't you getting tired of listening to this? It's time for a new playlist." Paige Cochran planted her heels in the dirt to shift the heavy barn door open. As usual, Paige dressed more as though she was going to a meeting at the investment firm she consulted for, not to visit her best friend's barn.

"I love this song," Liv muttered as she flicked through the playlists for something else to listen to.

"Here's the thing—"

"Don't say it. I can listen to whatever the hell I want to in my own damn barn."

"A little testy this morning?"

"I'm sick of people complaining about my music," Liv growled.

"People? What people? Who have you seen in the last few days other than Pooh and Micah?"

Pooh was a fourteen-year-old sweetheart of a mare. The Quarter Horse belonged to Renie, who stood firm on the name Pooh when they'd gotten the horse when she was ten. "You don't *know* Winnie the Pooh is a boy. He might be a girl."

"You're right," Liv had answered, rolling her eyes. "What was I thinking?"

The other horse, Micah, was Liv's baby. The four-year-old Appaloosa gelding showed promise as a barrel racer. Liv didn't want to part with him for proper training, and she couldn't train him herself. Those days were over for her. They had been since before Renie was born.

"You didn't answer me. What's going on?"

"Nothing. I'm getting tired of my own company. I'm bored, and sick of the cold weather. I'm ready for spring."

"I sent a text asking if you wanted to meet for breakfast, but you didn't answer."

"Sorry, I haven't checked my phone. I'm done out here. We can still go into town."

"Let's stay here. I know you have coffee and something fresh out of the oven that I shouldn't eat, but will anyway."

Liv made cinnamon scones before she came out to the barn that morning. With Renie away at college, she added most of what she baked to her already overloaded freezer.

"Aren't you overdressed to have coffee with me?"

"I intended to talk you into going to Denver with me later this morning. Although I see you're in no mood for it."

Paige managed to get herself involved in at least one new business venture a month. For someone semi-retired, she still worked fifty hours a week. If there was a deal to be made between Denver and Colorado Springs, Paige was usually on the inside edge of making it happen. She was very different from the room mom Liv met fifteen years ago when their daughters started kindergarten together.

"How about a different proposition? I'm going to Vegas next week. Mark said he'd horse-sit so you can come with me."

When Liv met them, Paige's husband, Mark, was traveling twenty-five days each month as the lead singer of a band. Diagnosed with cancer a year later, Mark retired and never looked back. Instead, he focused on their three children. Their youngest, Blythe, had remained Renie's best friend since their kindie days.

Mark still wrote music but spent most of his time picking up odd jobs, painting houses, or other handyman projects, often for friends. He never hesitated to help Liv, sometimes without her realizing she needed it.

Mark would come over to ride, but soon he'd be mending a fence, or heading into her house to fix something she hadn't noticed was broken. Liv didn't know what she'd do without the Cochrans. They were her lifeline now, with Renie at college.

"A trip to Vegas would help with the grouchy-bored thing, and get you away from the cold weather. Come with me. Sit in the sun. Get *ungrouchy*."

"I don't know."

"What's stopping you?"

Liv turned on her heel, grabbed her tablet, and headed in the direction of the house.

"I've come with a bribe."

"What's that, Paige?"

"CB Rice is playing at the House of Blues next Wednesday."

"Yes, I know."

"And you don't want to go?"

"That's *why* I don't want to go. I'm almost forty, too old for this stalker-groupie life I've been living the last few months."

It was bad enough that the universe threw the two of them together every time she turned around—but to put herself in his line of fire on purpose? He would start to think their random encounters weren't serendipitous at all, but rather her stalking him.

Six days later, Liv boarded an early morning flight, headed for a few days in Las Vegas and another not-so-chance meeting with CB Rice.

They weren't in Las Vegas often, but when they were, Liv and Paige stayed at the Delaney, part of the Mandalay Bay complex. Situated near the end of the Strip, it catered to a different clientele than the other resorts. The lights weren't as bright, the casino not as loud, the crowd more subdued. That suited Liv and

Paige fine. They didn't gamble. Paige had meetings scheduled, but otherwise they'd be camped out by one of the eleven-acre resort's pools.

"Maybe we'll bump into him in the elevator. Or he'll be at the bar tonight."

"Would you stop it? You're making me nervous. Didn't you say we're here to relax? Are you going to let me?"

"I see your eyes scanning the crowds."

"He's not here yet."

"How do you know?"

"Social media. He has a show tonight—at home."

Liv looked away. "Yep, I'm a stalker," she mumbled.

"We'll get the tickets on our way to the pool," Paige suggested. She put on sunglasses and grabbed her bag.

"No, let's wait."

"Why? It'll be one less thing to worry about."

"I haven't decided whether I want to go or not."

"Isn't that why we're here?"

"No. It's not. You're here for business meetings, and I tagged along because I would've been bored at home, and I wanted to relax and sit in the sun."

"Yeah, right."

"I'm serious, Paige. I don't know whether I want to go tomorrow night."

"You listen to his music almost non-stop, and he's playing a show while we're here. You're not making sense."

"I'm not kidding when I say he'll think I'm stalking him. I've 'run' into him twice in less than a year. This will be the third."

"But you're in Las Vegas, staying at the same complex as the House of Blues. Why wouldn't you get tickets? It makes more sense that you would go."

"I don't know. If I decide I want to, we can still get tickets tomorrow."

"Do you want a Bloody Mary?" Paige tapped Liv's shoulder an hour later.

"What? Oh, yes, a Bloody Mary, please."

"Were you sleeping?"

"I must've drifted off. Sorry."

"You're here to relax, as you keep reminding me, so quit apologizing. I'll be right back. And put on sunscreen before you fall asleep again."

Liv hadn't been asleep. She was thinking about Ben Rice, again. She pulled out her phone and checked the social media feeds. Nothing. He wasn't here yet; he had a show tonight. Wait, was it tonight, or last night? She checked again. Shit. It had been last night. Now she'd never relax. He may be there already.

4

Ben Rice had started skiing and playing guitar before he learned to read, as his dad and grandfather had before him. In high school he formed a band that he named CB Rice in honor of his hometown, Crested Butte, and his family. It confused people. They'd call him CB. That was his band; he was Ben. It didn't take long before he got used to it. If someone called him CB, they were a stranger. If they called him Ben, they were a friend.

All he'd ever wanted to do was make music. Twenty-five years, hundreds of shows, and a half-dozen albums later, he was still doing it. He loved it more than anything.

Performing, hearing the crowds, watching them get into his music—there wasn't much in life that did it for him the way being on stage did. He'd perform until the day he died. Yeah, that was attention you got addicted to. It was the only addiction he couldn't live without.

He toured as often as possible with his band. They averaged a hundred shows a year, most in Colorado, but he expected that to change. The band was solid. They'd even played Red Rocks last summer, which had been the fulfillment of a dream.

Ben considered himself an average guy, even if his grandfather had been one of the original developers of the Crested Butte ski area. He'd worked for his family all his life. He didn't mind hard work. When he wasn't touring, he spent a lot of time at The Goat, his family's bar and restaurant.

Ben learned the importance of giving back to the community from his parents and grandparents. He and the band played at countless fundraisers for medical research, and for patients faced with life-threatening illnesses, like cancer, who didn't have insurance.

When he was thirty-seven he had been diagnosed with cancer himself. That same year, he and his wife divorced. He fought the disease and an ugly custody battle at the same time. He'd gone through the standard treatments and, to this day, remained cancer-free. When he was home, his two boys lived with him half the time.

A little over a year ago, his family and bandmates staged an intervention. He spent a couple of weeks in rehab and quit drinking. Battling alcoholism was the hardest thing he'd ever done—harder than fighting cancer, harder than watching his marriage and family fall apart. But he had a year of sobriety under his belt, and he'd never felt better.

It was harder to fight the urge to drink when he was on the road with the band and they'd arrive at a gig to find a case of beer and a bottle of bourbon waiting for them. He didn't struggle with it as much at home, not even when he was at his family's bar. He'd get distracted by conversations, or if he was tempted to drink, he'd pick up his guitar and start to play. Once the crowd got into the music, the adrenaline rush took the cravings away.

Singing brought him back. It reminded him not to give up or forget how far he'd come. Performing reminded him not to give up on his kids, himself, or his life. Giving up on his marriage had been hard, but he and his ex were better off apart. Ben believed, deep in his soul, there was someone out there for him, someone he could spend the rest of his life with. Fate would put her in his path—all he had to do was keep his eyes open and recognize when it happened.

The band was in Las Vegas to play an event. It had started out as a fundraiser for a hometown girl who'd relocated from Crested Butte to Vegas. They'd gone to high school together, and she was a bartender at the House of Blues. When the manager found out how hard she struggled to make ends meet, he called Ben. Sandy Smith had lost her fight with the disease, but the event continued annually. In its fourth year, it raised funds for cancer research. The owners of the hotel complex kicked in a hefty amount, as did the House of Blues. Last year they'd raised over two million dollars. This year they were hoping to double it.

It would be an all-day event, and tickets were one hundred dollars each. CB Rice would go on right before the main headliner, who Ben had asked to play when they opened for them at Red Rocks. The lead singer's wife had battled cancer herself, so the band was quick to agree to participate.

He didn't have much to do today, but he flew in early anyway. It wasn't his event anymore, or even his fundraiser, yet he still took responsibility for it and wanted to be here to help if needed. It meant an extra day away from home, but it was for a good cause.

He pulled out his cell and dialed his son Jake's number as he walked through the casino in the direction of the pool.

"Hey, Dad."

"Hey, man, how's it going?"

"Okay."

Typical tween on the phone. He should have texted him. "I'm good. I'm headed out to the pool. This place is a giant water park. I should have brought you and your brother with me. Next year. Remind me, okay?"

"Okay, Dad. Sounds good. Wanna talk to Luke?"

"Yeah I do, but, Jake, wait. I miss you, and I love you."

"I love you too, Dad. I'll see you in a couple days."

"Okay, man. Behave."

"Dad?"

"Yeah?"

"It's not a big deal, okay? You'll be home day after tomorrow."

Jeez, his kid slayed him. "It's just two days too many."

"Yeah, here's Luke."

"Hey, Daddy. Where are you?"

Luke was nine and still had a little boy's voice. At twelve, Jake's voice was starting to change. Sometimes he sounded like a little boy and sometimes he sounded like a man. And then at other times, he sounded like a screeching prehistoric bird. God, he missed his kids.

"I'm in Las Vegas, buddy, and next year when I come to play this show, I'll bring you and your brother. You'd love this place. There are wave pools, a lazy river, all kinds of slides, and other stuff. There's even a beach."

Silence.

"Luke, are you there?"

"Yeah. I'm here. I miss you, Daddy."

"I miss you, too. I'll be home in a couple days."

"Okay. Bye." Click.

That was quick, but at least he talked to them for a few minutes.

He opened the camera app on his phone. He'd take a few shots, text them to the boys, and post a couple on social media sites. Tomorrow's show wasn't sold out, and he wanted it to be.

He turned in a circle, taking pictures. He was able to fit most of the poolside marquee announcing the show into one.

The band had a cabana reserved, and he wasn't the first one there. He grabbed a towel and threw it on one of the lounge chairs, tossed his phone on the table, and reached around to pull his shirt over his head. A couple of hours by the pool wouldn't hurt. He didn't remember the last time he had nothing to do.

Ben sat back down and picked up his phone, scrolling through the photos he'd taken. He texted several to Jake, and then scrolled back through, trying to decide which ones to post and which to delete.

Wait. He went back to the previous image, using two fingers on the screen to zoom in closer. There was a woman in the background who looked familiar. Who was she? He studied the picture, but it was too out of focus. He stood and looked around him, and then looked at the photo again, trying to figure out where she'd be sitting, based on other landmarks.

He wandered out of the cabana area, searching. Her familiarity tugged at him. He needed to find her.

Ben walked by the lazy river and waited as people floated by. He stood there until the same people floated by him, again and again. He turned to leave, and bumped into an inner tube.

"Oh, I'm so sorry. I can't see where I'm going." A tiny voice giggled from behind the giant pink tube. Ben lifted it out of the woman's hands and came face to face with her—Liv. Even with as out of focus as the photo was, he'd somehow known it was her. This was the third time in a year fate put her in his path. This time, he wouldn't let her go.

Liv gasped, and then got very dizzy. He set the inner tube down and put his hands on her shoulders.

"Liv, are you okay?"

She gazed into his big, blue eyes and couldn't decide whether she would die right there on the spot, or if she'd ever been as okay as she was at that moment.

"Hell-o? Liv? Anybody home?"

That was a different voice. Oh, that was Paige's voice. Those were Paige's hands waving in front of her face.

"What? Yes, I'm okay. I'm so sorry, I couldn't see where I was going." Liv turned to pick up the inner tube.

"Oh, no, you don't. You're not getting away this time." Ben picked up the tube and held it far enough away that she couldn't reach it. He was a foot taller than she was, so he didn't have to hold it very high.

"Liv, it's me, Ben."

"Hi, Ben. How are you?"

"*How am I?* Don't you think it's wild running into me? What are you doing here?"

"I'm here on business, and I made Liv come with me. I'm Paige. We met once before, briefly, at Red Rocks."

Paige was talking, so she didn't have to. Ben was answering her. More talking she didn't have to do. Now, if she could slink away without him noticing, she'd be fine. But wait, she wanted to listen to his voice a little longer. She loved his voice.

"Where are you going?"

Oh, crap. She'd backed away from him. And he noticed. "Come with me. You, too, Paige."

"Where are we going? Can you ease up a bit, please?"

Ben's grasp on her hand was tight. "I'm not letting go this time, Liv. If I do, I may never see you again."

Once they were within the confines of the cabana, Ben pulled out a chair and pointed at it. "Please, have a seat."

When she didn't sit, he took a step forward. "Liv, please." He sounded more exasperated than he intended. When she sat, he moved to the other side of the table, pulling a chair out for Paige.

He came back, sat next to Liv, and stared at her, wanting to memorize the lines of her face, the curve of her body. Here she was, sitting next to him, this woman who haunted his dreams.

She was a mystery. *Didn't she recognize him?* It sounded as though her friend did.

"Now that you may stay put...hi, Liv. How are you? It's nice bumping into you here."

"Ha, ha." She looked away.

He touched her cheek, turning her head so she'd look at him.

"Hi, Ben. It's nice bumping into you, too." She took a deep breath and added, "I'm surprised you remember me." She looked down again.

He didn't want her to look down; he wanted her to look at him. He moved his hand from her cheek to her chin and lifted her gaze to his.

"Why do you run from me?" he whispered.

Paige jumped up from her chair. "I'll get drinks. Liv? Ben? What would you like?"

"Paige, please sit back down," he stated without looking away from Liv. "We have cabana service. Tell me what you want, and I'll order it for you."

Paige sat back down.

"Liv, what can I order for you?"

"Lemonade?"

"Is that a question?"

"Lemonade, please."

"Paige?"

"I need something a little stronger. A Salty Dog, please."

"I'll be right back...I'm walking a couple feet away...I'm ordering drinks...do not get up from the table..." He kept his voice low and free of inflection, like a hypnotist.

He came back and pulled his chair closer to Liv. "So—let's start over, way back at the beginning. Why don't we talk about why you bolt away from me every time I start a conversation with you? Is there something about me you don't like?" He rubbed his head. "I'm bald. Is that it? You don't like bald guys."

"No, I like bald guys. I mean, I like everything about you. No, that isn't what I mean. See? I can't even put two thoughts together. I 'bolt,' as you put it, because I don't want you to realize I'm an idiot."

Ben leaned back and laughed. She was so damned cute. She made him laugh. If there was one thing he was certain of, she wouldn't be bolting away from him today.

She laughed, too. Then Paige did.

Ben put his hand on Liv's arm. "Better now?"

"Yes," she giggled. "I'm better now."

He talked them into ordering lunch, and when they finished, Paige excused herself to go to a meeting.

Liv got up from her chair. "I should go, too."

Ben stood and put his arm around Liv's shoulders. "No. Stay. Can you stay? Please?" He wasn't used to women trying so hard to get away from him. It was usually the other way around.

Liv looked at Paige, as if to ask for a reason to leave. "I'll be back for dinner. Stay. *Enjoy* yourself."

"Well, I guess…"

"There, it's settled. Liv, you're staying. And Paige, before you go, what are you doing for dinner?"

"We hadn't gotten that far."

"Good, then you'll both join me and the band. We have something special planned tonight. You'll enjoy it."

Liv and Ben had a nice, quiet afternoon. *Somewhat unexpected.* They sat on the steps of the pool and talked. He told her about his two boys, and she told him more about Renie. When he noticed her getting chill bumps, he led her to the hot tub. "Let's get warm."

She was plenty warm, overheated in fact, but she wouldn't admit it to him. Ben, with clothes on, made her blood boil. Without them, the sweat bubbled on the surface of her skin. She longed to have his powerful arms wrapped around her and to be close enough that she could feel his ripped chest against her.

He sat down first and pulled her to sit in front of him, as if he'd read her mind.

He ran his lips between her neck and shoulder. "God, Liv, what you do to me," he whispered, pulling her closer.

Liv heard a moan and wasn't sure if it came from him or her. She closed her eyes and leaned into him.

"That's my girl." He wrapped his arms around her waist and scooted her as close as she could get without sitting on his lap.

"Ben—"

"Shh…the music is starting to play. Listen." He started to hum, then sing softly.

The soft skin on your bones and the smile I would own.

He nuzzled into her hair and breathed in her scent. "You smell delicious. What is it?"

Liv couldn't wait a moment longer. Instead of answering, she turned far enough that her lips touched his.

When she did, his mouth devoured hers. She pulled back and bit her lip. Ben's hand slid into her hair and gripped a fistful, gentle, but firm, tugging her head back.

The steam rising off the warm water in the hot tub swirled around them. His arms moved back to her waist and tightened around her, pulling her even closer. He gave a rough groan as he lowered his head and kissed her again. His body felt big and solid against hers, and she sank into him. His kiss was heated, yet so tender. He slid his tongue over her bottom lip and nipped at it.

"I want you, Liv."

She pulled back, gasping to get air into her straining lungs.

"Let's go somewhere we can be alone," he said, his lips parted, his eyes dark and hungry. "I want to get you out of this bikini."

Liv shifted away from him. She wanted his lips back on hers, wanted him naked too, but...they needed to slow down. She moved away but held his gaze as they stared at each other.

"Too much?" he ventured.

"Too soon," she answered.

Ben insisted on walking her back to her room, to her door. "This way, if you run from me again, I'll know where to find you."

"Ben, I—"

"Shh…I'm sorry. I didn't mean to make you uncomfortable. I can't explain this attraction between us. It feels as though I've known you forever, not that I'm just getting to know you. That must sound crazy. I won't push so hard, I promise."

It wasn't that, she wanted the same thing he did. She didn't know how to tell him, though, how long it had been since she'd done this. *I hope it's like riding a bike.*

"Pretty much, but like no other bike you've ridden before, baby," he said, nuzzling her neck.

Oh no, did she say that out loud?

Ben leaned up against the wall outside Liv's hotel room. His body pulsed with lust, heart thundering, and his eyes closed. They opened and fixated on her. He could spend all day studying every inch of her.

Her skin was kissed by their day in the sun, and her hair hung in waves around her face. The thin cover-up that left her arms bare was so feminine, the way it wrapped around her slender body. And her eyes, the bluest he'd ever seen, were gazing at him apprehensively.

"I'm leaving now, Liv, and it's not because I want to. We have reservations at Charlie Palmer at eight. Would you like me to come back up later, and we can walk down together, or would you prefer to meet me in the lobby?"

"You're sure about this?"

"Of course I am. The band has a private dining room reserved for a special dinner tonight."

"Should you check with the band first?"

"No, Liv, it's my band. Which reminds me, do you have tickets for the show tomorrow night?"

"Um, no, we hadn't gotten around to getting them yet."

"Good. You'll be my guests."

His arms ached to hold her, to put his lips on hers, but he stopped himself. This was new for him, having to exercise such restraint. He wanted to reassure her, explain how he didn't care about anything else at that moment, besides being with her.

He was accustomed to reaching out and taking what he wanted, and that wouldn't work with this woman.

He ran his hand down her cheek. It felt velvety soft beneath his fingers, calloused from years of guitar playing. He pulled her back into his arms, bent his head, and found her mouth again with his. He'd show her how much he wanted to be with her when words weren't enough.

Dinner with the band was fun—and loud. Liv envied the way they all embraced life with *gusto*. Several members of the other bands were there, too. Before she realized it, it was after one in the morning.

Paige was more of a night owl than she. It didn't surprise Liv one bit that Paige was discussing record deals and song rights with the other guys in the band, or that she'd gone outside to smoke a cigar with them. It would never occur to Paige to be unfaithful to Mark; she just fit in wherever she happened to be. And if the conversation involved business, Paige was in her element.

Ben stroked his fingers up and down her arm, lulling her into a state of relaxation. "Tired?"

"A little," Liv answered as she stifled a yawn. "What about you? You have a big day tomorrow."

"Yeah, I do." He took the glass of wine she still held and set it on the table. He rose and took her hand, pulling her with him. He ran one finger from beneath her chin, down to the place where her dress met the top of her breasts. She breathed in, pushing herself closer to him.

"Come with me," he murmured, walking toward the door.

"I can't."

"You can. Let's take a walk in the moonlight."

"A walk, and then we have to say goodnight."

Ben started humming, then singing again.

The charm of your tease
When you make me say please
Your eyes and your hair
The look of your stare
The way that you laugh…

"Wooing me with your music; that's not playing fair."

Ben kept singing.

All I want is your mouth, and your lips
And your soft fingertips
The curve of your spine well it's gotta be mine
The warmth of your kiss when we're lying like
*   this*
The heat of your touch well it's never too
*   much.*

They shared a heated smile and walked in the direction of the elevators.

"My room is this way," he pulled her in the opposite direction.

"And my room is this way. Would you like to say goodnight here?"

"No, I wouldn't like that. But, if I walk you to your room—the room you're sharing with Paige—we won't have any privacy. If you come with me, we'll be alone all night."

"Which is why I'm going to my room. It's been a long day. Tomorrow will be, too. Goodnight, Ben."

"Not yet, Liv." He brought her hand up to his lips and kissed across her knuckles.

The elevator dinged. "Walk me to my room."

They were almost to her door when Ben stopped walking. "Liv, please, let me stay with you tonight."

She smiled, but shook her head. "Goodnight, Ben. Sweet dreams."

Ben put his forehead against the wall as the door clicked behind her. He doubted the sweetness of his dreams, but he didn't doubt how hot they'd be. He'd never wanted a woman the way he wanted her. How much of it was her resistance to him?

5

Liv hadn't heard Paige come in last night, or this morning, but she heard her in the shower. What time was it? Eleven? She never slept past eight, not ever.

"Good morning," said Paige, coming out of the bathroom door in a waft of steam, wearing one of the hotel's big, fluffy robes. "I wondered if you were going to sleep all day."

"You got in after I did. Why are you so chipper first thing this morning?"

"First thing? It's almost noon. I've been up since before nine. I got coffee, read for a while, and decided, if you were still asleep when I finished my shower, I would blast CB Rice songs through the iPod."

Liv rolled over and buried her head in the pillow. Paige sat down on the bed across from her.

"Spill. Tell me all the details. I'm dying of curiosity."

"He's so...hot."

"Yes. That part is obvious. What happened after you left the restaurant last night? Oh, before I forget, I found an envelope containing two tickets to the show slipped under our door this morning."

"Nothing happened. He walked me to the room. We said goodnight."

"That's it?"

"Paige, what did you expect? That I'd invite him in and have hot sex with a stranger?"

Paige looked dumbfounded.

"Paige? Is that what you thought?"

"Of course it's what I thought. I don't want to hurt your feelings, honey, but for God's sake, when *was* the last time you had sex? You have had sex since you conceived Renie, haven't you?"

"Of course I have."

"Wait, I better clarify. You have had sex since Scott died, haven't you?"

No response.

"Liv, that was twenty-one years ago!"

"Thank you for reminding me. It should be obvious why I didn't invite him inside."

Paige shook her head. "It's about as far from obvious as it gets." She started getting dressed. "No wonder you're so grouchy."

"Hey! Be nice. Just because someone isn't having sex doesn't make them grouchy. After a while, you get used to it. It's the idea of having sex again, and then not having it, that makes a person grouchy. And to be honest, I am *very* grouchy this morning."

"Again, why didn't you do something about it last night?"

"Argh—I told you why not. He's this hot, younger guy who wants to have sex with me. How long do you think that'll last when he finds out I'm a forty-year-old re-virgin?"

"Re-virgin? Is that a thing? I haven't heard about that. Is that what it's called?"

Liv buried her head back in the pillow. This was pointless. She couldn't get through to Paige, so why bother? That was last night. She'd missed her chance. Even if she saw him tonight, he'd be busy with the show—where there'd be younger, hotter women to compete with.

Oh, God. What had she done? She'd missed her one chance to have sex since before Renie was born. What if she never had sex again? She'd die a shriveled up old lady who hadn't gotten laid in sixty years. Maybe longer.

Liv jumped when the room phone rang. Who called on hotel phones anymore? Paige answered.

"Hello, yeah, good morning. Yep, she's right here."

"It's him," she mouthed.

"Huh?"

"It's Ben," she said out loud this time, her hand covering the receiver.

"Oh."

"Here, take it." Paige shoved the phone in her direction.

"Good morning."

"Good morning, yourself. I slept longer than I wanted to. Actually, I didn't sleep much at all, and it's your fault. I couldn't stop thinking about you. I drifted off around sunrise. I woke up and realized I missed my chance to have breakfast with you this morning."

"You didn't. Paige just woke me up too."

"Liv, tell me—did you dream about me?"

Silence.

"Liv? Are you there?"

"Mmm hmm."

"And? Tell me about your dreams."

"Not a chance."

"I'll get it out of you during breakfast. Or lunch. It's Vegas—you can get any meal you want, any time of day. How soon can you be ready?"

"I don't know. I should check with Paige."

Paige waved her hands, shaking her head. "Go with him. I have a meeting."

"Never mind, Paige has a meeting. I can be ready in a half hour."

"Okay, I'll be there in ten minutes."

"Wait. *What?* I said it would take me a half hour to get ready."

"Yeah, but I'm gonna help."

Silence. He hung up.

"What? What's happening? You're supposed to tell your best friend what's happening. I shouldn't have to force it out of you."

"He'll be here in ten minutes. He said he'd help me get ready."

Somehow Paige managed to finish getting dressed while Liv talked to Ben. She'd even put on makeup and pulled her hair back in a sleek ponytail.

"How did you do that? Five minutes ago you got out of the shower, and now you're ready to go. And you look great. How?"

Paige picked up her bag and briefcase and moved in the direction of the door. "See you later," she said as the door closed behind her.

"Wait! When? When will I see you later?" Too late. Liv would have to text her.

Oh, no! Ben was on his way. She hadn't even brushed her teeth. Did she have time to jump in the shower? She had to try.

When she climbed out of the shower, Ben was pounding on the door. He barged in as she opened it, and put his arms around her. When his hands moved to the sash on her robe, she stopped him.

"Liv, I'm sorry. Last night I told you I wouldn't push, but damn, I can't keep my hands off of you."

"I don't want you to. But, Ben, this is too much, too fast for me."

He backed up and leaned against the wall. "Do you want me to leave?"

Liv almost smiled. Ben's pout reminded her of Renie's when she was a little girl.

"No, I don't want you to leave, at least not without taking me with you."

Ben took a deep breath and smiled. "Do you have any idea how much I want you right now?"

She nodded and smiled too. "I do."

"Breakfast?"

"I'd love it."

Ben walked over to the window and looked out. "Maybe by the pool?"

"Sounds perfect. I'll be right back."

"You sure you don't need any help?"

Liv went into the other room to put on her bikini and cover up, hoping she was making the right decision. Paige had been shocked that she and Ben hadn't had sex, and here she was, turning him down again.

"Ready?" she asked, walking out to where Ben waited.

Ben closed his eyes and groaned. "You're killing me, woman. A red bikini? Seriously? I think you should put that big, fluffy robe back on."

When Liv turned to go change, Ben grabbed her around the waist. "I'm kidding, Liv. I love your red bikini." He ran his hand from her cheek, down her throat, to just under the top of her bikini, and then pulled his hand away and put his arm around her. "Come on. If it can't be me, let's get some breakfast in you." He winked and opened the hotel room door.

The pools were crowded, but Ben led Liv to the same cabana he'd reserved the day before. Towels scattered the chaise lounges, but no one from his band was there. Maybe they were setting up for the show. As soon as he and Liv ordered breakfast, Ben would call and see if they needed him.

"You look worried."

"I do? Yeah, I guess I am. I didn't think to check in this morning."

"Do it now."

"I will, as soon as we—"

Liv picked the phone up off the table where he'd set it, and handed it to him.

"Worry is seeping off of you, Ben. Make the call and figure it out so you can either leave or relax."

Ben threw his head back and laughed. "You're something else, sweetheart. Just when I think I've got your number, you go in a direction I never expected." He squeezed her and nuzzled her neck.

"Make the call." She squirmed against him.

"You keep that up, and I won't make the show later."

Ben called Jimmy, who was the bass guitarist but also managed the crew. "Hey," he said. "What's goin' on?"

Jimmy told him they were almost finished with sound check and didn't need him for at least another couple of hours.

"So," he said, pulling her down on the chaise in front of him. "Looks like I'm yours for a while longer. What should we do?"

"Breakfast?"

"That's right. I promised to feed you." He wiggled his eyebrows and smiled.

Paige and Liv sat near the center of the stage, in the first row of tables. They'd missed the first couple of opening bands, but got there in time to see the last one on the stage before CB Rice played.

She hadn't seen Ben since they left the pool and he walked her to her room.

He'd been sweet and flirty, never missing an opportunity to tell her how much he wanted her, but he hadn't pushed. Thinking about how much she wanted him, too, brought color to her cheeks.

"Whatcha' thinking about?" Paige smirked. "Did you have a nice afternoon while I slaved away in meetings?"

"Stop it. You don't slave. You talk and everyone else listens. And yes, I had a very nice afternoon."

"Tell me about it."

"Paige—I don't ask you to tell me about you and Mark!"

"We've been married forever. No one wants to hear about us. You, on the other hand, spent the day with Ben Rice. Everyone wants to hear about that."

"Shh, lower your voice. God, I'm so embarrassed."

"No one can hear me over the band. Why are you embarrassed? He's…"

"Hot. Very hot. Scorchingly hot."

"See?"

"And that's all you're getting out of me."

"Damn."

Liv looked in the direction of the bar and saw one of the guys she'd met at dinner. She thought it might be

Jimmy, but she wasn't sure. He waved and motioned for her to join him.

"I'll be right back."

As she walked up, she saw Ben standing with his back to her. He turned as she drew closer, and smiled that devastatingly perfect smile that made her want to slide into his arms and never leave.

His worn jeans, with holes and tears in all the right places, sat low on his hips. His Henley crept up as he reached his hand out in invitation, revealing a peek at his rock-hard abs. The True Grit plaid shirt he wore, open in the front, stretched across his broad shoulders, and his cowboy hat sat down low on his head, almost covering his eyes.

"Wow, look at you, all sexy and hanging out at the bar. Aren't you afraid your fans will mob you?" She stepped closer and breathed in the scent of him.

"Nah, I've been out here forty-five minutes, waiting for you. Nobody recognizes me."

"If I knew you were waiting for me, as hot as you are, I would've gotten here much sooner."

"Me? Look at you. You're fire and ice, baby." Liv's sleeveless red dress clung to every curve of her body. She wore a solitaire diamond on a long chain that hung low, resting in the hollow between her breasts. Her four-inch nude heels made her legs look impossibly long, and her wavy hair framed her face with perfectly placed blonde highlights.

Ben sat on a bar stool, put his arm around her waist, and pulled her closer to him. "I want to kiss you so bad, right here in the bar. Would that embarrass you?"

Liv rubbed her lips across his before pulling away.

"That isn't a real kiss. Come here. Give me more of that."

Before he could pull her closer, she stiffened her arm, keeping him at a distance. "Careful, your adoring fans may not like seeing you with me."

"What's goin' on with you?" Jimmy asked after Liv walked away.

"I wish to hell I knew. God, look at her." Ben breathed in deep. "I could eat her up. Have you ever seen a more beautiful woman?"

"I'm confused. Didn't you just meet her? You seem kinda' over the top."

"Yeah, I did. I mean, I met her last summer, after the show we played at Red Rocks."

"Oh, yeah. Now I remember. So you met her then, for five minutes, now she's coming to our shows? Hmm."

"Nah, it's not like that. I ran into her another time in January, and then at the pool yesterday. "

"She didn't *mean* to run into you? Come on."

No, she was different. She hadn't meant to run into him; fate kept putting her in his path. Liv had been fighting the attraction between them. She didn't recognize it for what it was. Something special, something unique.

"I'm tellin' you, it's not that way. I like her, so back the hell off."

Jimmy held up his hands. "Just sayin'."

Liv could not wait to see Ben on stage again. She'd loved watching him play at Red Rocks, and now, being so close, she'd be able to see those big, powerful hands on the guitar, and watch his eyes as he sang.

She fanned her face. Maybe she should go get some fresh air before they started. Wait, this was Las Vegas; there wasn't much fresh air, and what there was of it wouldn't cool her off.

One by one the band members took the stage—everyone but Ben—and the emcee came out. "Ladies and gentlemen, please welcome...C...B...R-i-i-i-c-e!" The place was packed, and the crowd roared. The band started to play, and seconds later, Ben came out, guitar in hand, already playing.

They were so close Liv could see the sweat on his brow. His eyes closed as he stepped forward, singing, "Twisted."

Can't blame it on the whiskey
Can't blame it on the smoke
Half of me's in heaven,
The other half's in hell.
I might be goin' crazy,
But I just can't tell.
She's got me twisted
All torn up.
There's nothin' I won't do
For her sweet, sweet love.

Ben's eyes met hers.

Paige elbowed her. "Jeez, this is as hot as he is. He's singing to you again."

Liv wanted to crawl under the table. It wasn't that she didn't like it. But anyone looking at her would surely know exactly what she was thinking about.

By the third song, Liv and Paige were dancing, along with everyone else. The band got people on their feet. Liv turned and surveyed the faces in the crowd, who were all mesmerized by Ben. She wasn't alone in that. He pulled people to him, made them sing along, hang on every word. He was magnetic.

They slowed things down with the next song, and the crowd settled back in their chairs, giving Liv an opportunity to watch Ben play. The muscles in his forearms flexed, the corners of his mouth turned down, his eyes closed, and his whole body moved with every sound coming out of his guitar. He threw his head back and got into it—the way she imagined he would if they had sex.

"Whatcha' thinking about now?" Paige elbowed her and grinned.

Liv grinned back. Being alone with him again. Never letting go once she did. That's what.

She didn't want to think about how soon they'd both get on a plane and go back to their normal lives. Her boring, lonely, sexless life. Nope, she didn't want to think about that.

When she looked up at Ben, he was watching her. His brow furrowed, as though he wondered where her mind was and why it wasn't on him.

It was silly of Liv to think his mind would be on her. He was performing for a room full of people. He was lost in his music, lost in his fans. She doubted he even remembered she was there.

They played for another hour, then came back out for three encores. During the break between CB Rice and the last band taking the stage, one of the guys from CB Rice came to their table.

"Ben asked if you'd come backstage with me. Paige, will you be okay by yourself for a few minutes? Liv won't be too long."

"Of course, go! I'm fine." Liv saw Paige had already struck up a conversation with the people at the table next to them. She never had to worry about her best friend. She'd never known a stranger, just friends she hadn't met yet.

"Come here, baby." Ben reached out for her. "No, wait. I'm all sweaty."

"I don't care," she said as she rested her body next to his. "I like it when you get me sweaty."

Ben pulled her closer, bent his head, and kissed her. Liv's mouth opened beneath his, and the kiss deepened. She put her hand on his cheek, and his hand went to her bottom, pulling her close. "God, you're so sexy."

"No, I'm not. But you—" Liv couldn't finish. Everything about him excited her. His fingertips drifted down to where her dress rested against the swell of her breasts, the way they had the night before.

"You have no idea, do you? What you do to me? What you were doing to me while I was on stage? All I thought about was being alone with you. Every song, every note, I'd close my eyes and see you there—writhing beneath me."

"You were thinking about me?"

"You weren't thinking about me? About us? Getting horizontal with me?" His arms wrapped around her waist, and he kissed the side of her neck, under her ear, down and over her shoulder. "I want to be alone with you so bad, Liv. I don't wanna share you with anyone else right now."

Like him, she'd like nothing better.

"We can't, though, sweetheart. At least not for a little while. I gotta go talk to the guys, hang out before they go on stage. They're setting up a roped off section for us. I can't come out before they start their set, but I'll be out right after that." He pulled her in again and ravaged her mouth with his. "Then later, it's you and me. Got it?"

"Mmm hmm." She nodded.

The guys in the final band were pros. Their horn section alone reverberated throughout the club. She'd seen them before when CB Rice opened for them at Red Rocks. The amphitheater had been filled with ten thousand people, and even in that setting, they were bigger than life. Seeing them in a small venue like this was something she was glad she hadn't missed.

The House of Blues closed its doors after the show, but with the number of bands that participated, the place remained crowded. Everyone wanted to talk to Ben, and Liv hadn't seen him for an hour. Paige was talking with a couple involved with Mandalay Bay management.

She didn't want to pout, but she was bored and tired. Exhausted, actually. She wanted to crawl into bed. The problem was, she didn't want to crawl into it alone. She wanted Ben as much as he said he wanted her.

She put her elbow on the table and rested her chin in her hand. Here she sat, alone. Why did she surround herself with people who were so much more interesting than she was? Ben, Paige, Scott, even her parents had been more interesting than she was.

***

Liv grew up *loving* Scott Fairchild. There wasn't a better or more handsome man alive. Her dad mentored Scott as a cadet at the Air Force Academy and helped guide his career, and he visited her parents regularly.

When Scott was promoted to captain, he planned to be in Colorado Springs, so Liv's father could be the one to do the honors. Her parents threw a small celebration dinner for him after his pinning on.

"He asks about you," her mother said.

"Who does?"

"Scott. He asked your father if he'd mind if he took you out while he was here."

"What did Dad say?"

"Dad said it was okay with him."

Liv was stunned. She was sure Scott hadn't ever thought of her as anything other than her father's little girl. She was eighteen, and Scott was eleven years older.

He took her out every night the rest of the time he was in town, and Liv was the happiest she'd ever been in her life. When he went back to his base, they'd talk every night on the phone. Scott spent the next Christmas with her family, and proposed. She said yes, and they married on Valentine's Day. Soon after, Liv realized she was pregnant.

In less than a year, she went from being a girl who graduated from high school a few months before, to a wife, soon to be a mother. Less than ten months after that, she was a widow. She and Scott hadn't been married a year when Scott was deployed to the Gulf War, where his plane was shot down.

Liv hadn't been with another man since Scott. She hadn't thought about it. Scott was the only man she'd ever had sex with. The truth was, she'd been too scared to let anyone close enough to share that part of herself again. The last time she opened herself up that way, her heart had been broken into a million pieces.

***

All these years, she believed if she kept her heart closed, she wouldn't ever have to experience that gut-wrenching pain again. The only person she ever loved who hadn't been taken away from her was Renie. And every day, Liv prayed that God would keep her safe.

She didn't know whether to thank Ben for awakening these feelings of desire in her, or curse him for it. This was different though; this wasn't about her heart. If she had sex with Ben, it wouldn't be about forever, not the way it was supposed to be with Scott. It would be a fling, a one night stand. Lots of people had sex with someone they'd never see again.

She stood, facing the bar, trying to decide whether to get Ben's attention or head up to the room, when his arms slid around her waist.

"There's my girl. Oooh, you feel good."

"Hi," she whispered, turning to wrap her arms around him.

"Let's get out of here. You ready?"

"Are you sure you can leave?"

"Yep. I can't wait another minute to be alone with you. Come on, let's go."

He pulled her with him, heading to the bank of elevators in the opposite direction of hers. "I want you with me tonight, Liv. Please, tell me you want the same thing."

Liv took a deep breath. She needed to keep reminding herself, *this wasn't about her heart; it was sex*. This time with him would give her memories she'd carry with her forever. They wouldn't keep her warm at night, back on her ranch, but at least she'd be able to say she'd done something a little wild, a little crazy, and maybe even had sex again after a twenty-one-year dry spell.

He crowded her in the corner of the elevator, covering her mouth with his. Ben's muscles tightened beneath her fingers when she put her hand under his shirt and touched his skin. He shifted so every inch of his long, hard body was up against hers.

"Liv," he whispered her name, "you are so beautiful."

"So are you," she whispered back. Her hand slid down his belly toward his hip. Her heart thudded faster as she leaned into him, her body pressing close to his.

"You're sure about this, Liv? Do you want me as much as I want you?"

"So much," she groaned.

The elevator stopped, the door opened, and they twisted out, neither letting go.

They were still in the hallway when Ben covered her breasts with his hands.

"Wait," she gasped. "Someone might see us."

He cupped the perfect mounds of flesh and stroked her hardened nipples with his thumbs. "I don't care." He moved his hands to her bottom and grabbed her, pressing against her.

Her back was to the door of the suite, and when he opened it, she almost tumbled to the floor. He pulled her back against him and pushed the door shut behind them.

"I can't keep my hands off you," he groaned. His lips trailed down her body. "I can't keep my lips off you." He reached for the zipper on her dress and pulled it down. It slid off her shoulders to the floor. He traced the lacy edge of her bra, his gaze riveted there.

"Your turn," she murmured, tugging at his shirt. He grinned and reached behind him, pulling it off in one swoop.

"Now this." His hand moved to her back to unfasten her bra with practiced ease. He removed the pale pink lace and dropped it to the floor. "Beautiful," he murmured. "Skin on skin. This is what I've been craving."

Liv ran her hands over his firm pecs, his chiseled abs, and down to the waistband of his jeans. She reached for his belt, but he caught her hand.

"You first." His hands moved to her panties and pulled them over her hips as she shimmied out of them.

She pressed her lips to his shoulder blade and ran her tongue over his skin.

His breath caught, and his abs tightened beneath her exploring lips.

"No more waiting," she said, reaching for his belt.

He unfastened it and jerked his pants off his own hips, let them fall to the floor, and stepped out of them.

He turned away from her, leading her by the hand.

"Your suite is much bigger than ours," she commented. "Must be a perk of being famous."

"No talking." He turned her around, walking her backward, belly-to-belly, into the large open area of the suite.

She looked up at him, and he caught her mouth in a deep kiss. She wrapped her arms around his neck and kissed him back. He grabbed her bottom in both large hands and pressed her more securely against him.

He moved her backward again, not stopping until her legs came in contact with the bed. Ben eased her down onto the mattress, never taking his lips from hers.

He moved her where he wanted her. "I want to look at you, Liv. I need to."

He sat next to her, his hip touching hers, and ran his fingers over her breasts, her belly, and down across the heated flesh between her thighs.

"Ben." She arched her back and swayed her hips, trying to position herself closer to him.

"Don't rush me," he said. "I'm still looking."

"Less looking. More touching," Liv groaned.

He moved so his body covered hers, wedging his knee between her thighs, opening her up to him.

"I can't wait."

She gasped and tried to stop him, then realized he already wore a condom. When had he put that on? Her thundering heart raced out of control. Who cared?

He moved so slowly at first, easing into her, waiting until her body adjusted to him being inside of her.

She'd forgotten the incredible feeling of fullness, of how complete her body felt. How had she gone so long without this? Why had she waited when Ben could've brought her to this nirvanic place yesterday?

She clenched around him, wanting to keep him there, a part of her, for as long as possible. Spasms of relief overtook her, spreading throughout her body as he moved over her, faster and faster, harder and harder, until she exploded.

"Again, Liv, let's figure out what else you like," he said as he trailed gentle kisses along her jaw.

Liv wrapped her arms and legs around him. The pressure began to build again inside her. Need engulfed her senses. Ben slowed and looked into her eyes. "I want to take my time with you, sweetheart, but I've wanted you so bad, I'm struggling to go slow."

Liv murmured and moved beneath him, slowly like he wanted, her mind memorizing how he felt against her, inside of her. When her pace quickened, she watched as Ben's expression changed.

"Now," he growled, as he threw his head back and closed his eyes, the way he had on stage.

As his movements slowed, he brought his lips to hers. "Even better than I thought it would be, Liv."

She kissed his temple as he murmured the sweetest sounds.

"Be right back."

He slid into bed and snuggled into her, pulling her closer so her back nestled against his front.

"I wish I wasn't so tired," he whispered. "I don't want to miss a moment of being with you."

"Mmm." Her eyes closed, and she fell asleep before he did.

Ben blinked himself awake and tried to get his bearings. He lifted his head from the pillow and felt Liv's body cuddled against his. When he shifted, she woke.

"Good morning, beautiful." He kissed the top of her head. He liked waking up with her next to him.

"What time is it?"

He shifted again, checking the clock on the nightstand. "Eleven."

"What? Eleven? Again? I never sleep this late." She snuggled back into him.

Her stomach rumbled, making him chuckle. "Hungry?"

"Yeah, I haven't eaten since yesterday afternoon."

"Liv, are you kidding? You must be starving." He lifted her off him and swung his legs over the side of the bed.

"No," she protested. "Don't go. Come back here."

"I'm ordering food, then you'll have my undivided attention. What do you want to eat?"

"Don't care. Need nourishment."

He called room service, and then he stretched his body out next to hers.

"What time's your flight?" he asked, wishing he didn't have to.

"Tomorrow morning. When's yours?"

"Seven."

She let out a groan that sounded more like a stifled sob.

"I can change it. What time is your flight tomorrow? I'll leave the same time you do."

"No, don't do that. You have to get home."

He sat back up.

"Wait—you promised me your undivided attention."

"I'll change my flight time."

"Don't. It's okay."

"It isn't a big deal; I can leave anytime I want to." He snuggled back into her. "If I could, I'd stay right here with you, and never leave. Are you trying to tell me you don't want to spend another night with me?"

"That isn't it."

"What is it, then, Liv?"

She couldn't think when he trailed kisses from just below her ear, down over her shoulder. "Your boys," she murmured. "You need to...um...see your...um...sons."

"If that's the only thing that's worrying you, if you promise that's it, I'm staying." She started to speak, and he put two fingers on her lips.

"If I left tonight, they'd be in bed long before I got home. And tomorrow is the day my boys hang with Grandma and Grandpa. Dad is not allowed to interfere with grandparent time. They'll be up and gone by sunrise. By the time they get home, I will be too. And, I'll get to spend another few hours with you."

"But..."

"Let go, Liv. Don't worry so much, and just enjoy this time we have together."

"It's just that…"

"What, Liv? Don't you like being with me? I sure like being with you." Ben smiled, but she could see his lingering tension.

"I have enjoyed being with you, Ben." Liv got up and climbed into her panties, looking for her bra.

He walked over to her, bringing his hand up to caress the side of her face. He tucked her hair behind her ear. "Talk to me. Tell me what you're thinking. Are you worried about Paige?"

"No. Paige travels all the time. She does her own thing. I don't need to worry about her."

"Then what is it?" He rubbed his head again. "We already determined you like the bald head. We discovered other things you like, too. Come on, give me somethin' here. You ready to run away from me again, Liv?"

If she left now, her pride would stay intact. She'd walk away, thank him for the wonderful memories, great sex, and ride off into the sunset, or at least to the elevator. If she said goodbye first, she might have more of a chance to keep her emotions in check and not make a fool of herself.

Ben stood with his arms crossed, less than a foot from her. "Liv, tell me. I can see the wheels turning. Talk to me."

"I have to go. It's been great…a great couple of days." What else had she planned to say? She couldn't think. "It's been, you know—fun. But it's time to get back to real life." She picked up her dress and looked for her shoes and bag.

"Uh-uh."

"What?"

"No. This isn't going down like this. You are not, I repeat, *not* running out of here. Even if I was leaving tonight—which I no longer am—I wouldn't let you leave now. Who knows how long it will be before we see each other again? We haven't even talked about that yet."

6

"Sure, that works. See you then." Liv ended the call.

"All set?"

She bit her lip. "I realize I said Paige is self-sufficient, but even as busy as she is and as much as she has to do, she'd never do this to me."

"Do what?"

"Leave me with no one to hang out with while we were traveling together."

"What did she say? Did she sound upset?"

"She said she wanted me to enjoy myself, more than anything, so…"

"What else did she say? So…what?"

"I wasn't so damned grouchy when we got home."

Ben's head tilted back and he laughed, again. She loved his laugh—he did it with his whole body. His whole body experienced the joy of the moment. And it wasn't just when he laughed; he reveled in joy all the time. On stage, and especially when they were having sex.

He pulled her back down on the bed and shifted so she was on top of him. "Skin on skin, baby. You know how much I like this." His hands worked their way up and down her back, pressing her closer to him.

"Can you sleep on the plane?"

"What did you say?"

"If we stay up all night, can you sleep on the plane tomorrow?"

Ben hired a car to take them to McCarran. "Fly back with me. It won't be a problem for us to fly into Centennial, drop you off, and then fly to Gunnison."

"I didn't realize you had your own plane when you said you were changing your flight." Liv felt peevish.

"Well, it's not mine; it's the band's, and we share time with my folks. My dad's a pilot too."

That got her attention. "My dad was a pilot. Air Force."

"My father got his pilot's license in his twenties, to ferry my grandfather back and forth from Denver. He was never a military guy."

"Oh."

"You sound disappointed. Does it matter?"

No, it didn't matter. But outside of their undeniable mutual attraction, how much did they really have in common?

Last night Ben insisted they talk about when they could see each other again. Liv had been purposely evasive. He didn't think she believed that he'd want to see her again, did he? He didn't need to placate her by promising he'd call. Did he think she wasn't smart enough to recognize this for what it was?

"I thought we might have that in common," she shrugged.

Ben looked at Paige, who shrugged too.

"Look, it's a nice offer, but we've got a car at DIA. Flying into Centennial will complicate things. Let's say goodbye here. It'll be easier that way."

Ben looked at Paige again. "I thought you said, if I stayed another night, she *wouldn't* be as grouchy."

Paige spit out her coffee as she laughed out loud.

"It isn't funny." Liv moved away from both of them. "I'll be back in a minute." She huffed off in the direction the ladies' room.

"What...in...the...hell?" Ben looked at Paige. Granted, he might be used to getting his own way. Maybe he was a little stubborn, and perhaps a tad controlling, but this woman wouldn't give *an inch*.

"Go easy on her. She's w-a-a-a-y out of her comfort zone with you. Let her be pissy, but like her anyway. She'll come around." Paige hesitated. "As long as you do."

"Is that it? She thinks I won't come around again?"

"She doesn't think it; she knows it. At least that's what she's convinced herself."

"How do you know all this? Did she get up in the middle of the night and call you?"

"No. But I know her. When I say she's out of her comfort zone, she isn't even on the same planet as her comfort zone when it comes to you. Cut her a little slack; understand what the motivation is behind her behavior. As I said, she'll come around as long as you do."

"Ready, Paige?" Liv touched Ben's arm, stood on her tiptoes, and kissed his cheek. "Bye, Ben. Thanks for everything. I had a lot of fun. Come on, Paige, it's time to leave." Liv turned and got two feet away from him, hoping he'd let her go.

Two long strides later, he grabbed Liv around the waist and spun her back to him. "Oh, no. We aren't doing *this* again. Come here, baby." Ben's mouth covered hers. His hand held the back of her head close; she couldn't have ended their kiss even if she wanted to. His other arm came around, and he squeezed her behind. And then he released her.

"I'll talk to you later, Liv. Have a safe flight." With that, he turned around and walked in the other direction.

Liv stood still, stunned, then looked at Paige. "Not. A. Word. Got it?"

"Got it." Paige giggled.

"You okay?" asked Paige twenty minutes into their flight.

"I'm fine. Why do you ask?"

"I'm not playing this game. You know why I asked. Now start talking...tell me about Ben, about what's happened, about all of it."

"I'm not playing games, Paige. When I say I'm fine, I mean it."

"Not buyin' it."

"Why not? Look—I lived out every woman's fantasy. I had a whirlwind romance with a guy completely out of my league. I had fantastic sex, and then he offered to fly me home on his private plane. Why wouldn't I be fine?"

"Because you said goodbye to him."

"What does that have to do with anything? I went into this with my eyes wide open. Not the first day, but you pointed something out to me that I hadn't considered. It changed my whole outlook."

"Which something?"

"That I hadn't had sex since Scott died. Do you realize how messed up that is? It's crazy abnormal in a freakishly weird way. If it weren't for Ben, who knows when, or if, I ever would've again. So, yeah, I'm fine."

"No regrets, no self-doubts, no wondering when you'll see him again?"

"None of the above. As far as seeing him again, I have no intention of allowing that to happen."

Liv turned her face toward the window and closed her eyes. Every time she did, she saw Ben. Yes, she had an ache in her heart, but what good would it do to allow herself to get absorbed by it? Not one bit. Ben had an exciting, bigger-than-life life. She had her ranch, and she was lucky to have it. Other than that and an amazing daughter who was out creating her own life, independent of her mother, there wasn't much more she brought to anyone's table.

"You don't fool me."

"Paige, please, let it go."

"No, I won't let it go. He wants to see you again."

"To what end?" Why wouldn't Paige drop it?

"Why do you keep yourself on the outskirts of life? It breaks my heart. You're an amazing woman, and yet it seems as though you're done. You raised your daughter and you've begun the descent. Your life isn't over, Liv. It's just beginning. Why won't you let yourself take a chance with this guy?"

"Enough, Paige! Why do you have to push so hard? I had a great time. I didn't fall in love, and I don't plan to ever again. Scott was it for me; the great love of my life. There, are you happy? You made me say it. Now leave me alone."

"Oh, sweetie…" Paige tried to comfort her, but Liv jerked her shoulder away.

She didn't tell Paige that when she turned her cell back on after the flight, there was a text from Ben, with a photo. And a voicemail from him, which she didn't intend to listen to until she got home.

He sent a picture of himself on the plane, pouting, and he wrote *I'm not letting go of this, Liv.*

She doubted their little fling amounted to much more than a blip on his radar. He probably kept a string of girls on the hook, one in every city—his hookup girls. She had no intention of being one of them. She wouldn't answer. He'd lose interest and go away.

Her phone beeped again; another text from him. *Hey, baby, how was your flight? Miss you already.* Oh, God, what was he doing? She powered down her phone and put it in her bag.

"Hear from him?"

"Nope, and I don't expect to," she lied to Paige, and she didn't have any idea why.

Liv dropped her bags inside the back door and went straight to the barn. She wanted to ride as hard, fast, and far as Micah would take her.

"Hey, sweet boy," she said as she walked into the stall. "Let's ride. What do you say?"

Micah nuzzled up against her.

"Did you miss me? I missed you." She scratched down his nose and led him out of the stall.

Ten minutes later, she had him saddled up and out on the trail. From her hundred-acre ranch off County Line Road, she had a perfect view of Pikes Peak and the rest of the Front Range. There was nothing like the wide-open spaces and blue skies of Colorado.

When her father retired, he bought this ranch, knowing how much Liv wanted a horse of her own. He'd promised her that, one day, they would live in a place where she could own one. They were an Air Force family, and that meant they moved every two or three years. Having a horse, or even a dog, had been out of the question given the life they led. Liv's mother hadn't been keen on the idea of living so far outside of town, but the Black Forest community was a tight-knit one, and the loneliness she'd expected from their secluded location never materialized.

They made friends with other ranchers, and almost every weekend, there was a social function either with them or with other retired Air Force families.

Liv was a freshman in high school when they moved to Colorado twenty-six years ago. She left briefly when she and Scott married. Now she considered it home and never planned to leave.

Micah wound his way through the heavily treed trail without much coaxing from Liv. Once they reached the top of the short incline, they came to a clearing and a wide-open meadow where he could run fast and hard.

"Ready, boy?" she asked, giving him a little kick, and Micah took off like a rocket. This was freedom. No worries, just her and her horse. She was thankful every day that her father bought this ranch.

Her parents died within a couple of years of each other. Her dad went first, ten years ago, followed by her mom. The ranch had no mortgage, and they'd left her a generous sum of money. Liv never had to worry about how she'd support herself and her daughter. But between the two of them, they decided to take in boarded horses anyway. It provided a bit of an income, but more, it provided company when the people boarding came to ride.

One of the neighboring ranches was owned by a couple who had become a second family to Liv. The Pattersons had been leasing Liv's ranch land for cattle since before Liv's father owned it. It added income like boarding did, provided for the care and maintenance of the land, and it also gave them a little excitement.

Calving season and branding gave her and Renie life experiences they wouldn't have otherwise known. Liv wasn't much of a ranch hand herself, but she would dish out a hot meal for the cowboys and wranglers at busy times of the year. Her pies became the dessert mainstay of Patterson Ranch barbecues.

She tied up Micah near the Pattersons' barn and walked in the back door.

"Hey-o, anybody here?" Liv never knocked first. Dottie would've been insulted if she had.

"In here, honey," Dottie answered from the kitchen.

Liv came in and let herself be surrounded by a hug like no one else gave but Dottie. Her eyes filled with tears.

"What's this?" Dottie asked, holding Liv at arm's length. "Sit down, and tell me why you're crying."

Liv told Dottie about Ben Rice, including the part about her not having sex since Scott died.

"Bill and I hoped one of the cowboys who worked our ranch would turn your head, but year after year, it never happened. Not for lack of trying on their part, either."

"What are you talking about? Whose part?"

"Well, now…there have been a slew of 'em trying for years to get your attention."

"Who?"

"Billy Junior, but he gave up years ago, honey. You wouldn't even look in his direction. The Morehouse boy, what was his name?"

"Brandon."

"That's right, Brandon. He had a fierce crush on you. There were others."

Liv was stunned. She'd never known this.

"Are you sure you aren't talking about someone else?"

"No, I'm not talking about someone else. I'm talking about you, Olivia. You've never been aware of your own beauty. That's one of the things that makes you so irresistible. And from the day she was born, you've been wrapped up in being the best mama to Renie. But sweetie, we've worried about you not realizing there's more to life."

"I hope I wasn't rude to anyone."

Dottie laughed. "A little. It made them want to follow you around all the more."

Liv hadn't been that interested in dating in high school; she'd already decided Scott was the only man for her. She supposed guys flirted with her, but she never paid attention.

"I didn't know."

"That was clear." Dottie chuckled again. "It's that way, isn't it? The girls who do the chasin', the boys don't want. The girls who don't know boys exist, the boys can't get enough of."

Dottie put her palm on Liv's cheek. "Open your heart a little. Let him in, honey."

"Who? Ben? He doesn't want in, Dottie. I'd be surprised if I heard from him again."

"You got your cell phone on you?"

"Yeah," she said, pulling it out of the pocket in her vest.

"Is it on?"

She hadn't remembered to turn it back on since she got home. She hit the power button and set it down on the table.

It chirped. She had new voice messages, and a couple of text messages, too. Liv picked up the phone to look. Her face turned red.

"That's what I thought. He called, didn't he?"

"Yes, but…"

A COWBOY FALLS

"I'm gonna excuse myself for a few minutes. You listen to those messages, and when I come back, you're gonna tell me what he said."

Ben didn't understand why Liv hadn't answered his texts or returned his calls. Maybe she hadn't charged her phone. Her flight landed a couple of hours ago. He figured she'd be home by now, although he had no idea how far it was from the airport to where she lived. Monument was somewhere between Denver and Colorado Springs, and if she had a ranch, it probably wouldn't be close to the highway.

He wished she would answer him. As it was, he couldn't think about anything else. He was beginning to think she was avoiding him, and this was uncharted territory for him—having a woman so far under his skin.

The door of his house flew open, and Luke came running toward him, followed by his brother.

"Daddy's home!" Luke shouted.

Ben lifted him and swung him around a couple of times before setting him down, grabbing Jake, and doing the same thing.

Jake gave his dad an exasperated sigh, but Ben didn't care. You never got too old for your dad to show you he loved you. At least he hadn't. Ben's mom and dad walked in the door behind the boys.

"There he is," his mom gave him a squeeze and a kiss on the cheek. "We missed you around here."

Ben's dad hugged him too. They were a family who had never been shy about affection, and Ben loved it.

"Hey, Dad, how are you?"

"I'm good. How were the bright lights of Las Vegas? Stayed a little longer than you thought. Were you winnin' big?"

"Nah, I never have been a gambler."

His father looked deep into his eyes. His dad wouldn't ask, but Ben answered anyway.

"Nothin' to report, Dad. Life is good."

Ben's father put his hand on his shoulder. "Glad to hear."

They worried whenever he went on the road, and they were right to. However, during the time he spent with Liv, he hadn't thought about drinking at all. Even at the show. Ben wanted her, but he hadn't wanted a drink.

The boys were racing around him, each vying for his attention, telling him what they'd been doing. That morning his dad had taken them fishing, and his mom grilled up what they caught for lunch.

"There's a rodeo in Gunnison, Dad. Can we go? This is the last year Luke can do mutton bustin'."

Luke was Ben's Tasmanian devil, Jake was the more cautious of his boys. The older Luke got, the more trouble he'd get into, the same way Ben had. That worried him more than a little.

"Of course we can go. Are Grandma and Grandpa coming along?"

"You bet."

Ben pulled his cell phone out to check the time and to see if he'd missed a call from Liv. He hadn't. "It's two-thirty. What time do we have to be there?"

"Check-in's at five o'clock," Jake answered. "Can we play video games until it's time to go?"

Ben laughed. "You can play video games for an hour, then you can play outside until it's time to go."

"Thanks, Daddy," said Luke, climbing up Ben's leg to give him a kiss. Ben picked him up and hugged him close. "I missed you, buddy."

"Me, too. Put me down now, Daddy. Jake's gonna pick out a game I don't want to play if you don't put me down."

"Okay, there you go, partner." He set Luke on his feet and turned back to his parents, who were studying him.

"What?" Ben looked behind him as if to ask what they were looking at.

"Good to see you, Ben," his mom said, kissing his cheek for the second time.

"What's goin' on? I was away for a couple of days. You're both acting as though I was away for a month."

"When you changed your flight plan, I have to admit, it made your mom and me worry."

"It's not what you think."

"What is it, then?"

"I met someone."

7

One of the new texts on her phone was from Ben. The others were from Paige and Renie. Paige wanted to make sure Liv was still speaking to her. Renie wanted to know how she enjoyed Las Vegas. Where to begin? How much should she tell her daughter?

Ben's said, *Are you okay? Answer me, Liv. Please.* His voicemails said much the same. But hearing it, rather than reading it, made it different. There was longing in his voice. He said he couldn't stop thinking about her, couldn't wait to see her again, couldn't wait to have her body next to his. Then he sang a little.

Liv put her elbows on the table and leaned her face into her hands. She didn't know how to respond. Did he want her to pick up and drive to Crested Butte? What did he expect? He wasn't specific.

Dottie shuffled back in and sat down next to her. "So?"

"He said he can't wait to see me again."

"And?"

"That's about it."

"What are you going to do about it?"
"I have no idea."

Liv rode Micah home, brushed him down, and went into her house for the first time in several days. Mark had left the mail on the kitchen counter and watered her plants. When was the last time she ate? She opened the refrigerator, but nothing appealed to her. She thought about opening a bottle of wine, but decided that wouldn't be a good idea, considering she had an empty stomach.

Her cell phone was in her pocket. It hadn't made any new noises, but that didn't mean she'd forgotten about it, nor had she forgotten the unanswered messages it contained. She pulled it out and called Renie.

"Hey, Mom. How was Vegas?"

"Good. Relaxing. We went to a CB Rice show while we were there."

"And?"

"And what?" What the heck? Had she been talking to Paige?

"Did he see you?"

Yep, he saw her. All of her.

"Mom, are you there?"

"I'm here. We, um, spent time together."

"What? You and Ben?"

"Me and Ben. We went out on a couple of, um, dates."

"Did you sleep with him?"

"Renie! That is not an appropriate question to ask me!"

"Why not, Mom? Jeez. I'm not a kid anymore."

"It's complicated."

"So you did. Good."

"Renie, honey, so you realize this up front, I am not as interested in discussing your sex life as you seem to be in mine. Just because we're having this conversation doesn't mean I'm opening the door to details. On either side."

Renie laughed. "Got it, Mom. I'm glad you had fun. When are you seeing him again?"

That was the million-dollar question, wasn't it?

They were halfway to Gunnison when Ben's cell phone rang.

"Hey."

"Hi, Ben. It's Liv. I'm sorry it took me so long to get back to you."

"It's okay. Well, it's not okay. Are you home?"

"I am. I didn't even go in the house when I got here. I went straight out to the barn and went for a ride."

"The barn? A ride? Do you have a horse?" She hadn't told him she had a horse. Had he asked her anything about herself? They'd talked about her daughter, but other than that, he knew nothing about her. Wait, her dad had been a pilot in the military. Had she said Air Force?

"I have two. One belongs to Renie, but since she's away at college, I have two. Micah's mine. He's not very old, so he needs a lot of exercise. Micah likes to get out and run. I also board horses."

"Speaking of horses, I'm on my way to a rodeo in Gunnison."

"Oh, I should let you go. Take care, Ben."

"Hold on, hold on, don't go hanging up yet. I told you so you realized we had something else in common. You seemed worried about it at the airport."

Ben was suddenly aware that the four people with him were listening to every word he said.

"Hey, it might be better if I call you back, since I'm driving. When I do, will you answer?"

Liv was quiet, so quiet he thought the call had dropped. "Liv, are you there?"

"I'm here." She went quiet again. "Um, it might be best if you didn't. I have a lot to get caught up on with the ranch, and I'm tired. It'll be an early night for me and a busy few days."

Ranch? She had a ranch? He was such an asshole. No wonder she didn't want to talk to him; he hadn't bothered to find out anything about her. He'd been too busy getting into her panties.

"Give me half an hour."

"Ben..."

"Half an hour, Liv, and I'll call you back."

He parked the truck after letting his parents and boys off at the main entrance. "Go check in and I'll meet you." He was so anxious to return Liv's call, he wanted them out of the truck—a fact not lost on his mom and dad.

The phone rang three times before she answered. Ben was almost beside himself by the time she did.

"It is so good to hear your voice, Liv."

"Yours, too."

"I'm sorry I couldn't talk earlier. My parents and the boys were in the truck. Every word I said was the most interesting thing they'd ever heard," he chuckled.

"It's okay. I bet they missed you."

"They did. But, Liv, I miss *you*."

"I'm not sure what to say. I had a nice time, but now we're back to our own lives. We shouldn't get into the habit of talking to each other."

"What do you mean? Why shouldn't we get into the habit of talking to each other?" Getting angry would push her away, but he couldn't help it. She pissed him off. "I'm sorry I raised my voice, Liv, but, Jesus. Are you serious?"

She didn't respond.

"Liv, come on. Don't do this."

"I'm not doing anything. We had fun."

"But now it's over?"

"How could something that didn't start be over? It's not over. It's…I don't know what. It just isn't."

"It isn't? It's not anything to you? It's something to me."

"Ben, go be with your kids. Enjoy your night at the rodeo. Enjoy your life."

Regardless of what he said next, she'd say goodbye. And then, if he called again, would she even pick up?

"I can't let go of this, Liv. You think you want me to, but I can't. More than that, I won't. So, I may hang up now, but I'll call you again, and if you don't answer, I'll keep calling until you do."

"Why, Ben?"

"Because this matters, and I plan to show you how much."

He said goodbye and hung up. If he hadn't, he might have resorted to begging to come see her. Ben's boys were with him until Monday morning. He'd give her a couple of days and call her again, if he was able to last that long. For the first time in several days, he wanted a drink.

Liv locked the back door and went into the bedroom. It was too early to sleep. If she did, she'd be wide awake at three a.m. But there wasn't anything she wanted to do. She turned on the television, but nothing interested her. She picked up her tablet to read. She wasn't interested in reading either. She swiped the music icon with her finger, and Ben's voice sang to her.

You've had a rough day,
Why don't I turn out the light.
Let down your hair,
It's gonna be all right.
If you need me to dry your tears,
Baby, I'll be right here.
Goodnight, blue eyes,
May your dreams come true.
Goodnight, blue eyes,
I love you.

Oh, God, what had she done? Why did she have sex with him? Why had she let herself get involved with him? Her ache of loneliness had been manageable—

she'd gotten to the point where she hardly noticed it. Now it was all she noticed.

She'd been alone all these years by choice, because she couldn't let herself risk falling in love again. When she loved people, they left her.

Ben might say he wanted to see her again, but he didn't realize that it would matter more to her than it would to him when he would turn out to be just another person who left her behind.

Instead of a CB Rice song, country music was playing when Paige walked into the barn Monday morning.

"Hell-o, Liv, are you in here?"

She came out of the stall at the end of the barn. "Hey, Paige, how are you? I'd hug you but…"

"Not necessary. What in the world are you doing? You're filthy."

"Cleaning the stall. A new horse is coming in at the end of the week. Might as well get ready now."

"You didn't call me back this weekend."

"I'm sorry."

"Are we okay?"

"We're fine." Liv walked closer to Paige and sat down on one of the barn stools. "I needed time to myself."

"You have too much time to yourself. That's the problem."

Liv glared at Paige.

"I'm not intimidated by you. Other people are, but I'm not. I have things to say, and you need to listen."

"When have I ever *not* listened to you? Jeez, Paige, you're one of the few people I do listen to."

"Have you talked to Ben?"

"We talked on Friday."

"Did you make plans?"

"Paige, we just got home! It hasn't been a week. No, we didn't make plans."

"Did he say he'd call again?"

"No. I mean, I thought he'd call again over the weekend. But he didn't. You know how the saying goes, 'be careful what you wish for.'"

"And what did you wish for?"

"To never see him again."

Paige sat down on one of the other stools. "Oh, honey. Why not?"

When Liv's eyes filled with tears, Paige walked over to hug her.

"I'm a mess. You don't want to hug me."

"I'm sure you have something I can change into when I decide I no longer want to smell like a horse. Come here."

"This is stupid. I expected it. I shouldn't be upset. What would a man like him want with a woman like me?"

"Isn't it a little early in the game to call it?"

Liv pulled away, and Paige sat back down on her stool.

"I pushed him away hard, Paige."

"Has that worked before?"

"Before? What before? We don't have a before."

"You tried to push him away in Vegas, and from what I remember, it didn't work."

"That was different."

"All I'm saying is give it a few days."

"And then what? What will be different? I'm still somebody he slept with while he was 'on tour,' or whatever he calls it. I'm sure he's forgotten my name by now."

Ben picked up the phone to call Liv at least a hundred times over the weekend, and each time he set it back down. He missed her so much his chest ached. He'd never missed anyone this much, besides his boys when they weren't with him. When he dropped them off at their mom's this morning, the ache multiplied.

He hated that he was divorced and that his boys didn't have the same family life he had. Ben and his brothers had been given the gift of a home in which his parents loved each other, and them, more than anything. There had never been a doubt in his mind that his parents would love each other and be together until the day one of them died. He failed in creating that for his boys.

Ben supposed he'd loved Christine at one point. If it had been up to him, they'd still be married. They'd be miserable, but they'd still be married. He was thankful she still lived in Crested Butte, that way the boys didn't get shuffled back and forth too much.

Christine had remarried not long after their divorce was final. He seemed like a nice guy, and always treated his boys well. Joe wasn't from Colorado, they'd met skiing, and soon after, he moved to Crested Butte.

She was good about making sure the boys spent time with him when he was in town. When they were married, he played clubs every weekend of the month. Now that they were divorced, he steered away from booking gigs on weekends. He wanted to spend as much time at home with his boys as he could. It had been a tough balance to maintain.

The boys were leaving town today and wouldn't be back for a week. Christine and Joe were taking them to the Grand Canyon for spring break. The trip had been planned for six months. He didn't want them to go. He'd be lonely without them, but the trip was for them, not him.

Ben had seven days with nowhere he needed to be and nothing he needed to do, and all he could think about was Liv. He liked her, a lot. He wanted to get to know her, spend time with her. The fact that she didn't seem to want to see him made the urge to win her over even stronger.

An hour later he was on the road. He wasn't sure where she lived, but he'd find out. If she didn't want to see him—well, he wouldn't accept that. He had no intention of giving up that easily. It was crazy, but he was doing it anyway.

Liv swung the gate open and led Micah into the pasture. They'd had a good ride, much more fun than her ride on Pooh had been. Pooh was getting older, and Liv didn't ride her enough. She planned to give one of the neighbors a call this afternoon to ask if her grandkids would consider riding the horse for her. She'd even pay them. That way, Pooh would get the exercise she needed, with the kind of rider she was used to, someone more like Renie.

Two more months and Renie would be home for the summer, and Liv couldn't wait. She'd planned to talk to her about an extended vacation, but they'd missed each other's calls.

Liv removed Micah's saddle and other tack. She'd let him relax in the pasture for a while and brush him later. She opened the gate, walked around the corner, and slammed the saddle into Ben's stomach.

"*Ow!* Shit, that hurt."

"Oh! You scared me. I'm so sorry." Liv dropped the saddle to the ground and was about to make sure Ben was okay when her tummy did a flip. "Wait. What are you doing here?"

Ben grabbed her and crushed his lips to hers. He didn't try to hold back. He wanted her. He'd planned to be sensible, to be civilized, to have a rational conversation with her. But now that she was in his arms he wanted to mark her, possess her, consume her.

Liv's hands fisted in his shirt, pulling him closer. Ben pulled back and looked into her eyes. Her pupils were dilated, and her lips were red and full from his assault. "I couldn't wait. I had to see you."

"I'm glad." She took his hand, leading him away from the barn and pasture.

"What about…" He pointed to the saddle, and then to the horse in the pasture.

"They'll be fine."

She led him in through the back door and into the kitchen. "Can I get you anything?"

"No, thanks. Come here." Ben wound his arm around her waist and pulled her closer to him.

"I couldn't stay away."

"I see that."

"You said you were glad I didn't wait."

Liv nodded, and he kissed her forehead.

"You're giving me mixed messages, sweetheart."

She pulled away from him and rested against the kitchen counter. "I don't know how to do this, Ben. I mean, I haven't."

"I haven't either, Liv."

She raised her eyebrows, and he smiled.

"Not like this. I've never felt this way before. As hard as that might be to believe, I'm telling you the truth."

"I don't know what that means."

"It means I think about you every minute of the day. It means that my arms ache with wanting you to be in them. Like now." He walked over to where she stood and put his arms around her.

"Ben, I—"

"Shh." He covered her mouth with his and kissed her hard. He didn't want to talk; he wanted her skin on his. Now that she was in front of him, he wanted to devour this woman that had been on his mind every waking hour and, when he slept, in his dreams.

His fingers trailed down the side of her neck, over her collarbone. As he unfastened the top buttons on her shirt, the backs of his fingers brushed the curve of her breast.

Without words, Liv took his hand and led him into the bedroom. His eyes took in the openness of her house as they walked through it. Big windows looked out at the prairie, and a massive two-sided stone fireplace separated the bedroom from the master bath. He put his arm around the back of her knees and back, lifting her, and setting her down on the fluffy, cream-colored, king-sized duvet. The bed looked enormous with Liv alone on it. He'd take care of that as quickly as he could.

He toed off his boots and lay next to her. She unfastened her buttons, finishing what he had started. He pushed the open shirt over her shoulders and drew back to look into her eyes.

"So beautiful." He kissed her mouth reverently.

Liv stared into his big, blue eyes, his long, thick eyelashes. She ran her hand over the stubble of darkness on his strong chin. When Ben smiled, the corners of his eyes crinkled. His laugh lines were deep because he smiled often. Her body tingled all the way from where his lips met hers to her toes. Ben's powerful leg stretched over the top of hers, pressing his hardness into her hip, and she reached for him.

His kisses grew stronger, making every nerve ending in her body hum. Heat rushed through her veins.

"Ben," she breathed.

They broke apart, each removing their own clothes. He wove his fingers through her hair and kissed his way over her lips, to her chin, then throat, and then to her breasts. His breath was warm on her stomach as he continued working his way down her body.

Sensation sizzled across her skin from the inferno building inside. She whimpered, and in a flash he was inside her. Once again she had no idea when he'd donned a condom.

"Don't move," he whispered. "Be still. Let me feel you."

She ached to move against him, but she willed her muscles to still, and let Ben lead her where he wanted her to go. She arched to him, and he moved faster and harder into her. Pleasure began to flow from her center out to her fingertips and toes, until the tension coiled inside her. He took her higher and higher until she burst and cried out.

"That's it," Ben groaned as he came apart with her.

They stayed that way, slumped together in the softness of the duvet. Her head spun as his lips began to work their way back up the side of her neck. They continued beneath her ear, across her chin, and up to brush over her lips.

"Liv," he breathed, as though it was a prayer. He kissed each of her eyelids, then back to her mouth, where he kissed each corner.

"How did you find my house?" She asked later.

"It's a secret."

"Paige?"

"As long as you won't be mad, yes, Paige."

"How long can you stay?"

"All week. Or as long as you'll have me."

"We'll see how it goes," she said as she stretched out on top of him, skin on skin, body on body.

"As much as I don't want to move, I need to take care of Micah. Can I interest you in a ride later? Around sunset?"

"Sounds like heaven." As long as he was with her, anything she wanted to do sounded like heaven. He wanted her, and he intended to have her. He was into this deeper than she was, but by the end of the week, he'd change that.

8

When they rode over the crest, they could see Dottie and Bill by the campfire. Bill stood up and waved.

"You don't mind, do you? They're family to me."

"Don't mind at all. If they mean something to you, there isn't anybody I'd rather meet."

It took them ten minutes to make their way down the rocky terrain. It was almost dark, so if they stayed any length of time, it would be better to leave the horses in the Pattersons' barn overnight and ask Bill to give them a ride back to her house.

They tied the horses off and walked over to the fire where Bill had chairs set up for them and a bottle of wine open.

"Bill and Dottie, I'd like you to meet Ben Rice."

"Pleasure to meet you." Ben reached out and shook Bill's hand. Dottie stood, and when Ben reached to shake her hand, she pulled him into a hug.

"I don't shake hands, Mr. Rice. Men will judge you by your handshake. I like to see what you young fellas have in the way of a good, strong hug. Tells you a lot about a man."

"Nobody hugs the way Dottie does," Liv sighed.

"You don't do too bad yourself, sugar." Ben kissed her forehead.

"I like him already," Dottie proclaimed.

"Glass of wine, Liv?"

"Sure, I'd love a glass."

"Dottie had me run in the house to get it when we saw you comin'. Livvie, here, loves Zinfandel. We keep it on hand for her. Before she taught us about wine we thought Zinfandel was the pink stuff. I thought she'd have a fit the first time we tried to serve it to her."

Liv turned pink. "That's me, always gracious."

"We love you anyway, darlin' girl." Bill pulled her near him. "When Livvie lost her parents so close together, Dottie and I adopted her. She's one of our own. Keep that in mind, young man."

She'd lost her parents? Another thing he hadn't known about her. He should start making a list of questions, so he didn't feel like such a jerk when someone else pointed out something he should already know.

"How about you, Ben, can I get you a glass?"

"No, thank you. Don't touch the stuff."

"Can I get you a beer?"

"No, sorry. I'm not a drinker. If you've got a coke or a bottle of water, I'll be fine."

He turned toward Liv. There was a flash of confusion on her face she quickly masked away. This was something he hadn't told her. Not that she'd asked. It hadn't seemed as though it was a big deal when they were in Las Vegas. She had a drink now and then, and it hadn't been necessary to point out he abstained.

"Have a seat, you two. Get comfortable."

An hour into their campfire and several rounds of s'mores later, Bill asked Ben to help him with the horses. "They're better off staying in our barn tonight, Livvie."

She smiled and nodded in response.

Ben put his arm around her shoulders and kissed her again. "Be right back, *Livvie*."

"Dottie and Bill are the only people who call me Livvie. And Billy, their son."

"I like it."

"I'd be lost without them," she sighed.

Ben nodded. "They're good people."

"The best," Liv murmured, sounding as though she was talking to herself more than him.

"How'd you and Livvie meet?" Bill asked Ben while they settled the horses.

"Fate kept throwing us together, and we started paying attention." Ben told Bill about meeting her at Red Rocks and again at his family's bar in Crested

Butte. He told him about bumping into her at the pool in Las Vegas, but that's as far as he took the story.

"You come back with her from Las Vegas, then?"

"Nope. I went home first and spent a couple days with my boys, then drove over this afternoon. I surprised her."

"Boys?"

"I have two. Jake is twelve and Luke is nine. Their mom and I have been divorced for a few years."

"I guess I'm transparent when it comes to my kids, and I consider Livvie one of 'em. She's not an easy one to get a fix on. Plenty boys 'round here would tell you that. My own son had a mad crush on her for years. He gave up, not for lack of trying." Bill chuckled. "Either she's real good at playing like she doesn't notice somethin', or she was clueless all them years."

He thought for a minute before he continued. "But don't go thinkin' she's not smart as a whip. She's one of the brightest women I've ever had the pleasure to know. Sad that she lost her husband so young. Renie wasn't even born yet."

Ben wanted to ask more, but how did he tell Bill that he was staying at Liv's house but didn't know about her husband, her parents, or even where she grew up?

"Did Livvie tell you Scott was shot down in the war? They'd only been married a few months. Tragic. I gotta tell you, for a long while I thought that man held her heart for good. We figured that was why she didn't pay any attention to men trying to catch her eye. Guess we were wrong."

Ben shook his head. Tonight, tomorrow, and every day after that, he planned to get to know her. As much as she would let him.

"You're awful quiet."

"She's a remarkable woman. One I want to spend as much time with as I can. I appreciate all you've told me, Bill."

"You care about her?"

"I do."

"Then you'll be all right with Dottie and me."

They walked back to the campfire, where Dottie and Liv were snuggled up under a blanket. Liv's head rested on Dottie's shoulder.

Ben stroked her cheek with his finger. "Tired?"

"Content." Liv stood and put her arms around his waist. "Ready to go back to the house?"

"Yes, ma'am."

Bill handed Ben a set of keys. "You take the old Ford. I'll come get it in the mornin'."

"Thanks, Bill. I'm glad you and Dottie got to meet Ben."

"We are, too. Ben, how long you in town for?" Dottie asked.

"Through the weekend. If she'll have me."

"Well, if she lets you stay, I expect the two of you for dinner on Friday night. You can take her out on Saturday for date night."

"I'll do that." Ben smiled and took Liv's hand in his.

"Can you drive a stick shift?" she asked as they walked up to the driveway.

"You're kidding, right?"

"Does that mean yes?"

"That means *of course*. I have to get you back to Crested Butte. You don't have any idea how much of a good ol' boy you've gotten yourself mixed up with."

"I noticed you didn't have any trouble finding your seat on a horse."

"Did I pass a test tonight?"

"You did."

"Will there be more?"

"Lots more, cowboy."

The next day, Ben followed Liv around like a mix between a newspaper reporter and a lost puppy. He wanted to know everything about her and didn't want to let her out of his sight.

By dinner, she was exhausted. They ate, cleaned up, and sat in the family room.

"This house is spectacular," Ben said, looking up at the cathedral ceilings and the rafters that looked as though they'd come from an old barn. "Did your father build it?"

"No more questions, Ben." She pushed him against the arm of the couch and put her hands on either side of his head.

"You're trying to distract me," Ben said as he pulled her in and kissed her deeply.

"Are you writing a book, Ben? Is this a 'This is Your Life' interview?"

"I want to know everything about you." He pushed the bottom of her shirt up and put his hand on her breast. "I want to memorize every curve of your body and every nuance of your soul, baby."

"Let's focus on the body for the rest of the night, okay?"

"You got it." Ben nuzzled under her ear and breathed in the scent of her. "You smell so good I want to bottle you and keep you with me all the time."

"Ben." That way she said his name made him want to devour her. He kissed her hard while his hands roamed wherever they reached.

Ben reared back from her. "Here or the bedroom, Liv?"

"Bedroom."

He pulled himself up and reached under her back and knees, picking her up as if she was no more than a pillow in his powerful arms. He carried her in and stood her by the bed. He broke their heart-stopping kiss to finish undressing her. When she stood before him naked, he said, "Now, me."

Liv's hands pulled at his shirt, trying to get it off over his head. "Lean down," she breathed.

Her hands were on his belt, pulling it loose, grabbing at the button on his jeans and pulling down the zipper.

He threw his head back. She leaned forward and licked across his throat, down over his sternum.

Ben groaned, "I need you now, Liv."

Her mouth slammed into his, cutting short his demands. His rough hands cupped her bottom and lifted her. Her legs circled his waist.

"Wait," he said, lowering her to the bed. He reached for a condom.

"I wondered how you got them on so quickly. I thought you had a magic trick."

His mouth was hard on hers again, picking her back up, putting his hands on the back of her thighs, helping her circle his waist again. "Shh, no talking, remember?"

With a quick snap of his hips, he was inside her. "Hold on to me," he demanded.

Liv wrapped her arms around his neck. He thrust hard, again and again, holding her firmly against him with both hands. He started humming, the deep vibration of his voice spread through her, and she trembled.

"Fall with me, Liv. Let yourself go." Liv gasped at his words and cried out.

As soon as her head stopped spinning, she opened her eyes, and he was gone. The bed shifted as he lay back down beside her.

"Wow."

"Liv, can I ask you something?"

She rolled to her stomach. "I thought we agreed, no more talking."

"This is different. I don't want anything to come between us. I don't want to use a condom when we're together."

Liv hesitated. "I'm not on birth control, Ben."

He put his arm across her back and kissed her shoulder. "Do you want to be?"

"By the time I do…"

"Finish the sentence, Liv."

"We might not…you know."

"What? Be together?"

Liv nodded.

Ben rolled to his back and looked up at the ceiling, taking a deep breath, gathering his thoughts before he spoke. "Have I given you the impression I wasn't in this all the way?"

"No, I guess not."

"Then why are you so hell-bent on ending this thing between us?"

Liv had to answer him. He would keep at her until she did. "I'm very independent, Ben."

He pulled her until she was stretched out on top of him, her head resting on his chest. "I'm not letting go of this, Liv. I haven't felt this way for a very long time. I'm not sure I've ever felt this way. I want to be with you every chance I get. Can you, please, accept that and quit fighting me on it?"

"I can try."

"That's all I can ask, but, Liv?"

"Yeah?"

"I want you to try a whole heck of a lot harder, okay? I want you to let go, let yourself fall for me."

"I'll try," she said again.

"Repeat after me, 'Ben, I will let myself fall for you.'"

Silence. "Come on, Liv, do it. Repeat after me."

"Ben, I will let myself fall for you."

"There, that wasn't so hard. Now keep repeating it in that beautiful head of yours."

"I'll try, Ben. I promise, I will."

He waited until her breathing evened. She fell asleep splayed on top of him, and his heart surged with joy. No more sleeping alone, that's what he was after with her. He sensed the road to it wouldn't be an easy one, but she was worth whatever it took to get them there.

He closed his eyes and let himself drift to sleep.

Ben wanted to make time stand still, but the week sped by too quickly. Wednesday night they had dinner in town with Paige and Mark, and then went back to their house. Ben had an acoustic guitar with him, and he and Mark went off to jam for a while.

"Was he on his way when we were in the barn Monday morning?"

"No, he called after I left your place. I wouldn't have lied to you about it. He wanted to surprise you, so you wouldn't tell him not to come and so he got an honest reaction out of you when you did see him." Paige poured Liv another glass of wine.

"He doesn't drink."

"I noticed that when we were in Las Vegas."

"I didn't."

"You were too busy paying attention to what the rest of his body was doing."

Liv blushed. "Don't get me wrong; it doesn't bother me, but he hasn't talked about it. He doesn't talk much about himself. He asks me plenty of questions, though."

"He wants to get to know you better."

"It's as though he wants to know everything right this minute. Why is he in such a hurry? It's not natural…he's forcing it."

"Have you told him that's the way you feel?"

Liv shook her head. "And that's the other thing. I'm not used to having to tell somebody how I feel all the time. I'm used to being alone, Paige. All this togetherness…"

"How long is he staying?"

"Through the weekend, he says. His boys are on vacation with their mom and stepdad."

"That's a lot of together time for you, isn't it?"

Liv didn't answer. She was enjoying the togetherness. Even after just a couple of days, she liked waking up with him, spending the day together, being a couple.

"What's he say?"

"About being together? That he wants us to do it as much as we can. I don't know how that looks, or how it feels, or what his expectations are."

"You should try asking a few questions of your own."

Liv woke up before Ben the next morning, put a pot of coffee on, and went out to the barn to feed the horses. Yesterday he had helped her; today she wanted time alone with her routine.

She stroked Micah's nose as she led him out of the stall. "Let's get you outside this morning. We'll take a ride a little later." She threw the lead up and over Micah's withers. "What do you think of him? Seems okay, right? And when he leaves, you'll still be here for me, won't ya, boy?"

Ben stood outside the barn door, listening to Liv confide in her horse. It sounded more as though she expected him to leave permanently, not just leave at the end of the week. He wasn't sure how to convince her he wanted more. Only time would show her that. Only a week ago, they were in Las Vegas and he was trying to convince her he wanted to see her again.

He was impatient when it came to her. The more she resisted, the harder he pushed. He didn't understand it himself, how could he explain it to her?

He came around the corner and cleared his throat. "Mornin'," he said as he wrapped his arms around her waist and kissed her cheek. "I was lonely when I woke up and you were gone."

"You used to having a woman next to you every morning when you wake up, Ben?"

Ouch. He hadn't expected that from her. "No, can't say as I am. I can say, though, that these last couple of mornings, I liked waking up next to you. Not any woman, Liv. You."

Liv pulled away, leading Micah toward the panel door at the back of the barn. "Be back in a minute."

Ben guessed that meant she didn't want him to follow. He walked in the opposite direction, and got his guitar out of the back of his truck. After he went back inside, he walked through the kitchen, and out the door to the deck that wrapped all the way around the southern side of her house.

The view was spectacular. In one direction were the big trees that made up the Black Forest, in the other direction, prairie. On a clear day, Ben would bet you could see all the way to Kansas, and most days in Colorado were clear.

He sat down and strummed his guitar. This is what he wanted to do when he was alone. Liv was probably used to quiet mornings taking care of her horses. He'd give her space; he understood her need for it.

Besides her daughter, Liv hadn't lived with anyone else since her mother died. Ben hadn't found out how long ago that had been yet, but decided that, today, he'd stop asking her questions and start telling her more about himself. For now, he'd play his guitar. There was a song inside him, itching to get out.

A while later, maybe as long as an hour, he heard her moving around in the kitchen. As tempted as he was to go in and wrap himself around her, he stayed put. He'd let her come to him when she was ready. His yellow pad was full of lyrics and notes. The song he was working on was coming together.

"Whatcha' doin'?" Liv sat down on the arm of the Adirondack chair next to him.

"There's my girl." Ben put his hand around the back of her neck and pulled her closer. His lips covered hers. What he intended to be a chaste and simple kiss turned into something much hotter.

He pulled back. "I'm sorry. I do that a lot, don't I?"

"Do what? Kiss me? Don't be sorry, I like it."

"I'm an affectionate guy. My mom and dad were. Still are. They never held back showin' each other how much they cared. They never held back with me or my brothers either. Not everybody is used to that, I guess."

"It's okay. I like it," she said again.

"But you're not used to it."

"Ben, I've been alone a long time. I've been alone a lot more than I've been with somebody. My husband died before I had a chance to learn how to live with someone that way. My mom and dad loved each other, and me, but you're right; they weren't as openly affectionate as even Dottie and Bill are."

"I like being here with you, Liv."

"I like having you here. I'm sorry about earlier."

Ben set his guitar down and patted his leg. "Come here." He pulled her down on his lap and snuggled her into him.

"This isn't a normal way of going about courtin' you, I admit that. I should be callin' you up, askin' you out on a date, givin' you a few days in between to decide whether you like me or not. But it hasn't been that way between us, has it? Here I am, invadin' your space, not givin' you much choice about it."

Liv didn't answer. She ran her finger up and down the back of his hand, lost in thought.

"Do you want me to leave?" He hated to ask. He was so afraid she'd say she did. He got here on Monday and dug his heels in, telling her he was staying rather than waiting for her to ask him to stay. He held his breath, waiting for her to answer.

"No, I want you to stay."

He let the breath out, so relieved he started to laugh. "God—what you do to me, girl."

"I don't know how to do this. I've never done anything like this. I've never had a man come and stay with me. Ben—wow, this is harder to say than I thought it would be. I should tell you…" She looked as though she wanted to jump up, run into the house, and lock the door.

"I haven't been with another man since Renie's father, and that was a long, long time ago."

Ben tightened his arm around her shoulder, keeping her close to him. Her muscles strained, but he wouldn't let her go. How did he say this? "I know."

"You do?" She tried to pull away from him again, and he held her tighter.

"It wasn't anything you did, or didn't do. Don't go getting all insecure on me. It was a feeling. I can't explain it."

"It's the re-virgin thing."

"The what?" When she smiled, he knew he hadn't hurt her.

"I told Paige it had been so long since I had sex I was a re-virgin."

He leaned his head back and laughed. He felt her muscles relax as she rested against him.

"Hungry?" she asked.

"Starving. Guess what I want to do?"

"What?"

"I want to cook in that *fantaspacular* kitchen you've got in there. I've been *jonesin'* for it since I saw it."

"You're on, cowboy. I'm going to give Paige a call and invite her to join us...if that's okay with you. Paige usually has breakfast with me a couple times a week. She's staying away on purpose."

"Please, Liv, it's your house; you don't need to check with me before you invite somebody to breakfast. Does Mark usually come along?"

"Sometimes. Would you like me to invite him?"

"Yeah, I would." Ben started to chuckle. "Mark's one of the funniest guys I've ever met. I had a good time last night at their place."

"Most people say that. And you're right. Most of the time I'm with them, I laugh so hard my stomach aches by the end of the night." Liv hugged him.

"What's that for? Although, you never need a reason to wrap yourself around me."

"You like my friends."

"Baby, I like a lot more than your friends."

9

"We should go out and do something today since it's going to be warm and sunny. Away from the ranch, I mean," Liv said as Ben and Mark were clearing the dishes. "I have a new horse coming in tomorrow to board. I should be here most of the day, to make sure he's settled."

"Tomorrow night we're having dinner with Bill and Dottie. Is that still on?"

"Yep, Dottie left a message on my cell, asking us to be there at six."

"Whatever you want to do is fine with me, baby."

Paige got up from the table and motioned for Liv to follow. They walked out on the deck, and Paige closed the door behind her.

"What's up, Paige?"

"I had to get out of there before I opened my big mouth and stuck my foot in it."

"Why? What's wrong?"

"Nothing's wrong. You're such a...couple."

Liv swatted at her. "Oh, stop it. We are not."

"You are. Making plans, figuring out your day. 'Whatever you want to do is fine with me, baby,'" Paige mimicked him.

"He's being polite. Stop it." Liv got up to go back inside.

"Wait. It's nice to see you this way."

"It's nice to feel this way." Liv turned and faced Paige. "I won't like it when he leaves."

"You'll cross that bridge when you get to it. Enjoy your time with him, and then make plans for the next time you'll be together."

"But what if—"

"Really? You're going to go there?"

"No, I guess I better not."

Since it was unseasonably warm and dry for late March, Ben and Mark made plans to take Mark's four-wheel drive up one of the mountain roads. They were like two little boys when they talked about it.

"What do you say? Liv? Paige?" Mark asked.

"Liv will be in; I will not," answered Paige. "I have too much to do anyway. Go enjoy yourselves."

"Liv, you're sure you want to go?" Ben asked.

"Liv loves to ride in Mark's Jeep and get all dirty, don't ya?" Paige answered for her.

"Nothing I like more than getting dirty," she smirked.

After a late lunch, they decided to take a different fireroad back home. Before they got on the road again, Mark popped a CD into the player. A CB Rice CD.

"One of my favorite people gave me this CD," Mark told Ben. "I like it, but she *lurves* it, so I'm humoring her."

Mark turned toward her. "Been on any of their social media sites lately?"

"I could throttle you," Liv muttered.

Ben didn't know what to say. It was cute that she followed him on social media. It wasn't a surprise; he'd seen her name and her picture. He didn't want to freak her out by contacting her, but he'd thought about it. That was after he met her again in Crested Butte, but before Vegas.

"W-e-e-l-l, I guess I said the wrong thing." Mark joked.

"Have you, Liv?" Ben figured the best way to make her more comfortable was to talk about it.

"I haven't." She hadn't even thought about it. Why would she? He was *with* her. Ben rubbed her shoulder, but Liv remained silent the rest of the ride home.

"It's nothing to be embarrassed about," Ben said after Mark dropped them off at her house.

"You must think I'm a stalker."

"Why? Were you?" Ben tickled her. "Were you stalkin' me, baby? Did you run into me with your inner tube on purpose, just to get me into bed?"

She rolled her eyes and scooted away. "No, I didn't. But, we did plan to go to your show."

"What show? The fundraiser?"

"Yeah. Paige and I were planning to go. I mean, before she talked me into going to Vegas with her, we talked about getting tickets."

"Nothin' wrong with that, is there?"

"I did check out your social media pages, too."

"That's how I knew you were there," Ben admitted.

"Where?"

"At the pool that day. I saw you in one of the photos."

"What are you talking about?"

"I took a few photos that day at the pool. First I sent them to Jake. Then I posted a couple on our site. As I went through them, trying to decide which ones to use, I saw you. When you ran into me, I was trying to find you."

"You were? You're not saying that to make me feel like less of a dork?"

"Who's the stalker now, baby? Sounds as though I am."

She loved him for teasing her. Wait. She *loved* him? *Oh God*, where had that come from? She stopped laughing and turned away. There was no way she would let herself fall in love with him. Nope, wasn't happening.

She'd experienced pain worse than she ever thought possible, once before in her life, and she promised herself then, she'd never let anyone other than her daughter close enough to risk it happening again. Her heart was closed, and it was going to stay that way.

"Whoa, what happened?" Ben tried to get her to turn back to him, but her muscles were rigid.

"Nothing."

"It isn't nothing. Your face went from laughing to full-on thundercloud. What did I say?"

"It's nothing. I'm fine. You didn't say anything." What could she say? No big deal, *I just realized I'm falling in love with you.*

"Come on, Liv, don't do this. We've had a great day. We've had a great week. You've had fun, haven't you?"

"I've had a great time, Ben. Everything is fine. I remembered something I have to do. I'll be right back."

Liv went out the back door and into the barn as fast as her feet would carry her. She checked on the horses, put a few things away, and made sure the stall was ready for the new horse arriving tomorrow. She ran out of things to do and had no choice but to go back and hope Ben let it go.

When she walked back inside, Ben was still in the kitchen, where she'd left him. He obviously hadn't let it go.

"Liv, please, sit. We need to talk."

"Ben, we've done nothing but talk."

"Liv, sit. Please."

She sat.

"This is hard for you. I've invaded your space and followed you around. I won't let you alone for five minutes without wanting to touch you, or kiss you, or get so close to you that we're one, not two. I like being with you. A lot. I like you a lot. When you do that thing you do—what you just did—it makes me crazy. You close yourself off from me and then you bolt."

"It was *nothing*."

"It wasn't. Don't *lie* to me about it. Talk to me." As much as his instincts told him to hide his anger from her, if he did, he'd be doing the same thing that made him angry with her.

"Maybe you should—"

"*Don't*," he shouted. "Don't tell me I should leave." He scrubbed his hand over his face and continued to pace the kitchen.

"That wasn't what I was going to say."

"What, then? What were you going to say?" His voice was still raised.

"I was going to say you should sit down."

Shit. What was wrong with him? He hardly recognized himself. She had him so tied up in knots he was acting like somebody he didn't know. He wanted a drink. *Fuck, no*. Where had that come from? He needed to leave. He stormed out of the back door in the direction of his truck.

"Ben, *wait!*"

Thank God she was following him. What would he have done if she hadn't? He turned back.

She threw her arms around him and crushed herself against him. "I'm sorry. Please don't leave."

"Liv, I'm an alcoholic."

She tightened her hold on him.

"And right then, for one of the first times since I've been with you, including in Vegas, I wanted to take a drink."

"I'm sorry, Ben."

He took her hands from around his waist and moved away from her. There were tears in her eyes.

"It happens; it's not you. I think about drinking. But when I'm with you, I don't. That's why it freaked me out. All week, even when Bill asked if I wanted a beer, or when we were at Paige and Mark's and they served wine. Not once did I have this horrible craving."

"I'm so sorry," she said again.

"No, Liv, listen—it's not you. You need to understand that. It's not you, and it has nothing to do with you. No, that's not right. It does, but in the opposite way. I love being with you. There, I said it. *I love being with you.* And this will make you bolt for sure. I think I'm falling in love with you. How's that for putting pressure on you?" He let go of her hands and walked toward his truck.

"Where are you going?" Liv asked.

"I'm not going anywhere. That's the thing. I can't."

"What do you mean?"

"If I got in my truck right now and left, I wouldn't make it as far as the highway before I turned around and came back."

"Then come inside with me." She put her arm around his waist and led him in the direction of the house.

He slung his arm around her shoulders and brought her head closer to him. "I'm sorry, baby."

"Don't be, Ben. I'm glad you talked to me about it."

"After dinner I need to call Renie. She and I have been playing phone tag since Saturday, and I need to talk to her."

"Where does she go to school?"

"Dartmouth."

"Holy crap."

"What?"

"It's a long way away, and damn, it's a hard school to get into."

"You're right. It's both of those. I miss her so much. This is one of her last summer vacations before she graduates. I want to see if she'd like to travel."

Ben did his best not to react, praying the expression on his face didn't change. They'd known each other a little over a week, longer than that, but a week. Her making plans that didn't involve him was the most natural thing in the world. His pang of jealousy was the most unnatural.

"Where are you going?" He hoped his voice sounded interested, not interrogatory.

"I want to take her to Europe, but anywhere she wants to go would be fine with me. All I care about is getting to spend time with her."

That's what I want with you, he wanted to say, but didn't. "Tell you what, why don't you give her a call now, and I'll make dinner."

She smiled. "You wouldn't mind?"

"I told you, I love your kitchen. I might even apply to be your full-time cook."

"How good at it are you?"

"Oh, baby, you wait and see."

Ben liked his kitchen at home, but Liv's was out of a magazine. A large cedar beam, similar to those in the family room, was the focal point of the space. Lighting fixtures hung down from it over the island where there was a seven-burner cooktop. Even more impressive were the bells and whistles hidden away. Electrical outlets and an exhaust panel were hidden within the rough-edged granite, and popped up at the push of a button. He'd seen her do it when they made breakfast.

On the other side of the kitchen, a cutting board was built into the surface of the countertop. A wine storage refrigerator sat next to the double-wide Sub-Zero. Double-stacked convection ovens were in the wall to the left of the old farmhouse-style sink, which was made of stone. And from there, three big windows looked out over the deck and a view of the prairie. Farther on the other side, in the opposite direction of the ovens, was another double-sided stone fireplace, similar to the one in the master bedroom. This faced the family room on the opposite side.

If Ben had been given the chance to redesign his house, he'd design it similar to hers.

He pulled out a chicken and decided to make a twist on *coq au vin*. His mother came up with the recipe that used Balsamic vinegar in place of wine. He found a cold-storage bin, similar to an in-kitchen root cellar where Liv kept potatoes, carrots, and onions.

"Go." Ben gently pushed her out of the kitchen. "It'll be at least an hour before dinner's ready. Talk to Renie as long as you want."

"Hey, Mama. Whatcha' doin'?"
"Well...I have a lot to tell you."
"Yeah, what's up?"
"Ben's here."

She heard her daughter's phone drop, followed by a lot of hooting and hollering.

"You better not be joking," Renie said when she picked up the phone.

"Not joking."

"When? Why? For how long?"

"He got here on Monday—"

"Which is why I haven't been able to reach you. Okay, keep talking."

"He's staying through the weekend."

The phone dropped again, followed by more loud celebratory noises.

"For goodness sake, Renie," she said when her daughter came back. "It isn't that big of a deal."

"No, Mom, it's a huge deal. Do you have any idea how happy this makes me?"

"Nowhere near as happy as it makes me."

"I'll refrain from dancing around my room again until we've finished our phone call, but, Mom, this is great. I'm so happy for you, I really mean that."

"We didn't get married. This may be just…a fling."

"If it's a fling, and it makes you happy, I'm all for it. This is so cool."

"It is. But listen, I called to talk to you about more than that."

"Okay, I'm all ears."

"I was wondering if you want to take a trip with me this summer?"

"Of course I would; I love to travel with you. Where should we go?"

"How about Europe? Two or three weeks in Tuscany, and take side trips from there. Then France for a couple weeks, and end up in England for the same amount of time. Unless you want to try to fit Spain or Germany in too."

"That's a big trip."

"It is, but I figured, once you graduate, we won't have the opportunity to take a trip like this. You'll either start working, or go to graduate school. Either way, you won't be able to take a couple of months off to travel."

"I love it. It sounds wonderful."

"But?"

"What about Ben?"

"What about him? I'm not planning my life around him."

"Why not?"

"Why would I? Renie, stop this. This thing between Ben and me is very new. Your summer break starts in less than two months. If we're going to do this, I need to start planning now. I'll have to hire someone to take care of the horses. I'm sure Bill and Dottie would be happy to recommend someone."

"You've given this a lot of thought."

"I have. It'll be our last big mother-daughter trip for quite a while, sweetie. I want to do it up big."

"I'd love to go with you, Mom. As long as you're sure."

"Of course I am. Oh, Renie, I'm so excited! I can't wait to start planning. I'll email you websites. There's a place I have in mind in Tuscany, which is why I want to go there first."

"This is exciting…we'll have so much fun. And, Mom?"

"Yes, sweet girl?"

"It thrills me that you sound so happy and so excited."

"You make it sound as though it's unusual."

"It is. I don't want to hurt your feelings, and it's not as though you're miserable or anything, but…you're not happy either."

"That hurt a little, but I'll take it in the spirit you meant it. Let's focus on the positive, not the negative."

"That's right. I love you, Mom."

"I love you, too. I'll call you in a few days, and we can talk more about our plans."

Liv danced her way back to the kitchen.

"Good conversation?" Ben asked, opening the oven to stir the stew.

"The best. I worried Renie might say she didn't want to hang out with me this summer, and it would've crushed me. I wouldn't have said so, but I'm relieved to say she's all in."

Then it wouldn't be a good idea to tell her *he* was crushed. "So, tell me what you're planning."

"We'll leave at the end of May, a few days after she gets home." Liv continued to tell Ben what she'd told Renie. "We should be back early to mid-August, plenty of time before she goes back to Dartmouth."

Ben's mind raced. Liv would be gone all summer. He couldn't wrap his head around the idea. "What about the horses?"

"That's not too hard to work out. Bill and Dottie have so many people working their ranch, a few who are part-time. There will be one or two interested in picking up extra cash and who are more than qualified to man my little operation. I may even let them board here themselves if we can work out the arrangements."

"In your house?"

"No, in the barn. Of course, in the house, silly."

"You'd let a stranger come and stay in your house?"

Liv raised an eyebrow.

"This is different."

"You're right," she said. "It's different. I won't be here when the other stranger comes to stay."

She was happy. He wouldn't spoil it, but maybe he should leave earlier than planned. He needed to get his head back on straight and stop trying to figure out what came next for them. He'd even considered asking her to come back with him on Sunday. What an idiot.

"When will dinner be ready, *mon chef*?"

"*En quinze minutes, mon amour.*"

"Wow, I should take you with me. Do you speak Italian too? You'll be my translator as well as my chef."

"Is that all you'd have me for? Not your lover too?"

"*Mais, oui; mon amoureux d'abord.*"

"Your lover *first,* until what? You grow weary of me?"

"I will never grow weary of you, Ben."

She wouldn't? He was relieved to hear it. Liv had him wrapped around her finger so tight, he didn't recognize himself. Never had a woman affected him this way. He controlled the situation, got what he wanted, pulled away when he wanted. He'd never had a woman turn the tables on him, and he didn't like it. Not one bit.

Liv walked over to the wine cooler, pulled out a bottle, and then put it back. She went to the refrigerator and pulled out a bottle of water.

"You can have a glass of wine. Do what you would usually do. If you'd have wine with dinner, have it. I'm very comfortable in my sobriety, Liv."

"Are you sure?"

"I work in my family's bar, and tour with a band. I needed to learn how to live my life being around alcohol. I just can't drink it."

"This is another thing I don't know how to do."

"Do what you'd normally do, Liv, and everything will be fine. If I'm having a problem, I'll say so. Deal?"

"Deal." She walked back to the wine cooler. "What's for dinner?"

"Balsamic chicken."

"Hmm…" She pulled out a bottle of Bordeaux and opened it. "You make it so easy on me. Everything. Are you this way all the time?"

He laughed. "I'm *never* this way. I have an ex-wife who'd be more than happy to confirm it."

"So this won't last?" As soon as she said the words, she wanted to take them back. "That isn't what I meant. It came out wrong."

"I'll see if I can figure out a way you can make it up to me." He put his lips on hers, pulling her against him. "After dinner."

Liv rested her elbows on the table. "You weren't kidding, were you? You would make a great chef. It would be a tragic waste of the rest of your talents, but wow, you can cook. I'm beginning to realize you're extraordinarily good at everything."

"Like this? Am I good at this?" Ben pulled her up from the table and set her on top of the wide, cold, granite island. His hands went straight to the button on her jeans and pulled them off in one swoop. He grabbed the hem of her shirt, pushed it up, and then pulled it over her head. Next, he reached behind her and unfastened her bra. All she had left on were her panties, and they were the next to go. "Lift up," he said as he pulled them from under her bottom, tossing them into the pile of clothes scattered on her kitchen floor.

"I'm ready for dessert," he said as he lowered her until she rested on the granite. He stood in front of her and spread her legs.

"Ben."

"Shh, the no talking rule is back in effect."

He kissed down her stomach, and then moved to the inside of her thighs. First one and then the other. She breathed in deeply, arching her back away from the coldness of the counter, bending into his warmth as he buried his mouth inside her.

"It's such a beautiful night. Should we go for a walk in the moonlight?" She and Ben were sitting in front of the fire in the family room.

"Let's stay right here…and talk." He laughed to himself. When had he become such a big talker?

"What do you want to talk about?"

"I should head home tomorrow."

"Okay."

"Okay. That's it?"

"What do you want me to say?"

"Ask me to stay. Tell me you want me to stay."

"Please, stay. And, Ben, I do want you here with me."

Friday and Saturday were a blur. They had dinner with Dottie and Bill but, otherwise, spent most of the two days getting to know each other better.

Ben stopped asking her questions and started telling her more about him. He told her that, while she was in Europe with Renie, he and the band would be on the road touring the majority of the time. Their new album was ready to release, and the record company had been pushing them to get out and promote it.

He hadn't said anything about when they might see each other again. When he jokingly told her to check the CB Rice website for the tour dates, dread settled in the pit of her stomach.

When she woke up Sunday morning, for the first time since he arrived, Ben wasn't asleep next to her. She got out of bed and went into the bathroom. There was no sign of him; his toiletry kit no longer sat on her counter. She walked back into the bedroom; his clothes and his duffel bag were gone, too.

She pulled on jeans and a sweatshirt, put her hair in a ponytail, put on a pair of socks, and went in search of her boots. There was no sign of him in the living room or the kitchen either.

She put on her boots, and went out the back door, holding her breath, willing his truck to be in her driveway. It wasn't.

She wrapped her arms around her waist, putting one foot in front of the other, making herself walk in the direction of the barn. Halfway there she started to cry. By the time she reached Micah's stall, she let it all out. All the pent-up emotion she'd been holding in the last few days worked its way to the surface, and she cried.

Ben was gone, and he'd left without saying goodbye.

10

She cried so hard she didn't hear the truck pull in the driveway, or the barn door open.

"Liv! What's wrong? Did something happen to Renie?"

"Ben?" She wiped at her tears. "I thought you left."

He held her close and stroked the back of her hair. "I'm right here. Shh now." He leaned back and kissed each of her eyelids. "I wouldn't just leave."

She hiccupped. "But your stuff. I woke up and you were gone, and your stuff was gone, and your truck was gone."

Ben held her tightly, stroking her hair, telling her again and again everything was okay. He tried to stop himself from...smiling. What kind of asshole did it make him that he wanted to smile? And not a little smile; he wanted to grin from ear to ear. She thought he'd left, and it wrecked her. And that made him *happy*. God, he was a sadistic bastard.

"Liv, I wouldn't have left without saying goodbye. When I woke up, you were sound asleep, sunshine. Your body took the rest it needed. So instead of waking you up, I came out and fed the horses. When I finished, you still weren't awake, so I put gas in the truck."

"But the last couple of days…"

"What? I haven't pushed as much? Haven't made you as crazy hanging on you, asking you to promise me your heart, and begging you to let me stay forever?"

"Are you trying to be funny?"

"Half-funny. Listen, it's been what? A couple of weeks? Yeah, I realize I've been pushin' you real hard, real fast. No matter what I say, you won't believe that I'm not usually this way, 'cause, for whatever reason, with you *I am* this way." He laughed, but then got serious. "I'm not gonna lie to you, Liv. Leaving, today, won't be easy. Every part of me wants to figure out a reason to stay, or beg you to come with me. And before you say anything, I know how crazy that sounds."

Liv's head rested against his chest, but he wanted to see her face. "Look at me, baby. I'm not letting go of this. Not at all. But I am going home to give us both time to breathe, time to figure out what this means. It definitely means something to me. Does it mean something to you, Liv? I want you to be honest with me. If it doesn't, I need to hear it."

"It does. Ben, I was *sobbing* because I thought you left. I feel more than a little foolish," she whispered.

Ben put his hands on each side of her face, turning her to him again. "Don't. Don't be afraid to show me you care."

Liv closed her eyes and listened to his heartbeat. She was stunned by her reaction to thinking he was gone. This had been a whirlwind between them. She'd miss him. A lot. And instead of trying to play it off as if it didn't matter, she should tell him that it did.

"I'd rather have waited to rest after you left."

"I have a little time before I have to get on the road if you want me to wear you out again?"

"I guess you're packed. Would the condoms be hard to find?"

"Not at all, darlin'. I left 'em in the drawer of your nightstand. And I counted 'em; there better be the same number left in there when I get back."

"You're coming back?"

"Soon as I can, baby. Soon as you'll let me."

Ben wanted to go slow. He wanted every inch of her skin against his, to savor being with her. In the days to come, he'd remember this, every moment of it. But he couldn't stop himself, his desire for her was all-consuming. His need to possess her overtook him. "Liv—"

The words wouldn't come. He longed to tell her that he loved her, but he didn't. She'd never believe him. But he did, as he'd never loved before.

"I need you," he said.

"I'm right here," she answered, her eyes burning into his, questioning.

"Come with me. Come home with me." *Give in to me, give yourself over to me,* he wanted to demand.

"Ben—"

He brought his head closer, his lips hovering right above hers, her hair still twisted in his hands.

"Come home with me, Liv," he demanded again. "I need you," he breathed.

He'd never had such an overwhelming need for a woman. He brought his lips to hers again. He broke their kiss, needing to take another moment, again, to look at her. When he closed his eyes he wanted to be able to see her face. He wanted the image seared in his memory.

Her long hair fanned out around her, and she gripped the back of his head, pulling him closer as their lips met again.

"Ben." The way she said his name, every time, was as though she reached in and squeezed his heart.

They'd gotten dressed, and Ben was out on the deck, on his cell phone, the door between them closed. He paced as he spoke, his hand rubbing over the top of his head.

She trusted Ben had handled the horses fine earlier, but she needed something to do with herself. The nervous energy was eating her alive. She longed to saddle Micah and take him out for a long, hard run, but she'd wait until Ben was gone. The thought filled her with an ache.

She went out the back door, walked to the fence where Micah stood, expecting she'd have a treat for him. She reached in her jacket pocket and pulled out a strand of red licorice. She didn't like it herself, red or black, but for her horses, there seemed to be no better treat. He nuzzled up against her, as though he realized she needed his affection.

She heard the back door close, and turned around to see Ben walking toward her. The way he looked at her, with such passion in his eyes, and when he smiled—Lord, help her—her knees went weak. Did all women react to him this way? And was he aware of it?

"Time to go?" She wanted to be the one who said it first.

"Yeah, as much as I don't want to. I'm already getting a late start. If I don't get on the road, I'll want to stay another night." He pulled her hard against him, so hard it almost hurt. But even then, the hurt inside overpowered it.

"Come home with me."

"I'm already home, Ben. This is my home."

"Come for a few days. I'll fly you back when you're ready."

"You said it yourself yesterday, Ben. You're going home to give us both time to breathe, time to figure out what this means." She stroked the side of his face and reached up to brush her lips over his.

He held her so tight she couldn't breathe. When he kissed her again, he took the rest of the air out of her lungs. She was dizzy, but it didn't have anything to do with breathing. It was him.

Liv didn't watch his truck leave the driveway. It might have been nicer of her to turn and wave him off, but she didn't. Instead, she walked in the opposite direction.

She brought Micah into the barn and saddled him. They went east, away from the sunset and rode and rode and rode.

When they got back to the barn, she was ridden out. She got Micah settled and brought the other horses into the barn, swept it out, and walked around. She needed to keep busy. She pulled up a barn stool and read through the week-old newspaper someone had left behind.

She ran out of things to occupy herself. She had to go inside the house, but it was the last place she wanted to be.

Ben pulled up to his house a few minutes before ten. He thought about stopping at his parents' place, but when he drove by, all the lights were off, so he didn't. He considered going back into town and swinging by The Goat, but it would be slow on a Sunday night this late in the ski season. Without a big crowd to distract him, being there would make him think of Liv. Everything did.

He went inside and slung his bag on the floor of the laundry room. He walked into his kitchen and was disappointed, in it and the loneliness of his house.

Tomorrow his boys would be home, and he hoped their antics would be enough to distract him. He was present with them, the same way his father had been with him. His boys were his world, the two most important humans on the planet to him. But now there was another human, a woman, and he thought about her all the time.

His arms felt empty. He longed to hold her. He'd gotten used to being able to hold her whenever he wanted.

He went back into the laundry room and picked up his bag. He took it into his bedroom, threw it on the bed, and sat down next to it. He opened the zipper, pulling out the last thing he had packed. One of her scarves. He'd meant to tell her he took it before he left, but it slipped his mind. He wondered if she'd found his shirt, the one he left hanging on the knob on the back of her closet door. He'd left it for her on purpose.

He brought the scarf up to his nose and inhaled deeply. He loved her smell. He closed his eyes and imagined her with him. Scent was the most powerful of the senses when it came to remembering. He rested his head back on the pillow, holding her scarf close to him, and drifted to sleep.

Liv climbed into bed and slid under the sheets. They smelled of them, him and her together. She nestled into the pillow, breathing in the scent he left there.

She rolled to where her cell phone sat on the nightstand, and for the first time in almost a week, she checked the various social media sites. Nothing. She scrolled through photos he'd posted before, many from months ago. There were several of him playing the guitar. In some, he smiled straight at the camera. Those were her favorite.

She wondered if he made it home yet, or if he was still out on the road. She hadn't heard from him since he left, but she hadn't expected to. And she had no idea when she would again.

11

It had been three weeks since Ben left Liv's house. They had now been apart longer than they'd been together. In his first few days home, he thought about calling or texting her at least once an hour. She answered when he sent her a text, but never sent one on her own, one that wasn't in response to something he'd said. He called; she'd answer, and they'd talk. Sometimes, when he called, he got her voicemail. She'd call him back, but she never called him otherwise.

He kept her scarf tucked under his pillow, and now it smelled more of him than it did of her. He still missed her as much as he had the first day he'd been home.

The first week, Ben kept busy with his boys. His mornings became about making breakfast, dropping them off at school, and coming home to try to get work done in the hours until he picked them up. At night, they worked on homework, ate dinner, and wrestled with bedtimes.

A week later, when it came time to take the boys to their mom's, Ben wanted nothing more than to pack a bag and head over the mountain to Liv's. But he didn't.

He spent the next few days thinking hard about whether his feelings for her were as strong as he believed them to be. Was it because she held herself back from him; did that only make him want her more? Was she a conquest he didn't want to give up on until he won? Or was his need for her just a symptom of his loneliness?

He'd been so lonely after he'd gotten divorced that, often, he sought the comfort of any warm, feminine body. He hated to think that Liv was nothing more than someone to soothe that kind of ache. He didn't think she was; he believed it was more than that. But if she wasn't feeling what he was, how hard could he push? He needed to back off and give himself as much time to think as he was giving her.

In six weeks, he and the band would leave on tour. Next week all hell would break loose when the dates would be announced. He had so much work to do between now and then; even if he wanted to go and see her, he wouldn't be able to.

The band was scheduled to play the Paramount in Denver at the beginning of June, but she'd be in Europe with Renie by then. He couldn't imagine not seeing her before she left, but he didn't know what to do about it.

One of the other guys in the band took over their social media. The record company told them it should be less about Ben and more about CB Rice, so he'd stopped posting anything at all. He wondered if Liv had noticed.

Since Ben left, Liv had been hibernating. She avoided everyone to the point where even Paige stopped dropping by. She still called and texted, but Liv rarely responded with more than a one- or two-word answer.

Mark drove out to see if she needed anything. "Liv, there's no music playing. I've never been here when you are, that there wasn't music playing."

"Silence is my music these days," she answered.

When Liv reached the one-month mark *AB*—"after Ben"—Paige showed up at the barn.

She walked in and took Liv by the shoulders. "Enough! You either go and see him or let him come here, but this has to stop. You're behaving as though you're in mourning, and, Liv—he isn't dead. This isn't you. You need to snap out of it."

"That's where you're wrong; this *is* me. I am a very solitary person, Paige, I have been for years. I don't have any experience with this kind of relationship."

"Listen to me. Go and see him. Call him, right now, and go and see him."

"I...can't..."

"Why in the world not? Nothing is stopping you, other than your own stubbornness. He wants to see you."

Liv got up and walked to the front of the barn.

"Liv, are you listening to me?"

"Have you talked to him?"

"No, I haven't. It's not my place to. But I don't need to; I know you well enough to know exactly what's happening."

"And what is that?"

"You're living in limbo. You're waiting for Renie to come home so the two of you can leave for Europe. In the meantime, you're waking up, and you're sleeping, without much else in between. Remember when we came back from Las Vegas and I told you I thought you kept yourself on the outskirts of life?"

Liv nodded.

"It's gotten *worse*, if that's even possible. Call him, Liv. I'm not leaving until you do. Call him and tell him you want to see him."

"The horses."

"The horses will be fine. Mark will come out and take care of the damn horses. Call him, Liv, right now."

"What if—"

"Don't. No 'what ifs.' Call him."

"Okay. I'll call him."

"Now. I told you, I'm not leaving until you do."

Liv took her cell phone out of her back pocket and called.

Ben jotted lyrics down and absentmindedly hit the talk button when his phone rang.

"Yeah," he answered.

"Ben?"

"Liv?"

"Hi, uh, are you in the middle of something?"

"Yes…no…I mean, I'm sorry I was so abrupt."

"Do you need to get back to it?"

"No, of course I don't. I'm so glad you called. How are you? What's up?"

"I wondered…" Ben heard another voice in the background, but didn't catch what the other person said.

"I was thinking…"

She was killing him. What was she trying to say? "Liv? What is it?"

"I wondered if you'd like some company."

Ben was in shock. "I would like company, very much, as long as you're the company."

"I wouldn't be intruding?"

"Liv, you're welcome here anytime."

"Your boys?"

"They're with their mom this week, but they'd love to meet you."

"You're sure about this?"

"Never more sure of anything. When?"

"I hadn't gotten that far."

He heard the voice in the background again and laughed. "Sounds like Paige is there."

She laughed too. "Your first clue?"

"Today?"

"Tomorrow."

"It's a long drive, Liv, especially by yourself. Say the word, and I'll be there in less than an hour by plane."

"I'm not sure…"

"I wouldn't keep you prisoner here, Liv. I'll fly you back when you want to leave. I promise."

"It isn't that."

"Then what is it?"

Liv walked out of the barn, so Paige couldn't hear her. "I'm scared," she whispered.

"I'm scared too, baby." He wasn't about to let her change her mind though. "Four o'clock. Ask Paige if she can give you a ride to the airport."

"When?"

"Today. And if she can't, I'll rent a car and come down and get you."

"No, not today. Tomorrow."

A COWBOY FALLS

"Liv, I'm flying over this afternoon. If you don't want to leave today, I'll come and help you pack."

After he and Liv hung up, Ben called his mom. "I need to talk to you and Dad."

"Anytime, you know that."

"Okay, I'll be right there."

The Flying R Ranch had been in the Rice family since 1853. They owned over twelve-hundred acres in the East River Valley on the south side of Mount Crested Butte. Ben and his brothers, one older and one younger, grew up on the ranch. It had been, and would remain their home for the rest of their lives.

When Ben's oldest brother, Matt, turned twenty-five, their father gave him a fifty-acre parcel where Matt built his house. When Ben and his younger brother, Will, turned twenty-five, their father gave them each fifty acres. An aerial view would show the boys' houses sat at the farthest points from the center of the ranch. Which was where their parents' house and outbuildings were located.

The parcels were situated in such a way that, when their parents passed away, the operation could be split into three large parcels, four hundred acres each. It was up to the three of them to decide whether they wanted to keep it as one working ranch, or divide it and work each parcel on their own. Ben and his brothers had decided long ago that it would never be divided; they would always run it as a single entity.

It only took Ben a few minutes to drive to his parents' house. He pulled up and joined them on the porch, where they were waiting for him.

"I'm gonna need the plane this afternoon," Ben began.

"Not a problem. Where are you going?" his dad asked.

"Centennial, and then flying back."

"What's this about, Ben?"

"I told you I met someone in Las Vegas. Her name is Liv, and she's the woman I went to see last month. She's coming here."

"What about the boys?"

"I don't have the boys this week, but if she stays through the weekend, they'll be fine with it."

His father raised his eyebrows but didn't say anything.

"Dad, I told the boys about her."

"What did you tell them?"

"When they came back from the Grand Canyon, I told them that I had been on vacation while they were gone. I told them I visited someone very important to me, and I told them about her."

"Think you jumped the gun a bit?"

"It sounds crazy, but I care about this woman. There's something about her…you're gonna think this is crazy, but I love her, Dad. I needed to tell them about her."

Ben turned to his mother, who hadn't said a word. "You're awful quiet."

"Hmm? I'm thinking."

"What about?"

"The apple never falls as far from the tree as we think, does it, Bud?"

"What are you talking about, Mom?"

"Do you want to tell him or should I?" she asked her husband.

"You'll tell it better than I would."

"When we went on our very first date, your father told me we were meant to be together. He said it was fate. It took me a year to believe him, but he was right. He's my soulmate and no other man would've been right for me."

Just like Liv was his soulmate. Ben was sure he had loved Christine, but the feelings he had for Liv were so much stronger. They were meant to be together—he only needed to convince Liv of it.

Ben and his dad were waiting in the small terminal when Paige delivered Liv to the airport in Centennial. When she walked in the double doors, he was struck again by her beauty, and how she seemed so unaware of it. In all the time they'd spent together, Liv never primped or preened. She was comfortable in her own skin, and he found it irresistibly sexy.

Ben walked forward, savoring the sight of her. When she stepped into his arms, her body melded against his, reminding him how well they fit together.

He closed his eyes and held her close, brushing his lips across hers. There was no awkwardness between them. It was as though they were coming home. He longed to kiss her deeply, ravish her, but they'd have plenty of time for that later.

"I missed this," she said.

"Me, too. I've been…empty, not being able to hold you in my arms." Ben's hand came to her cheek, his fingers stroking it. "There's someone I want you to meet."

They walked to where his dad was waiting. "Dad, this is Liv. And Liv, this is my father, Bud Rice."

"It's a pleasure to meet you, Liv," his father said. "My son speaks very highly of you."

Liv's cheeks turned pink as she shook his father's hand. "It's a pleasure to meet you, too."

His heart was full as he watched his father make conversation with her. It struck him then—and he was surprised it hadn't before—Liv reminded him of his mother. Beautiful, gracious, and refined, yet so down-to-earth that she made those around her immediately feel more comfortable. He was in awe of her.

Ben gave Paige a hug hello, whispering thanks in her ear, and introduced her to his father. He doubted Liv would've agreed to this trip without Paige's prompting.

"Shall we get back in the air?" his father asked.

Liv hugged Paige and told her she'd be in touch. They hadn't talked about how long she'd stay with him, and he didn't want to. The last thing he wanted to think about was her leaving and them being apart again.

With clear skies, the fifty-minute flight back to Gunnison went quickly. Liv was no stranger to the area. With plenty of beginner and intermediate slopes, it was their favorite place to ski when Renie was growing up. And then, when she got better, there was enough challenging terrain that they never got bored.

The valley at the base of Mount Crested Butte was surrounded by the most spectacular scenery in the Rocky Mountains. Roads led to remote canyons where groves of Aspens splattered the hillsides. Driving in from Gunnison, the butte rose majestically to the east.

"I love Crested Butte," she murmured as they drove into town.

"My grandfather played an important role in the town's development," answered Ben.

"I have to admit, my daughter filled me in on the Rice family's role in the history of the town." Liv laughed. "She gave me a lecture about not ever reading the magazines left in our hotel rooms." She sighed and grinned. "That was the night I met you for the second time, at The Goat." Her cheeks turned pink again.

"Nice memory?" his father asked.

"An embarrassing one," she laughed.

"What was it that made you run from me?" he whispered.

She smiled, but didn't answer.

They turned onto a remote road before they got all the way into town.

"Where are we going?" Liv asked.

"The Flying R Ranch, darlin'. This is our family's ranch." Ben answered. "We'll stop in at my parents' place and drop my dad off. My mom will want us to stay, but I told them we'd be having dinner at my house tonight."

He watched as she studied the scenery of the ranch, and thought back to one of their first telephone conversations, when she told him she'd gone riding and that she had a ranch. He remembered beating himself up for not asking her about herself, but now he realized that he'd never told her much about where he lived, or that he came from a ranching family.

Looking east from the entrance to the Flying R, the valley of tall grasses opened up to a perfect view of the south side of the butte. The Rices kept cattle on the north side of the river that ran through the center of the valley, and horses to the south.

It was beautiful in the winter, but in the spring, the entire valley bloomed in an artist's palette of color. The deep blue sky, touched with billowing white clouds, looked like a pastel painting, and the land, as far as the eye could see, belonged to the Rice family.

"It's breathtaking."

Ben experienced the same awe he heard in Liv's voice every time he drove these roads.

"Wow," she gasped when they pulled up in front of his parents' house. "It's wonderful."

Ben had to admit the ranch house was idyllic. Built of dark wood, it was as though it had been there forever, part of the surrounding land. The wraparound porch offered views of the valley in three directions and the peak of Mount Crested Butte in the fourth.

Ben's mom came out to greet them.

"Mom, this is Liv."

"It's nice to meet you, ma'am," Liv said as she extended her hand in greeting.

"Please, call me Ginny, and come here, give me a hug, sweet girl. I don't shake hands."

Liv looked at Ben and they both laughed.

"Dottie," Ben said and Liv nodded.

"Who's Dottie?" Ginny asked.

"Someone who reminded me very much of you, Mom" Ben answered.

"She doesn't shake hands either," added Liv.

Ben was antsy. There would be time for his parents to get to know Liv better tomorrow, or the day after that. Right now all he wanted to do was be alone with her. He longed to hold her close, skin on skin, and sink his body into hers.

As it was, he couldn't take his hands off her. He stroked her arm, and then pulled her in closer, kissing the soft skin right along her hairline. She smelled so good, like lavender and something else he couldn't place, but it was Liv.

"These kids would like to be on their way, Ginny," his father interjected, sensing his son's impatience.

"What's your hurry?" Ginny winked at Liv.

Ben stood and held his hand out to Liv, who wrapped her fingers through his. "We'll see you soon, Mom," he winked back.

"It was so nice to meet you both," Liv said, walking over to hug his father.

"And you too. We hope to see more of you during your visit." Ginny hugged her. "We're so happy you're here."

"Where do you live?" Liv asked when they got in the truck.

"Over this hill a little ways." He pointed in the direction of his house.

"On the ranch?"

"Yep. I guess I didn't tell you that, did I?"

"No, you didn't mention it."

He told her about his brothers then, and pointed in the direction of their places. He explained how his dad had divided up the parcels for each of his three sons.

"No sisters?"

"Sisters-in-law, but no, no sisters." Ben realized again how little he'd told her about himself.

"Oh, Ben," she said as they approached his house. It was a more modern version of his parents' place, built from the same dark wood, with weathered corrugated steel roofing and accents. He loved his house, but he had to admit, he loved hers more.

"I'm warning you, my kitchen isn't half as nice as yours. And I have one fireplace, not one in every room."

"I don't have a fireplace in every room, Ben."

"Just about," he teased.

They made it through the front door, but giving her a tour now was out of the question. He'd waited long enough to hold her, touch her, explore every inch of the body he'd spent so many days and nights longing to feel next to him.

Ben cupped the back of her neck, touching his mouth to hers, warm, barely there at first, then firmer. He parted her lips, angling his head, trying to get closer to her. His hands pulled her jacket away from her shoulders and tossed it on the floor. "I need you naked now, Liv," he groaned.

A flush warmed her skin as he nipped at her earlobe. "You taste so good."

A groan escaped her lips as she ran her hands over his shoulders, down, caressing his solid chest, moving lower, to unfasten his belt.

Before she did, Ben picked her up and carried her up the stairs. "Once you're in my bed, it will be a long, long time before I let you out of it."

He took her mouth again, hungrily. His hands traveled over her back, lingering as they slowly moved down the length of her spine, over her bottom, pressing her closer into him. The mere touch of her body lit him on fire.

Liv's eyes bored into his as he slid his fingers into her long hair, holding her still, and feasting on her lips.

"Talk to me, Liv. Tell me. Did you miss me? Did you miss this?"

"I missed you so much," she whispered. She took off the rest of her clothes while Ben watched. He cupped her chin and kissed her mouth, trailing his lips down her body, over the swell of her breast, softly kissing the curve of her stomach, then her hip.

Ben lifted her on the bed and pushed her gently so she spread out in front of him. He reached behind and pulled his shirt over his head, then took off his jeans. He reached for the drawer in the nightstand, and Liv sat up and stopped his hand with hers.

"No, it's okay. Nothing between us tonight, Ben."

"God, Liv, I need you. All of you. I want your eyes on me, watching what I do to you."

Liv didn't say a word, nor did she move from where she was. Her eyes stayed locked on his, never wavering as Ben's slow rhythm took them both over the edge.

12

"Are you feeling as though you're a hostage yet?" Ben asked two days later. They hadn't seen another person since they'd left Ben's parents' house the night she got there, but they hadn't spent the entire time in bed either.

Ben drove her around the ranch, somewhat stupefied that they didn't run into one of his brothers, or even the other ranch hands. He wondered if his dad had warned everyone to be scarce.

"Not at all. Although…"

"Don't tell me; let me guess. You want to go riding today."

Liv stared at him. "How did you know?"

"When you're nervous, you like to ride."

"Am I nervous?"

"We won't be able to avoid seeing other humans much longer, which means you may meet more of my family. And that makes you nervous."

"What about your boys, Ben?"

"Is that what you're most nervous about?"

"I understand if you don't want me to meet them."

"They already know about you, Liv, and I want you to meet them more than anything. They won't be back here, with me, until Monday, but I thought it would be nice to have dinner with them Saturday or Sunday. So it's not too overwhelming."

"For me, or for them?" She laughed.

"You have a charming daughter. I have two rough-and-tumble boys. One is at the beginning stages of puberty, so he'll be as awkward as humanly possible around anyone of the opposite sex. The other is still a little boy. He will crawl into your lap and never want to leave." Luke was his rascal, but also his cuddler, the one who never wanted to sleep in his own bed, wanted five more minutes of talk time, or another story at bedtime.

"Will I meet their mother?"

Ah, there it was. That's what bothered her, meeting his ex-wife. Her husband had died, but if they were divorced instead, he would've been nervous about meeting someone important enough to father her child.

"We should talk about them."

"Who them?"

"Your husband, my ex-wife. I want you to tell me about him. What made you fall in love with him, your life then."

"Scott and I weren't married very long before he died."

"It's still part of who you are. In a way, it's harder. With my ex, we decided we didn't want to be together anymore; she didn't die. I worry sometimes about living up to his memory. Particularly given how he died."

Liv hadn't seen this one coming. She never talked to anyone about Scott. She painted a picture for Renie, but it wasn't based on reality. Most of what she told her daughter was how she imagined Scott would've been as a father. He wasn't a father yet when he died.

As much as he wasn't sure about living up to Scott's memory, at least Scott wasn't a living, breathing, human being. He still saw his ex-wife at least once a week. How could she compete with that?

"Liv?"

Why did he want to talk about everything all the time? She didn't remember her father ever being so *talkative*. "I heard you. But, Ben, I don't want to talk about him, and I don't want to hear about her."

"Come on, Liv, tell me about him. How did you meet?"

***

Scott was what her mom referred to as a "flyboy," an F-15 fighter pilot. He was the most handsome man she had ever seen, and he was a gentleman. She worshiped him from the day she met him. The happiest day of her life was the day she found out Scott looked at her as a woman.

The first time he took her out, he opened doors and pulled out her chair. He asked her what she wanted for dinner and ordered for her. He'd been her prince charming. In fact, he'd called her his princess, and rather than Liv, he always called her Olivia.

They started seeing each other when he was in town for his promotion to captain, two months after she turned eighteen. He took her out every night that week, and when he went back to his base, he called her every night at eight o'clock. Funny she remembered it so well, waiting for him to call, and that he was so punctual.

They'd kissed, but Scott never pushed her to go any further. She'd been so innocent then, that she hadn't thought about it, but now she wondered why he hadn't. He asked her one night, during one of their phone calls, if she was a virgin. She remembered being aghast that he'd asked. She hadn't told him she'd been saving herself for him, but she had been, in every way.

He came back at Christmas and spent it with her family. He proposed on Christmas Eve in front of the Christmas tree, with her parents watching. She hadn't questioned it then, but remembered now how happy her mother and father had been. She wondered now if they'd been happy for her, or happy that she landed such a "catch."

She visited his base soon after they were engaged. Scott took her around, introducing her to his friends, most already married, with families. She remembered how he always asked if Liv wasn't the most beautiful woman they'd ever seen.

One evening during her visit, they went out for dinner with several other couples. One of the wives asked Liv about her hobbies and what she liked to do. Liv told her she had a horse and that she dreamed of being a barrel racer.

Later, when Scott dropped her off at her hotel, he sat her down and told her he didn't want to hear any more talk of barrel racing. She would be too busy as an Air Force wife for such foolishness, and he wanted to start a family as soon as they were married. She'd loved him so much that giving up her dream to be with him didn't seem like a sacrifice.

When she got home and talked to her mother about it, her mom assured her that life with Scott would be an unimaginable series of adventures. She'd travel the world and have opportunities as the wife of a pilot that few dreamed about. Rodeos and barrel racing were for women of a different caliber than Liv, her mother said that night.

The next month was a flurry of activity as they rushed to plan the wedding. They held the ceremony at the Air Force Academy chapel, and the reception at their ranch. Liv remembered knowing very few people at her own wedding—most were Scott's friends, or friends of her parents.

For their honeymoon, Scott took her to Hawaii and treated her like a queen. He was charming, romantic, and made her feel as though she was the most special woman who ever lived. He was gentle when they made love, and patient as he taught her how to please him. She'd never dreamed sex could be so spectacular.

While they were in Hawaii, he made sure they did everything she wanted to do. They went sailing, whale-watching, hiking, and snorkeling. He took her to each of the islands, and when they were in Kauai, they made love on a beach, under the stars.

As a captain and a fighter pilot, Scott arranged for a very nice home for the two of them, off base. Not nearly as nice as her parents' home, but Liv hadn't expected it to be. She missed her horse, but being with Scott meant everything to her.

Liv was accustomed to the life of an Air Force officer, she'd seen and learned it all from her mother. There'd be wives' clubs to join, dinner parties to host, and functions to attend.

In early April, Liv found out she was pregnant. Scott was thrilled. If she'd felt like a princess before, now she felt doubly so. He was attentive and caring, making sure she had everything she wanted or needed.

Each month, on the fourteenth, he gave her a gift to celebrate their anniversary. In March, he gave her an emerald four-leaf clover necklace. In April, a pair of diamond earrings, in honor of her birthday, April 17.

In May, he gave her tickets for the two of them to visit her parents for Memorial Day, and in June, he gave her a bracelet that belonged to his grandmother.

Scott never failed to tell her his sun rose and set with her, and she'd loved him, heart and soul.

In August he was deployed, and by November, he was gone. Those had been very dark days for Liv. Her world had ended when they told her Scott died.

Her parents flew in right away and took care of everything. She wondered now if her father knew Scott was shot down before she did. She moved home to live with them. She remembered Scott's funeral, the day they buried him at the academy cemetery. Everyone told her she should be so proud, her husband was a hero.

Irene Louise Fairchild was born a few weeks later, and Liv's world went from revolving around Scott to revolving around her daughter.

* * *

Ben watched the expressions on Liv's face change as she told him the story of her life with Scott. She had been so young, so innocent, but it sounded as though he had been a decent man, and good to her. And she'd loved him, completely. Which made it easier to understand why she'd never remarried.

"When Renie was little, I had no desire to do anything but be her mom. My parents would've been happy to watch her if I had ever wanted to go out, but I never did. I believed that Scott was it for me. I shut off that part of me. The day Renie started school, I met Paige. Her daughter, Blythe, was in the same kindergarten class."

Soon Liv became busy with mother-daughter play dates, helping in Renie's classroom and on field trips. When that happened, her parents started traveling more. Liv never realized how much they'd put their lives on hold to help her.

When Renie turned ten, Liv's father had a heart attack. He died the next day, without ever regaining consciousness. Liv got Pooh, Renie's horse, as a way to distract her daughter from the pain of losing her grandfather. Two years later, her mother passed away from breast cancer. The time between her diagnosis and her passing had been brief.

Between then and now, Liv had had her hands full raising her daughter. Paige and Mark tried to fix her up with different guys, but there had never been anyone who held a candle to Scott. She enjoyed the time she spent with Renie. They were as much friends as they were parent and child.

"I guess you didn't ask me to tell you my life story, but it's hard to tell you about Scott without doing so. The truth is, we were together such a short amount of time. Even so, he was my life, and he impacted the rest of it in a profound way. It's hard to separate one from the other."

Wow—her life story. First a daughter, then a wife, and then a mother. Until tonight, when she summed it up so succinctly for Ben, she hadn't realized her whole life she'd been someone's something. Liv had never been anything all on her own.

What bothered Ben the most about everything Liv had told him, was hearing her birthday had been a little over a week ago, and he hadn't known. Had she celebrated alone? He hoped Paige and Mark had done something nice for her.

"Are you getting hungry?" They were sitting out on Ben's deck. The sun was going down, and he turned on one of the outdoor heat lamps.

"I am. What should we make?"

"Let's go out tonight. How does sushi sound?" Ben wanted to take her into town to celebrate her birthday.

"Fabulous. I love sushi; I would eat it every day if I didn't have to drive so far. Um…what should I wear?"

"Something comfortable. I'd be happy if you wore nothin' at all, baby, but then I wouldn't want to leave the house." Ben snuggled her closer to him. "Thanks for telling me about Scott."

"I'm still not sure I want to hear about your ex-wife, Ben."

He needed to tell her about Christine, but more, he needed to tell her about himself, which included the things that led to the demise of their marriage. He didn't want to keep any secrets from her. He wasn't proud of the way he'd lived his life back then, but getting beyond it made him a better man. At least he hoped it had.

"Tell you what, let's leave that story for another day. I want to take you out on a date tonight. And show you off a bit."

The thought filled Liv with dread. Had Ben dated much? How many other women would they be running into that he'd slept with? Was she just another one of Ben's conquests? This was all so new to her.

The dates she'd gone on had never been with anyone she cared about. When she had dinner with Ben and the band in Las Vegas, she hadn't given much thought to other women in his life. The next night, before the concert, she worried about it more, but at that point, Liv still considered the thing between them a fling, something that would last a day or two. She no longer saw it that way.

She wished she'd brought something nicer to wear, but she made do with a sleek cashmere sweater, wool pants, and the black boots with the four-inch heels she remembered to throw in at the last minute.

He waited on the deck, leaning on the railing with his back to her. God, he looked hot, even from behind. His jeans, slung effortlessly low, hugged his tight behind and rock-hard thighs. The sweater he wore taut over his broad shoulders made her reconsider the cashmere. She was overly warm already.

Ben turned as Liv walked by the fireplace inside, the light from it casting a warm glow around her. He had never seen anyone more beautiful in his life.

"Look at you," he said when she came out on the deck. He took her hands in his but stood back, his eyes gazing over her. "Remember when I said I wouldn't want to leave the house if you wore nothing at all? This counts, too. You are so hot; I want to keep you all to myself."

"Uh-uh," she said. "You promised me sushi, and I'm holding you to it."

They stopped first at the Dogwood Cocktail Cabin. It was dimly lit and very romantic.

"Where to begin," Liv said, studying the menu. "These are the swankiest cocktails I've ever seen."

She decided on the Bee Sting, a mix of tequila, honey, mint, and lemon, with a splash of habanero. Ben ordered a Latin Lover—hot cocoa, habanero, and whipped cream, but he asked them to hold the tequila on his.

"I thought you might enjoy this place," he said. "It seems like a good place to start a date."

"Is this where you start all your dates?"

Ben pulled her close and nibbled on her earlobe. "You're the first woman I've brought here, Liv, and you'll be the last. It's you and me, baby. I thought you knew that by now."

She turned her head and brushed her mouth across his. Ben cupped the back of her neck, holding her close, and nibbling her bottom lip.

"Do you know what you do to me?" he whispered. "You make me crazy with wanting you."

Liv brought her hand up and stroked the side of his face. "I've never wanted anyone the way I want you," she whispered in his ear.

"Ben? What are you doing here?" Ben didn't have to look to know that his ex stood next to their table.

Every muscle in Liv's body tightened in an instant. She tried to pull her hands away, but he tightened his grip. Before he spoke, he brushed his lips against hers one more time.

"Shh," he whispered.

He kept his eyes fixed on hers, not even blinking. "Liv, this is my ex-wife, Christine."

She tried again to wriggle her hands free from his, but he wouldn't let go.

"Christine," he said, eyes not leaving Liv's. "What brings you out tonight?"

"Drinks with the girls. I didn't expect to run into you here. Who's your friend?"

Ben's gaze remained fixed on Liv's. Every instinct told him Liv would pull away from him, and he wasn't going to let her.

"This is Liv," he said.

"Oh, uh, nice to meet you." Neither Liv nor Ben looked at Christine. "I guess I'll let you get back to it."

Ben wanted to breathe a sigh of relief when Christine walked away, but Liv's body remained so taut, he was afraid to let out a single breath. "Liv, honey, what's goin' on?"

Her hands relaxed, and she took her eyes from his.

"She's stunning," Liv murmured.

"She doesn't hold a candle to you," he answered, keeping his voice soft, hoping to soothe her.

"Don't be ridiculous; she's gorgeous."

"You don't have any idea how beautiful *you* are, do you?"

"For an older woman, who spends more of her time with horses than humans."

He dropped her hands and sat back. "Liv, how much younger than you do you think I am?"

She shrugged, trying to be nonchalant. "Ten years?"

"How old are you?" he asked.

"Forty."

Ben shook his head. "I'm three years older than you are," he laughed. "Not that it makes any difference. I thought you should know, since it seemed to bother you."

"You are not."

"I am, and I'll prove it." He dug out his wallet and handed her his driver's license.

"I don't need to see that," she said, while at the same time taking it out of his hand. "Wow. You look damn good for your age, Benjamin Caldwell Rice."

"Let's see yours, Olivia."

"Not on your life. Your picture is way better than mine."

Ben let himself breathe that sigh of relief he'd been holding in. Liv was fine. The awkward moment had passed, thank God.

He brushed his lips across her knuckles. "Wanna get out of here?"

"More than anything."

Ben threw a fifty on the table, and they walked out before their drinks were even delivered.

They walked, hand in hand, around the corner and downstairs to the sushi restaurant. It was crowded, as usual, but there were four open seats at the bar. Ben led Liv over, pulling out a stool for her.

"Shouldn't we check in with someone?" she asked.

"There he is," she heard a deep male voice say. "This must be Liv."

Ben hugged the man and slapped him on the back. "Good to see you, big brother. Liv, I'd like you to meet Matt. Matt, this is Liv."

Matt took her hand in his and brought it to his lips. "The magnificent Liv. I've heard so much about you." He turned to Ben. "She's even more beautiful than you said."

"Back off, brother," Ben said, taking Liv's hand from Matt's and tucking it in his.

Matt threw his head back and laughed, the same hearty, whole-body, soulful laugh as Ben's.

"This is Matt's place," Ben explained. He waved his hand over the corner section where they were seated. "Reserved for family, no matter how crowded it gets."

Matt stayed and chatted with them for a few minutes, and then excused himself to seat open tables. Less than ten minutes later, Will, Ben's youngest brother, joined them.

"Is this a coincidence?" Ben asked as Will pulled out the stool on the other side of Liv and sat down. "Or did Matthew give you the word we were here?"

"I had to come and meet Liv," Will answered. "Who knows if you'll leave your house again while she's here? Liv," he turned to her, "I'm Will, Ben's younger, handsomer, more romantic brother."

"Will, it's nice to meet you," Liv responded. "Ben, didn't you say you had 'sisters-in-law,' plural? Do you have more brothers?"

"Damn," said Will. "You already told her I'm married?"

They both laughed. "Seriously, I'm Will, and I am all the things I said before, as well as happily married."

"It's nice to meet you, Will."

"Speaking of which, Maeve wanted me to invite you to dinner while Liv's here."

A few minutes later, two women approached, both gorgeous. Liv stiffened again, but relaxed when Will stood.

"And there she is. Hey, darlin', fancy running into you here."

"Will Rice," said the woman with coal black hair, and the palest, but most beautiful skin Liv had ever seen. "Don't pretend you didn't call me to come and meet her. Hi," she turned in Liv's direction, "I'm Maeve, Will's wife, and this is Allison, Matt's wife."

Will and Ben pulled more stools over to the bar. When the couple around the corner from them left, the group took over the whole far end of the crowded bar.

Ben watched Liv interact with his family. She fit, he thought, as she talked and laughed with them. She fit perfectly.

They never ordered, the guys behind the bar kept the sushi and other house specialties coming without them needing to. Matt was showing off, thought Ben with a smile.

"Oh, I'm so full," Liv said, putting her hand on her stomach.

Moments later the lights around the bar dimmed as the group broke into a rousing version of "Happy Birthday."

He could tell Liv was trying to figure out who they were singing for, until someone set a dish of mochi ice cream in front of her.

"Happy birthday, baby," Ben said, brushing his lips against hers. "Make a wish."

13

When Ben woke, the heat of Liv's body next to his flooded him with a sense of calm. He loved having her here with him, just as he loved being with her at her place. As long as she was next to him, he was at peace.

He wanted to talk to her about running into Christine last night, and her reaction. He hoped Liv understood that he and Christine were co-parents now, and nothing more.

Before any of that, though, he needed to tell Liv more about himself. He wasn't proud of most of his past, but he'd overcome a lot of his demons and made significant changes in his life.

Living at home and living on tour, as he soon would be doing, were very different things, though. Time on the road was crazy—a different city every night, sometimes several nights in a row. They'd have a day off here and there, but never enough time to come home and regroup. He wished again that she wasn't going to Europe with Renie, and that he could take her on the road with him. That wouldn't be fair to her, though. He didn't need or want a babysitter; he wanted a lover, a mate…someday a wife.

Liv shifted so her back faced his front, and he wrapped his arms around her, nestling her close. As someone who slept alone as many years as she had, he wondered if his constant need to touch her bothered her. Even in his sleep, he clung to her. Awake he wanted to bury himself in her every chance he had.

"Sweet Liv," he whispered in her ear, hoping to wake her gently.

"Hmm, is it morning?"

"It's almost nine. You can sleep longer if you want to."

"No, I'm awake."

Now or never. "I need to tell you the not-so-nice stories," he said.

Her muscles tightened, and he kissed across her back, from one shoulder to the other. He hoped he could get through it and be honest with her. He'd never be free with her unless he told her all of it.

"Okay," she said.

"A little over a year ago, I hit rock bottom. Will, Matt, and I had been snowboarding all day, and I'd been drinking, a lot. They took away my keys and drove me home, where they figured I'd pass out and sleep it off. Unfortunately, I didn't. I got my hands on a set of keys to one of the ranch trucks. I drove to Will's, prepared to give him shit, I guess. I don't remember anything about that night.

"When I got there, I must've passed out in one of the bedrooms. Something woke me up, and I went out into the living room. Maeve, Will's wife, was sitting on the couch. I don't know where Will was. Anyway, I sat down and started a conversation with her.

"Will came out and started screaming at me, asking what the fuck was wrong with me. Then he apologized to Maeve, and he got her out of there, fast. I don't remember much of this, but I do remember the last thing he said to me. 'You need to straighten your shit out, dude, or get the fuck out of my life.'"

Ben took a deep breath. He punched the pillow behind his head a little higher. He wanted to see at least part of Liv's face. If he went too far, he hoped he'd be able to tell.

"The reason Will was so done with me, that day, was because I came out, sat down, and started talking to his wife, naked. On top of that, I must've fallen, or I ran into something before I got there. By the time Maeve saw me, I looked as though I had been in a fight. I scared the hell out of her."

Ben tightened the hold he had around her. He hoped that, if he held her as close to him as possible, he'd be able to tell her everything he needed to.

"Before that night, there was a long, ugly road of random acts of misery I left in a trail behind me."

Ben told her that he'd started drinking as a teenager, hanging out at the ski area. It got worse when he started the band, worse still when he got married, and almost killed him when he got divorced.

"That night, Will took Maeve to my parents' place. He called Matt, who rounded up Jimmy and Phil. You met them, they're in the band, and I've been friends with them since we were in first grade. They all came back to Will's with my mom and dad and told me that they were taking me to rehab. I mean, there was a lot more to it, but, Liv, the sad part is there isn't much I remember about it. The only reason I can tell you what happened with Maeve is because I've been told the story so many times."

"Keep talking," Liv said, almost a whisper.

"When I met Christine, the band was hot. We'd released a couple of albums and were playing all over Colorado. We had a sold-out show at the Belly Up in Aspen. The crowd was crazy that night, and I saw her in the front row. I expected I'd be getting her under me sometime that night, but she wanted nothin' to do with me." Ben laughed, in an uncomfortable way, and rubbed his eyes. "God, this is sounding too familiar, even to me."

He kissed Liv's neck. "Are you all right; is it okay for me to go on?"

"Mmm hmm, keep going."

"She came to a lot of our shows. Young guys, hot band; girls followed us. She never got together with any of the other guys; she never got together with me, but she was always there. We had a few days off, and I asked her to spend time with me when we weren't performing. That was the first time she said yes to anything I asked her."

Ben told her that he and Christine partied, nonstop, for a week. She drank more than he did, and did a lot of coke, which he hadn't until then. During their weeklong bender, they had sex, and he'd been too drunk, too stoned, or too high to remember to use condoms.

"You can guess what I'm gonna tell you next. Christine came into The Goat, trying to find me a couple months later. I didn't recognize her. She'd put on weight, which I later found out was because she'd stopped doing coke. She was also pregnant and scared out of her mind that there would be something wrong with the baby."

Both Ben and Christine saw the pregnancy as a wake-up call. She stopped partying. Ben stopped too. He moved her into his house, and rather than *asking* her to marry him, he *told* her they were getting married.

"I tried to play it off as though I was a responsible guy who'd fallen in love, gotten my girl pregnant, and we were getting married, but I realize now that my parents knew what was happening. They were onto my shit the entire time. I think they played along, hoping it would be the thing that would make me stop drinking and maybe make me start acting like the grownup I was old enough to be."

Ben shifted again. Liv turned around, wrapped her arm around his waist, and put her head on his chest, right above his heart.

"Thankfully, Jake was okay when he was born. There were never any signs that he was adversely affected by Christine's lifestyle.

"We played house for a couple of years and did our best to find a common ground that didn't have anything to do with partying. I had to hand it to her then, she changed when she got pregnant, and she's always been a good mother to Jake and Luke.

"Not as much changed for me as it did for her. I still played clubs almost every weekend. I stopped doing drugs and convinced myself that, as long as I only drank, I'd be fine."

He told her the benders stopped, but in between Jake's birth and when Christine got pregnant with Luke, he'd slept with a lot of other women. Whenever they played out of town, they'd stay until the next morning. No matter where they were, Ben never slept alone. He'd learned his lesson about unprotected sex though, and he never went without a condom.

He and Christine had major problems, mainly because he was never home. Living out on the ranch was hard on her because she was so isolated. His mother was always nice to Christine, but they were never close.

In an effort to repair their marriage, they did the thing everyone says not to do, and had another baby. It didn't take long for Christine to get pregnant, but if she thought Ben would make changes in his life because of it, she was wrong. And that didn't make her happy.

At home, all they did was fight. Ben realized, in rehab, that most everything that went wrong between them was his doing. He hadn't been committed to the relationship, ever. He loved her more as the mother of his kids. She was beautiful, no question. But he wasn't the man she wanted him to be, and he realized now, she wasn't the woman he wanted her to be, either.

Liv shifted when he said it, but kept her arm around his waist and didn't try to move away from him. He kissed her forehead and started to run a trail of kisses down the side of her face.

"Keep talking," she whispered.

She was right. He'd better get through it before he lost the nerve to tell her the whole story.

Two years after Luke was born, Ben made arrangements to record the band's next album in Los Angeles. Christine wanted to go and bring the boys, but Ben said no. He told her it wasn't a good environment for them to be in. The truth was, he hadn't wanted her there.

When he left, she told him she wouldn't be there when he got back. Ben had no idea where she'd go. He'd never met her family, never heard a single thing about them, even after they'd gotten married and had two kids, so he didn't take her threat seriously.

He and the band had been in LA a week when a knock on the hotel room door, early one morning, woke him. Hungover, it took him a while to answer. When he did, Christine stood on the other side of it. She held Luke in one arm and held Jake's hand with the other.

He'd answered the door naked and had little choice but to let her push her way inside. When she did, she practically threw Luke in his arms before she attacked the woman still asleep in Ben's bed.

Ben still prayed Jake, who was five at the time, had no memory of that day.

Trying to manage a two-year-old and a five-year-old, both of them screaming, and rein Christine in was more than he was able to handle. Ben put Luke down on the floor and tried to get Jake settled, while also trying to keep their mother from pummeling the woman in his bed. Jimmy heard the commotion and came to help, but it was still ugly.

He got the woman out of the room and the kids settled with another member of the band. Once they were alone, Christine told him she was done. She wanted a divorce, and she wanted full custody of the kids. On top of that, she wanted a hell of a lot of money.

"I didn't know a lot about my financial situation then. I had money, but I didn't really understand how much. I also married her without a prenup and didn't know whether I'd put the ranch at stake."

He flew home with Christine and the boys, dropping them off at the house while he stayed with his parents.

"I know I looked like hell, between the shit with Christine, the band trying to cut a record with a detached producer, and the non-stop partying. I felt like I wanted to die. That's when I found out I was sick."

Less than a month later, he was diagnosed with cancer. The record went on hold, the divorce did not. He went through a tough surgery, followed by both chemo and radiation therapy. He stayed at his parents' place through it all while Christine and the boys remained in the house. She was adamant that she wanted full custody of their boys, and she used his illness to fuel her fight.

He learned later that his dad intervened and made a deal with her to finalize the divorce. In exchange for giving up all claims to the ranch and other family holdings, Ben's family would take care of her for the rest of her life. It would continue, provided she never tried to take Ben's boys away from him. If she ever tried, she'd lose everything.

The negotiations his father worked out on his behalf included a joint custody agreement. Christine moved into a house in town, and Ben went back to his place on the ranch as soon as he was well enough.

"You'd think with all that happened, the way Christine and I got together, the boys, the divorce, the cancer…that I would've stopped drinking, but I didn't. I drank more."

Ben and the band went back to LA to finish the album, and it wasn't long before he started picking up old habits. He continued to drink, and self-destruct, for another five years.

"That brings me back to the beginning of the story. When I nakedly terrorized my sister-in-law." Ben tried to put a lighthearted spin on the words he spoke, but there was nothing lighthearted about the story he told Liv.

"What happened between now and then?"

"With Christine?"

Liv nodded.

"The years before I got sober were tough. She tried to do the best for our boys. Sometimes I was easy to get along with and other times—not."

Once he got sober, Ben asked Christine to go to counseling with him so they'd be better co-parents. They'd been able to work through a lot in those sessions, and came out of it far better than when they'd started.

Now they managed to be friends. Christine met a guy not too long after they divorced and married him. Ben told Liv he didn't know a lot about Joe. He seemed to be good to his boys, his life with Christine, stable.

The scene from the night before still plagued him. Christine knew, as well as he did, that casual drinking would never be an option for them. Christine had been going to AA since she got pregnant with Jake. Granted, he'd been in the same bar, but he wasn't drinking. Maybe she hadn't been either. Apart from how it affected Jake and Luke, what Christine did, or didn't do, wasn't any of his business. Something else he needed to let go of.

"Addicts tend to be very sensitive people, Liv. We have a need to be in control, which should mean control of ourselves, but sometimes it spills onto other people in our lives.

"We also talk about everything, at least most of us do. We've learned that talking things through, acknowledging how we're feeling, is the key to our sobriety. As soon as I stop thinking through the decisions I make, I run the risk of making bad ones."

Ben pulled her close to him. "Please, tell me what you're thinking, sweetheart."

Liv tried to wrap her head around everything Ben told her. So much of it was foreign to anything she'd encountered in life. It sounded almost absurd, but she didn't think she'd ever known another alcoholic. Her parents drank, but in moderation. She'd never seen them drunk.

There were occasions when Scott may have had more to drink than he should have. But never enough that it worried her, or that she'd even noticed. And drugs had never been a part of her life, not in any way.

She didn't have a way to relate to so much of what he told her. She didn't understand what drove someone to do the things he did.

His desire to talk about everything made more sense, so did his impulsiveness, and his insecurity. Above all, she understood his need for control better than she had before.

But nothing about his life, before his sobriety or since, explained his attraction to her. They had an undeniable sexual attraction, but other than that, what did they have in common?

She began to worry that Ben might see her as safe, or innocent, the same way Scott had. She wasn't anyone's savior, not Scott's, not Ben's, not even her own.

She was a normal woman, who led a very simple life. She rarely took risks of any kind, rarely even stepped out of her comfort zone.

What if Ben needed her to be someone she couldn't be, and she failed him? What would happen then? Would he start drinking again? Would he blame her?

He knew her story—she lived with her parents most of her life, except when she and Scott were married. And when her parents passed away, Liv inherited everything. Everything had been handed to her. She never had to worry about working or providing for her daughter.

Ben also knew that Scott told her to let go of her dream of being a barrel racer, and she had, for him.

Did he expect her to do the same thing now as she did for Scott—give up her life for his? She couldn't. If she did, she'd never know who *she* was. Ultimately she'd resent him, and when she didn't live up to his expectations, he'd resent her too.

She'd questioned this thing between them so many times, but none more than she did now.

How did Ben see them continuing? He was going on tour with his band. She felt tension spread from her shoulders throughout the rest of her body. Ben was going to ask her to go with him. She could feel it, and she wouldn't do it. She couldn't.

She was at a crossroads, and she saw her history repeating. She'd given up her life, once, for love. She couldn't do it again.

He had opened her eyes to new possibilities, not just the possibility of having love in her life again, but so much more.

Ben knew the moment, the very instant, Liv disconnected from him. Her head remained next to his heart, but his heart hurt worse than he ever imagined.

"We can't get beyond this, can we?" he ventured.

"It isn't that, Ben."

"What is it, then?"

"I'm going to ask you something, and I want you to be completely honest with me."

"Go ahead."

Liv looked into his eyes so deeply, it was as though she was about to crawl inside of him.

"Close your eyes."

He smiled and did.

"Tell me what you see when you think about us."

Ben's smile grew.

"Not that. What else do you see? Think about our future."

He thought hard about what she was asking of him and knew the point she was trying to make. He saw her with him. *With him.* Logically, he knew it would be wrong to ask it of her, but when he closed his eyes and imagined their future, she was with him, on tour with the band.

As hard as it was for him to admit, she'd asked him to be honest with her. He opened his eyes.

"I get it, Liv."

"I can't do it, Ben. Not again. I've lost myself too many times."

"Where does that leave us? You go to Europe, I go out on tour, and maybe we'll see each other again someday?"

"No, Ben. I'm not going to Europe."

14

Once she got home from Crested Butte, Liv knew exactly who to talk to. She saddled up Micah and took off at a breakneck pace. When she got to the Pattersons' she prayed Dottie was home. She needed to talk to her now. Right now.

"Hey-o," she shouted when she walked in the back door.

"In here," Dottie shouted back from the kitchen.

"How come you're always in the kitchen when I come over?"

"There's my sweet girl! How are you, Liv? I have missed you something awful."

"Dottie, I have something important to talk to you about. You may call me crazy, but there's something I want to do, and I want you to help me."

Dottie listened as Liv spelled out her plans. "I know just the person you need to go see," Dottie said. She got up from the table and pulled out her address book.

"Her name is Jolene Baxter, and she'll help with everything you need. You may have to go to Texas for a spell, but it'll be worth it in the long run."

"I'll have to hire someone to work the boarding stables while I'm gone."

"I've got just the fella. Wait for a minute, and I'll give you his number too before you leave."

Liv rode Micah home and went into the house to call Renie. Her daughter would be disappointed, but Liv had to do this.

"Hey, honey, how are you?" Liv asked when Renie answered.

"Good, Mom, how are you?"

"I'm fine. You sound tired."

"Finals. Ugh. Two more weeks. I can't wait to be finished and on my way home…"

"Listen, that's why I'm calling. I have to cancel our trip to Europe."

Silence.

"Renie? Are you there?"

"Mom, is this about Ben?"

"No, honey. This isn't about Ben. This is about me. And before you ask, I'm fine."

"Okay, so what's going on?"

"There's something I have to do, and it means I'll have to be away from home for a while. I can't afford the time away to go to Europe and do this."

"Okay…you're being very cryptic."

"We'll talk more when you get home in a couple weeks. That is, if you're still coming home."

"Where else would I go? Is it okay if I come home?"

"Of course it's okay, but you don't have to. If you're coming home for me, don't. If there's something you'd rather do, you should do it."

"All right, crazy person. Whoever you are, can you please ask my mom to call me when you see her again?"

Liv laughed. "I miss you, sweetie, and I can't wait to see you. Oh, and I hope you're not too disappointed about our vacation."

"No, I'm okay. But, Mom—what happened with you and Ben?"

"We both have to live our own lives, sweetheart. I care a lot about him, but I care about me more."

Two weeks later, Liv picked Renie up from the airport and told her what she planned to do.

"Can I go with you?" Renie asked.

"Of course you can, but it won't be very exciting. I have a lot of hard work ahead of me."

"Maybe I can help. There's something else I want to talk over with you. About school."

"What's that?"

"I've been considering this for a long time."

"What?"

"I'm transferring to Colorado State University's College of Veterinary Medicine. Next year."

"You are?"

"I'm not cut out to be a people doc, Mom."

Renie had been on a biomedical track at Dartmouth but seemed ambivalent about what she might do with it. She wondered for a while if her daughter would take a couple of years off and continue with the graduate portion of her education after she decided what she wanted to do with her life.

"Large animal vet, huh?"

"It's what I'm meant to be, Mom. It's so obvious."

"Have you started the transfer process?"

"It's done. Which is one of the reasons I wanted to come home this week. I need to go to Fort Collins and complete the paperwork. I can do that tomorrow, and we can still leave for Texas the day after."

Ben thought about canceling the show in Denver, but that would go against everything he and Liv promised each other. Besides, it had sold out three hours after the tickets went on sale.

As hard as it was for him to let her go, the things Liv said made sense. Asking her to give up her life to travel with him was as ludicrous an idea as her asking him to give up his career for her.

They both agreed it would be best to focus on themselves for the next few months. As Liv reminded him, the record company had high hopes for their new album, and the tour they'd scheduled included venues Ben had once only dreamed of playing.

When they talked earlier in the week, he'd almost asked her to come home for this show, but he'd stopped himself. It had taken him forty-three years to get to the point where he considered someone else's feelings as much as his own—or more. He was determined to be the kind of man a woman like Liv could eventually see herself spending the rest of her life with.

"Believe in us, Ben," she'd asked of him. "If we're meant to be, we'll find our way back to each other. In the meantime, we both have to chase our own dreams."

It was especially difficult for him to do when, every night, his dreams were about being with her.

He was sitting in the dressing room when Jimmy knocked. "There's someone here to see you. Remember that woman from Las Vegas? She's here."

Ben's heart stopped. "Liv?"

"No, the other one, Paige."

"Let her come back." Ben tried to rub the ache in his chest away, but it wasn't on the surface; it was deep inside.

"Hey," he said, standing to greet Paige and give her a hug. Mark stood behind her.

"Come in, have a seat. How have you been? Glad you came to the show."

He tried to sound enthusiastic, but after thinking Liv was here, it was impossible for him to hide his disappointment.

Mark made small talk, but Paige was antsy.

"Spill, Paige."

"Are you going to Texas?"

"No, Paige. I'm not. Not until she asks me to."

"Argh. You're both so stubborn."

Racing legend Mary Beth Wilson agreed to train Micah, while Jolene Baxter trained Liv. No one Liv had spoken to thought forty too old to start barrel racing. Jolene had won nine world title championships in her career, the last at fifty-eight—and barrel racing didn't have age classifications. Jolene competed against eighteen-year-olds, twenty-six-year-olds, fifty-year-olds, and everything in between.

"There's a lot more to barrel racing than people think," Jolene told her. "It's all about making sure you have control of the horse's poll, neck, shoulder, barrel, and hind end. You're a solid rider. What you need to do now is be a sponge. Squeeze every bit of knowledge you can out of the horse you're gonna train on. Then shower it on Micah when he's ready."

Liv and Micah started training, and when they did, Liv tried her hardest to put everything else, and everyone, out of her head.

It wasn't easy when, every night, she dreamed about being with Ben.

"*No, no, no,*" Jolene yelled at Liv. "You're not focusing. You need to *blast* home. Micah knows it. Where is your self-confidence today? Come on, do it again."

"Whaddaya think?" Mary Beth asked Jolene.

"She's got it in her. There are days she just doesn't believe in herself. She knows that horse, no question about it, and they have a strong connection. It's her head that's giving her trouble. I wanna get her in the game."

"You think she's ready?"

"Yes, I do, and this'll show her. That's the only piece she's missing—enough confidence in herself. She's almost all the way there, and then somethin' makes her get back in her head."

"I'll get her into Woodward. The people are friendly, and it has real good ground condition."

"Yep, that'll be the perfect start for our Livvie." Bill Patterson drove down the day before, with Dottie, to check on Liv's progress, and was eavesdropping on Jolene and Mary Beth's conversation.

He was astounded by what he saw when he watched Liv, enough that he'd wager anyone who would take the bet that she'd finish in the top three at the Woodward rodeo, and then she'd be in the money.

He'd known Jolene Baxter almost all his life. Dottie had been a bridesmaid in Jolene's wedding to Larry, who was the best farrier Bill knew. Dottie did good, getting their girl set up with these folks.

"What's goin' on in that sweet head of yours, darlin' girl?" Dottie asked as Liv walked Micah.

"I dunno. Not on my game today, I guess. I'm missin' Renie. And Paige texted. Too many distractions."

"I hope you aren't countin' Bill and me as a distraction. I'd hate for us to be the reason you can't get your focus."

"No, not you and Bill, not ever. I don't know how to thank you for this, Dottie. It's because of you that I'm doin' this."

"No, it's not. It's because of you that you're doin' this, and don't you ever forget it."

"A little bird told me that Livvie is competin' in her first rodeo this weekend," said Bill, joining them.

"Bill Patterson, are you tellin' the truth? Our Livvie is gonna be barrel racin' in a rodeo this weekend?"

Liv bent over with her hands on her knees, took in a deep breath, stood, and threw her hat into the air. "*Woohoo!* Micah, did you hear that?" She nuzzled up against him. "We're ready, boy."

She wished Renie would come this weekend to see her mom in her first barrel race, but she'd be too busy getting ready to go back to school in two weeks.

Oh, the hell with that, thought Liv. Her first barrel race—Renie damn well better come down for it.

She wished Ben could come too, but he was the reason she lost her focus today. She'd dreamed about him last night, and this morning she couldn't get him off her mind. Dreaming about him wasn't unusual; she did almost every night. Last night was different, though. She and Ben were having sex, and the dream was so vivid, she swore he was in the room with her when she woke up, sweating.

She missed him more than she thought possible, but asking him to come to her first rodeo would go against what they'd promised each other. Ben's focus was on the band; her focus was on barrel racing. It wouldn't be fair to either of them if one pressured the other to put their dreams second.

It had been two months and twenty-eight days since she last saw him. She counted the hours too. He was on tour now, and the photos she saw on social media were amazing. He looked good, sexy as ever, with that smile that made her knees weak. As much as she tried to tell herself she didn't love him, she did. They hadn't said the words, but she'd always love him, and she knew he loved her. She only hoped their combined love was strong enough to carry them through to a time they could be together without either of them sacrificing their own life.

Ben wanted to kill Paige Cochran.

How much time do you have off before the next show? She texted him.

Five days. Why?

Woodward, Oklahoma is 9 hours and 48 minutes from Crested Butte.

Huh?

Get in your truck and DRIVE, cowboy. Mark and I will meet you there.

This had to have something to do with Liv, but why would Paige tell him to go to Oklahoma when Liv was in Texas?

When he texted and asked, she didn't answer. Something, though, pulled at him to get in his truck and do what Paige was telling him to do.

There were at least ten different times during the drive when Ben thought about turning his truck around and heading home. But that same feeling in his gut told him to keep driving. Paige was a live wire, no question about it. But if she wanted him to come to Woodward, Oklahoma, home of exactly *nothing*, it must have something to do with Liv.

He only hoped that, when he got there, she'd be happy to see him.

15

He was fiddling with the radio, trying to find a station, when the road sign caught his attention. "Hope, next exit," it said. As with everything, he convinced himself it meant something. Something about Liv.

Where are you? His phone pinged with another text from Paige.

Filling up the gas tank in a place called Hope, he answered.

You're close. Hurry.

Ben swore Paige would be the death of him one day. But she connected him to Liv. He'd put up with her until he took his last breath if he had to.

Ben got back on the highway and drove to Woodward. As his internet search had predicted, there was nothing there, except a rodeo taking place tonight. He parked the truck and texted Paige.

At the rodeo, is this where I'm supposed to be?

Ticket waiting at will call for you.

Yep, she was a laugh a minute, that Paige.

Ben saw Paige and Mark sitting in the center section of the stands, halfway up. Renie was sitting with them.

He gave Paige a kiss on the cheek when he got to his seat and whispered, "This better be good."

"Oh, it will be," she answered. "I guarantee it."

Mark shook his hand and shook his head. Renie waved at him. He supposed there'd be time for talking later.

"Ladies and gentlemen, our next event tonight is barrel racing." The announcement came through the loudspeaker. "We've got a lineup of a few of the finest barrel racers in the state of Oklahoma. Y'all are in for a real treat. And, I'm told two of the grand dames of the sport are with us tonight, with one of their protégé riders. Everybody, give a big round of applause for Ms. Mary Beth Wilson and Ms. Jolene Baxter."

The crowd stood and cheered while the two women rode the arena loop and the announcer listed their impressive achievements in barrel racing.

"First up tonight is a little lady out of Monument, Colorado. Ms. Mary Beth and Ms. Jolene have been workin' this girl hard, and they tell us they expect her in Las Vegas come the end of the year. Everybody, give a big welcome to Olivia Fairchild, ridin' Micah."

Every bit of air left Ben's lungs as he saw Liv and Micah fly out of the alley, heading for the first barrel in the pattern. Micah went left around it, then right. Both barrels were standing as Liv guided him to the third and final one. He rounded it perfectly, and she headed home, urging him for more speed to the timer.

"Ladies and gentlemen, coming in with a time of sixteen point eight is the little lady from Colorado. That is an unbelievable time for a first-time racer. Let's give her and Micah a big round of applause. Wow! I'd say Mary Beth and Jolene have trained a champion, wouldn't you, folks?"

The crowd stood again. Everyone except Ben, who was still trying to find the air he needed to breathe. He looked up at Renie, who met his gaze. They both had tears in their eyes.

"She's amazing, isn't she?" Renie came and sat next to him.

"So amazing." He wiped his eyes, but it didn't seem to do any good. There were so many reasons he wanted to cry. He was so proud of Liv he couldn't contain his emotions.

"You must think I'm…"

"I don't think you're anything, except in love with my mom." Renie put her hand on Ben's. "I don't know what happened, but this change in her is because of you."

He shook his head, still unable to speak.

"I've never seen my mom so determined about anything. Or passionate. I never knew she had it in her, is that terrible for me to say?"

"Your mom is one of the most passionate people I've ever known. And I don't mean that in the way you're assuming I do."

Renie laughed out loud. "I'm not assuming anything, Ben." The smile it brought to her face stayed there.

"I better get going."

"What do you mean?"

"Are you saying your mom knows I'm here?"

"No. She doesn't."

"This is her night. Not mine. I don't know what your mom told you, but we made a promise to each other. Unless she asked me to be here, I'm not supposed to be."

"That's silly, she'd—"

Ben held up his hand. "Renie, your mom and I have an agreement, and if I don't honor it, how do you think she'll feel?"

"She doesn't know Paige and Mark are here, either."

"It's different, and you know it."

Ben squeezed Paige's hand and winked. There weren't tears in her eyes until their eyes met.

"Thank you," he mouthed before he stood, shook Mark's hand, and left the stands, hands in his pockets.

A COWBOY FALLS

He only hoped he could get out of there, and into his truck, without completely breaking down. He was so damn proud of her. When they talked last night, she hadn't said a word about competing this weekend, and that was why he didn't understand Paige's text. If she had wanted him to be here, she would've said so.

Something by the barn caught his eye. *Liv.* He watched her run into the arms of a cowboy who picked her up and spun her around in a circle. The look on her face was pure joy. The cowboy's too. *Joy.*

He forgot about trying not to cry—now he worried he wouldn't make it to the truck before his chest cracked open with the pain burning in it. He had his answer. The reason Liv hadn't invited him to be here was because she was with someone else.

"Olivia Fairchild, am I ever proud of you!" Billy Patterson hooted at her before he swept her off her feet and spun her in a circle.

"Can you believe it? I got a sixteen point eight? I thought there was something wrong with the clock and I would be disqualified. *Shit,* Billy, sixteen point eight!"

"My mom and dad said you worked hard for it, girl. They're damn proud of you. And I hope you don't mind me sayin' I am too."

"Thanks, Billy. That means a lot to me."

"Whaddaya say we go do a little celebratin' tonight, just you and me?"

"Billy—"

"I'm just messin' around, but it was worth a try. Thought maybe you're so delirious with happiness that you forgot I don't do it for ya. God, Livvie, I've loved you most of my life."

"There are plenty of girls you do it for, Billy Patterson. Plenty. And you never loved me. I'm somebody safe you flirted with."

"Come out with us later. I'm meeting up with your folks and some friends." She winked at him.

"Whoo-wee, you keep that up, girl, and I'll be flirtin' with you all night long."

Liv turned to walk Micah back to the barns. There was another round tomorrow night, and if she did well, she might be in the money on Sunday—at her first rodeo.

She walked back out, after Micah was settled, and looked up at the stars. "Ben, are you seeing the same night sky I am?" She put her arms around her waist, as though she held him close to her. "What I would've given to have you here tonight. I wonder what you would've thought about all this?"

She knew damn well what he would've thought. Ben would've been proud of her. She missed him so much, it hurt deep down in her soul.

Don't go home, the text from Paige said. What the hell? If heartbreak didn't kill him, the heart attack Paige gave him would.

Ben pulled off the road. He couldn't drive home, at least not tonight. He needed to find a place to stay, sleep, and leave in the morning.

Don't go home, the text came through again.

I'm not, he wrote back.

Where are you?

Couple blocks away.

Meet us at Blue Water on Main.

Enough with the texts. He called her.

"Hey," she answered.

"Paige, I gotta tell you, I haven't been this close to havin' a drink in a year. You have to let up on me a bit. You mean well, but…"

"She knows you're here."

"What are you talking about?"

"Renie decided she needed to know."

Fuck. Now what? Ben laid his head against the steering wheel. He never should have come. Liv would not be happy about this. No matter what he did next, it would be the wrong thing.

"I saw her, Paige. She was with someone else. I can't see her and pretend like I don't know." He hit the off button on the phone and threw it against the passenger window, hoping it would break. Why had he come?

"Hey, sweet Mama," Renie said, meeting her mother outside the barn. "Do you have any idea how proud I am of you? How happy I am for you?"

"There were people in the stands tonight, cheering you on, that you didn't expect to be here."

Liv's eyes flew open, and she tried to catch her breath.

"Mom, are you okay?" Renie started slapping Liv on the back.

"Stop! Stop it. I'm okay; it went down the wrong pipe." Liv coughed a couple of times, trying to get her breath back. "Who?"

"Paige and Mark came down; you probably figured they would. And you already knew that Dottie and Bill were here. There was another person you didn't expect."

Liv wanted to strangle her daughter. "Who, Renie? Quit playing games and tell me."

"Ben."

Liv turned and walked back toward the barn.

"Mom, come back. Don't run away."

"Where is he?" Liv looked back at her daughter but kept her feet firmly planted where they were. "You shouldn't have interfered in this." She walked into the barn. As much as she'd wanted him to be here, she hadn't asked. How could she? Would it be fair to ask him to come and see her when she wouldn't do the same for him?

"We promised, Renie…" A tear rolled down Liv's cheek.

"He told me. You should have seen his face, though. He had tears in his eyes he was so proud of you."

"He did?" Liv whispered.

"Yes, he did."

"Where is he?"

"Paige is trying to keep him from leaving."

"I don't know what to do." It came out somewhere between a gasp and a whisper. She held onto her daughter's arm. "What should I do?"

"Call him."

Liv dug out her cell phone and called. "Huh. It went straight to voicemail."

"Leave him a message."

"Uh, hi, Ben. It's Liv. Renie told me you're here. I'm …uh…so happy you are." Why was she so tongue-tied? "Call me back. I…uh…can't wait to see you."

Ben picked his phone up off the floor of his truck and hit the "on" button. Nothing. He'd done it. He broke it. Wasn't that his intention? That way Paige wouldn't be able to reach him, but now he had no way of knowing if Liv wanted to see him. What the hell was he thinking?

He'd never get the image out of his head, of the cowboy's arms around her, and the look on her face. Even if she did want to see him, would it only be to say their final goodbye? Should he just get it over with—see her one last time and let her break his heart for good? Or should he just walk away and try to forget her, like she'd forgotten him?

16

Ben got out of the truck and paced along the side of the road. He didn't know what the hell to do.

Paige told him to come to Blue Water on Main. He assumed that was a restaurant, or a bar. He could find Main Street, since there were only two roads in the whole town and he was on the other one.

He finally decided to rip the bandage off, let Liv have her say, and drive home in the morning, if heartbreak didn't kill him while he slept tonight.

Ben walked into the restaurant but didn't see Paige or Mark. He didn't see Renie or Liv either. Or even Dottie or Bill.

"Is there another Blue Water in town?" he asked the bartender, who laughed at him.

He ordered a soda water and rubbed his hands over his face. He sat with his back to the door; he was too anxious to turn around and watch for her. If Liv walked into this bar and wanted to talk to him, she'd know he was there.

"I told him where we'd be," Paige said to Renie on the phone. "I don't know whether he'll come or not. He said something really strange about seeing her with another man. It didn't make any sense."

"Who?"

"I don't know. He hung up before I had a chance to ask."

"Have you tried calling him again?"

"Only once a minute. It keeps going to voicemail."

"She left him a message too, but he hasn't called her back. She's gonna be wrecked if he doesn't show. We handled this wrong."

"Thanks, Renie. I appreciate you saying 'we,' but this is all on me. I handled this wrong."

"Nope, you're not taking all the blame. It was my idea to tell her he was here. If I hadn't, he would've left. My mom never would've known he was here. Instead of looking as though she's gonna throw up any minute, she'd still be celebrating."

"Where is she?"

"She's walking toward me. Gotta go."

"Ready?" Renie said to her mom.

"Where are we going?"

"We're going to Blue Water on Main. Paige, Mark, the Pattersons, Jolene, and Mary Beth are coming. And, Mom, we're celebrating tonight, one way or another."

Liv smiled, although inside she was anything but. Why hadn't Ben called her back? And if he came all this way, why didn't he tell her he was coming? And why did Renie say Paige was trying to keep him from leaving?

"I'm sorry, Mom."

Liv went into mom-mode. "It's okay, baby girl. This thing between Ben and me is complicated. I realize everyone wants to help, but some things just have to happen on their own. Come on, let's go celebrate. Your mama is a barrel racer after all."

Everyone, except Ben, was waiting under the bright light near the front door when Renie and Liv pulled into the parking lot.

There were so many shouts and cheers, people picking her up and hugging her, Liv almost, for a second, forgot about Ben. Not a whole second, but part of one.

"Let's go eat," Bill said. "Dottie's treat."

Dottie slugged him. "That's right, big spender, make your wife buy your dinner, and everybody else's too."

"I'm just kiddin', sweetie," Bill said as he nuzzled up to Dottie. Watching them made Liv wish Ben was here even more.

Bill went in to get a table, followed by the rest of the group.

Paige grabbed Liv's arm and held her back. "Walk in with me," she said and hooked her arm through Liv's.

Renie was right in front of them, and Mark was right behind them. Liv wondered if they thought she would back out, so they had her surrounded.

It took a minute for her eyes to adjust to the darkness, but as soon as they did, she saw him. His back was to her, but he was there. She stopped where she was and took her arm from Paige's.

"Go ahead," she said. "I'll meet you in there."

Ben turned around. He felt her. The only thing he could do was smile; he was so damn happy to see her.

He stood, held out his arms, and she walked into them. When her mouth sought his, he crushed into hers. His arms were around her waist, and he pulled her body as close as he could to his.

The noisy restaurant went silent. He could only hear his own heart pounding and Liv's soft, quiet whimpers as she kissed him. Her lips tore at his as she ravaged him. Not the other way.

"Ben."

It was the only word he wanted to hear.

"There's my girl."

"I'm so happy you're here. I heard you watched me chase the cans."

"You were magnificent."

She looked down, and even as dark as it was in the bar, he knew her cheeks were pink.

He put his finger on her chin and tilted her head so her eyes met his. "Magnificent."

Her smile left her face, and her eyes bored into his. "I missed you so much."

"I know, baby, me too."

"I'm so glad you're here, but—"

"Shh. No 'buts.'"

He smiled and kissed her again. "Let's go join your party, darlin'."

Ben stood back and watched Liv as she circled the table, greeting each person there to celebrate with her. He pulled out a chair at the end of the table and sat next to Mark.

"You didn't go home."

"I sat next to you because I thought you were the only person at the table who wouldn't try to talk to me about Liv. Can't we talk about guitar strings, or baseball, or another random topic you're so good at pullin' out of thin air?"

"You got it, buddy." Mark pulled out his cell phone and started to show Ben videos on YouTube. The guy had the sense of humor of a fourteen-year-old, and sometimes that was a very good thing.

"Tomorrow's another day of training, as it would be back home. Don't go gettin' all full of yourself tonight, thinkin' you have this in the bag," Jolene said to Liv.

Dottie stood up in Liv's defense. "Oh, Jolene, can't you give the girl a break? Give Cinderella a midnight curfew if you have to, but let her enjoy the ball while she's here."

"You don't win world titles enjoying the balls," the gruff sixty-five-year-old spit out.

Mark picked it up and ran with it.

"What did she say? Liv isn't allowed to enjoy the balls? Bummer for you, dude."

"Yep. You're fourteen. A fourteen-year-old with gray hair."

As Liv moved from person to person at the table, she'd look at him and smile. Was she checking to make sure he was still there, or that he was okay, or was she wondering if he was watching her?

Too soon and yet not soon enough, Liv came and sat in the open chair next to him.

"This is so much…more," she said to him. "More than I ever imagined, more than I expected, more than I dreamed of."

"Which part, the barrels, or the celebration?"

"All of it. I'm not used to being the center of attention. I'm not used to having a reason to be."

"You're completely unaware of your significance in the lives of the people sitting at this table." Ben stroked her cheek with his finger. "If you only knew."

As much as he dreaded it, at some point he'd have to ask her about the cowboy he saw her with.

"What are you thinking about, Ben? You don't look happy all of a sudden. Do you regret coming?"

"No, Liv. Not for a minute." Questions could wait. The cowboy wasn't here with her; he was, and she seemed happy. "There isn't anywhere in the world I'd rather be than right here with my girl."

"The things you say, sweet talker. Sometimes they sound as though they should be in a song."

He laughed. "And sometimes they are, or they work their way into one."

Liv rested her head against him. Her breath warmed the curve between his neck and shoulder. When she shifted far enough that her lips were where her breath had been, he thought he'd come apart. "Liv—"

"Will you stay with me tonight, Ben?"

His blood heated, and he longed to carry her out to his truck and plunder her in the parking lot. He brushed his lips across hers, then moved so no part of her body touched his.

"Ben?"

He leaned over and whispered in her ear, trying to keep himself from touching her as he did. "I'm ready to throw you over my shoulder and carry you out of here, caveman-style. So unless you don't care what anyone at this table thinks of that, you gotta stop touching me."

He didn't miss the little grin she tried hard to hide, or the way her eyes drifted closed as she breathed in deeply.

"I know, sweetheart," he murmured.

Dottie got up on her feet and pulled Liv with her. "Come on, girls, I wanna dance."

Oh, Lord, Dottie wanted to dance, and all Liv could think about was getting out of this bar, and Ben out of his clothes. With Bill and Mark head-to-head at the jukebox, Liv wasn't sure what to expect.

"Come on, Paige, you're in on this too."

The heavy sounds of a guitar filled the room, something about saving a horse and riding a cowboy. She'd kill Mark, if Paige didn't do it first.

Dottie, Jolene, and Mary Beth were woo-hooing it up. "Save a horse, Livvie!" They pulled her in to dance with them.

She'd had a damn good day, one of the best of her life. What the hell, she deserved to have some fun.

They danced, and danced, and danced. Liv needed a drink, something tall and cool and wet. *Ben.* She'd rather have him than a drink.

"One more song, Livvie," Billy Junior hollered out. "This one's a slow one."

The fiddle started to play as Zac Brown's "Free" drifted through the speakers in the bar.

"I love this song," Liv said to no one in particular right before Billy swung his arm around her waist and proceeded to move her around the dance floor.

Ben lasted all of twenty seconds before he was on his feet. He recognized the cowboy about to put his arms around Liv. "Pardon me, but you're dancin' with *my* girl."

"She was my girl before you came along…"

"Billy, you don't want to start this." Liv kissed his cheek. "You'll ruin my night."

Billy stepped aside, and Ben pulled Liv in close. As much as he didn't want to do this here and now, he couldn't help himself.

"Who is he, Liv? Someone special?"

"Haven't you met Billy? He's Dottie and Bill's son."

Ben's arms tightened around her. "What's he to you, Liv?"

"I don't know. Like a brother, I guess."

Ben stopped moving and pulled far enough back that he could look in her eyes. "You're sure there's nothing more between you?"

"Don't be ridiculous." Liv pulled him closer. "You don't seem like the jealous type, Ben."

"As long as he keeps his hands off you, I won't be."

Liv put her hand on the back of his neck and pulled his mouth closer to hers. "This is the first time you've held me in your arms and danced with me. Do you realize that?"

"It's good, isn't it?"

"Dancing?"

"You, in my arms."

He pulled back so he could see her face, and hated that he couldn't get the image of her and Junior out of his head.

"You think anyone would mind if you carried me out of here now? Remember that caveman thing?" She was talking so damn seductively; it was almost as though she was purring at him. He didn't care if anyone noticed; it was time for them to leave.

He danced her over near Dottie and Bill.

"We're gonna call it a night. Thanks for everything," he said to them.

"You better ask Jolene what time Livvie's supposed to be at the barn in the mornin', Ben. Won't be good for her to be showin' up late." Bill shook his finger at them as he said it.

"Jolene, what time does Livvie have to be at the barn?"

She was dancing with Mark, God love him. Ben wasn't sure she heard him.

Jolene glared at Ben, and then looked at Liv. "Not a minute later than nine, little girl. We gotta make sure you're *focused*."

"She's a tough one," he said.

"She's my hero," Liv whispered.

Ben put his arm around her and moved her in the direction of the door. "Are you gonna stay awake long enough to tell me where we're staying tonight?"

"Oh, you don't need to worry about me stayin' awake, *cowboy*."

Ben didn't waste a second once they got to his truck. His hands fisted in her hair as he backed her up against the door. His lips rubbed against hers, nibbling and teasing, followed by his warm tongue invading her mouth. Her stomach did a little flip as he first groaned, then growled when her hands dug into his chest beneath his shirt. He took over, imprisoning her hips with his. She loved having the length of his body against hers.

His hands gripped her hips as he kissed her harder, and stroked the soft skin where her shirt rode up. He angled his head, changing his kiss. He was gentle, so gentle, sweet, but she wanted so much more from him.

"I can't think straight for wanting you, Liv." He nuzzled her cheek then, realizing his stubble probably scratched her, he reached up and softly rubbed his fingers where his face had been.

He pulled her away from the door and unlocked it. "I want you too much for it to be this way."

She climbed into the passenger seat, and he leaned in, laying his face against her breast, his fingers squeezing the inside of her thigh. His hand came up, and he gripped her chin.

"You are so beautiful."

When Liv looked away from him, Ben brushed her cheek with his fingers. "No, don't look away. You are so beautiful, but you are so much more than that. You're everything. Do you understand? You're everything to me."

He pulled away and closed the door, stopping to take a deep breath before he walked around the back of the truck. He got to his door and stopped again, and took another deep breath. God, he hoped he could drive. It wasn't as though he'd been drinking—it was Liv who intoxicated him.

As soon as they were in the hotel room, Ben worked the buttons on Liv's blouse free, running his fingers along each sliver of her skin. Once her shirt hung open, he slid it off her shoulders and let it fall to the floor.

His eyes darkened with heat as his lips followed where his tongue had been. He dropped to his knees, and his tongue licked across her middle. His fingers popped the button on her jeans. He lowered the zipper, and his warm mouth softly kissed along the top edge of her panties. He tugged her jeans until they were down below her knees. She was almost naked, and Ben was still fully clothed.

"On the bed, Liv." He placed his hands on her knees. "Let me in."

He leaned in close enough that his jeans rubbed against her skin while his hands slid up her thighs, around her hips, up her back and around to the clasp of her bra.

"You're too good at that," she groaned.

He palmed her breasts, and she arched, letting her head fall back. And then he was gone. She opened her eyes as he yanked his shirt over his head. She watched as he unhooked his belt buckle, unfastened the button, and unzipped his jeans.

"Do I need a condom, Liv?"

"No, you don't."

"Is it for me, only me?"

"Only you, Ben." She tried to stifle her cry. There was no one else for her. There never would be.

He swooped down and fused his mouth to hers, kissing her hard, and rough, and eager. His lips followed the line of her jaw, up to her ear. "I need you, baby."

She didn't answer with words but arched against him. And at that moment, he went still, right before he buried himself inside her. Slowly. So slowly.

There was no better feeling in the world than her body joined together with his.

"You're mine, all mine, Liv." He started to move faster, harder. "Tell me. Let me hear you say it."

"I'm yours, Ben, all yours."

Later, Ben waited until her breathing became more even. He moved her hand off his hip and whispered her name, to see if she was asleep.

"You're all I ever wanted, Olivia. Since the moment I laid eyes on you. You're it. I love you, heart and soul, with everything I am."

He rolled to his back and stared up at the ceiling. "And why is it that I can only say this to you when you're sleeping?"

Liv shifted again; her arm came across his waist, she turned part way to her side, and her body nuzzled up against his. She brought her head up and laid it on his chest. Her eyes never opened; her breathing never changed. In her sleep Liv's body sought his; she got close to him…when they made love, and when she slept.

Liv felt Ben's body next to her, and this time, she wasn't dreaming. Soft light filtered in through the window coverings, letting her know it was still early. She drifted back to sleep for a moment, then shook herself awake again. She wanted this time awake, while he slept.

Her eyes drifted over his face, slowly, as though they were her fingers, so slowly she let them wander. They lingered on the lines at the corner of his eye, etched there because of his smile, the one he gave so generously. They moved to the crease in the hollow above his eyes, between his eyebrows, as though, as he slept, stress stayed, furrowed there, not allowing his brow to be completely at rest. His mouth called her eyes to move to its pout. The corners turned down in his sleep, the same way they did when he played guitar and got lost in it, forgetting where he was. He slept with his mouth closed. Did everyone?

Had Scott? Liv didn't remember. She closed her eyes and pulled at her memory. It wouldn't bring Scott into focus. He'd faded, her mind no longer remembering how he slept or how he looked. She opened her eyes again, to continue her study of Ben's face. His eyes were open, studying her.

His hand came up, joining his eyes. His fingers feathered strokes on her cheek. His eyes added to the caress.

Liv let her eyes wander back to where they'd been, on his mouth. Then let them slowly drift over his chin that jutted strongly when he concentrated on something. As her eyes moved lower, she saw the pulse beating in his neck. He swallowed, and she watched the way the muscles changed when he did. Down, they continued, over his chest. At rest now, it looked softer; her fingers longed to run through the downy hair scattered over it. But this feast was for her eyes.

She let them move to his arm, shifting back to see him better, without her body lying against it. His square shoulder never rounded. Had he been a swimmer? She tilted her head to look at his forearm, his wrist, and his hand. Masculine hands with big, firm fingers, symmetrically calloused from their continued use on the strings of his guitar.

She looked back up to his chest. It rose and fell with a stronger rhythm, as if his heart was driving it harder and faster.

Back to his face, his eyes were half-lidded, getting darker and hungrier as his breathing accelerated. His mouth opened slightly, but he didn't speak.

Liv's hand slowly moved the sheet that kept the rest of him hidden. Her eyes needed to take in all of him. Would he stay still and let them? He didn't move.

Her eyes lingered on his torso, watching as his body changed the longer her eyes studied him, as though they were speaking to him. Urging him on, to feel their heat.

More movement. The muscles in his thighs beckoned her attention. His leg shifted; his knee bent slightly. Her gaze drifted over his calf, his ankle, and to his feet. She loved his feet. Feet said a lot about a man. His were strong and sturdy. They carried so much, his feet.

She let her hands find their way back up the slow trail her eyes had just taken, softly stroking his skin as they went. He breathed in deeply, almost a gasp. Her lips longed to finish the journey. She brought her mouth to his skin and continued the path, slowly easing back over each spot her eyes had rested on.

Ben was so still, the pace of his breathing measured against his stillness. Liv climbed up and laid her entire body against his. Body on body, skin on skin.

She loved it as much as he did. Her hand took his, and she gently set it against her hip, giving him permission to move, to let his body begin to take part in the exploration hers began.

His other hand came up on its own, but as slowly as the first had. At first still, they started to move along her sides. Soft fingers trailed from each hip, to the side of her breasts, and then up, slowly, over her shoulders, hardening as they got to her neck. Grasping as they reached her face, pulling as they brought her lips to his. At the same time his mouth joined with hers, his body did too. They fit together with such ease.

Liv raised up, her hands digging into his chest, the place her eyes had kept selfishly to themselves only a few minutes ago. Her eyes took their place in his, searching for the thing they needed to see. Longing, love—there it was. She kept them there as she moved, bringing them both to the place where their bodies answered the need in their eyes.

When Liv got out of the shower, Ben was sitting in the chair by the window, guitar in his arms, singing.

To see you here then, it tickles me crazy.
To see you here in the midst of your fall.

A COWBOY FALLS

I know your fear, I know your tears.
But that smile, so sweet, that longing so deep.

He stopped when he realized she stood outside the bathroom door. She smiled, leaned against the wall, and closed her eyes.

Your eyes burn into my heart,
my love, my joy, my fall.

She wanted him to keep singing; she wanted him to finish. But she couldn't wait. Ben, seeming to sense it, leaned his guitar on the floor, next to the table, as she stalked toward him.

He stood, and she launched herself into him.

"You're gonna be late, baby…"

"Don't care."

17

"Can you stay, or do you need to get back?" Liv asked Ben as he drove her back to the rodeo grounds.

"Waitin' for you to ask me. Figured I already pulled the 'I'm here, and I'm stayin' whether you want me to or not,' card. Gotta let it be up to you sometimes."

"Can you handle giving up all that control?"

Ben threw his head back, in that way he did, and laughed. "For an hour or two, probably my limit."

"I'll be riding and working with Micah most of the day. Jolene has a horse whisperer approach she wants me to try. But it's gotta be me doing it. He only responds to me."

"Kinda like me."

Liv was lost in thought about Micah and what they needed to work on. He went left, every time. Right he hesitated, yet all her instincts told her to push him that way. Even that split-second hesitation carried tension into her shoulders. That's what they needed to focus on today.

She realized Ben was watching her, smiling. "Where'd you go?"

She felt the warmth in her cheeks. "Turn two."

"I like you this way. All sweet and cowgirly."

"Never underestimate a cowgirl, Ben. We're rarely sweet."

Liv jumped out of Ben's truck, waving her hand as she walked away. She never looked back. It was a little thing, but he started to realize she did it every time. Most people looked back. She never did.

He drove to the outskirts of town and found a shady place to sit for a while. He wanted to finish the song he started this morning.

When he went to check the time, Ben remembered he broke his phone last night. *Shit*. He better get to town and get a replacement, but he doubted there'd be anything in Woodward. He'd have to go farther, maybe back to Hope. He needed to check in with the band, his kids, and his parents. When he left yesterday morning, he hadn't told anyone where he was going, considering he hadn't known that part himself.

The first call he made was to Jimmy. They wouldn't head back out on the road until Tuesday morning, but he needed to be home sometime tomorrow to pack things up and get ready.

"Where are you again?" Jimmy asked.

"Woodward, Oklahoma."

"I don't even wanna ask."

"Yeah, there's not much here, except a rodeo. And pheasant hunters."

"Huh?"

When Ben was brushing his teeth that morning, he'd noticed the sign over the sink that said, "No cleaning pheasants in sink." It stuck with him; might be a song in there somewhere.

"Whatever, never mind that. When are you coming back?"

"I was wondering if you guys could handle packing up for next week?" Ben wanted to stay through the end of the rodeo on Sunday night, to watch Liv wrap up her first showing. He'd drive back Monday and meet up with them.

"Yeah, I guess."

Ben heard the hesitation in Jimmy's voice. "What?"

"Nothin'. Can't say no, since you never ask. What's so important in middle-a-nowhere Oklahoma?"

Ben hesitated.

"Oh. No."

"What?"

"It's her, isn't it?"

"Yeah, whatever. See you Monday night." Ben ended the call.

A slew of texts started coming through on his phone, including one from Jake, who was fighting with his brother. His mom sent one saying she left a container of soup in his refrigerator, and then another asking when he'd be home.

The last texts were from Paige, one that she'd sent after he broke his phone. There was one from today, asking if he was still in town.

He answered and asked where she and Mark were. Ben wouldn't mind hanging out with him today. Maybe they'd go pheasant hunting.

There was a voicemail, too. It was from Liv, telling him she was happy he was here, and she couldn't wait to see him. He listened to it a couple of times. He'd never delete it.

"How is she?" Paige asked as soon as Ben sat down in the booth with them at the diner.

"Mad as hell at you," he teased and smiled. He watched her face go from panicked to irritated.

"I'm not gonna let you two hang out together anymore," she said, glaring at Mark.

"How did I get involved in this?" he asked.

Truth was, Ben had never seen a guy who was more of an innocent bystander than Mark. He and Paige had been married for thirty years, so Mark had to be used to it.

"When are you going back?"

"Thinkin' Monday morning."

"Things must be goin' well, then."

"If it's none of her business, you gotta say so. Until you do, she's gonna keep probing for more information," Mark said without raising his head.

Ben looked at her, "Paige, it's none of your business."

"You should be thanking me."

"Thank you, Paige," he smirked.

"Can I join you?" asked Renie.

"Of course," said Paige, motioning for Ben to scoot over.

Renie sat down, put her arm on the back of the booth, and turned to face him. "So. You're still here."

"Renie," Ben said with a killer smile, "it's none of your business." Mark high-fived him.

Liv rode Micah around and around in the warm-up arena, trying to keep her thoughts on the barrels and off of Ben. She pulled a slot further down tonight, so she wouldn't be first out of the chute. That was good and bad.

One of the bareback bronc riders had stopped by the barn today to introduce himself, and Liv noticed him riding the warm-up arena, trying to stay close to her.

"Hey, cowgirl, you chasin' the cans again tonight?"

She grinned over her shoulder. "You know it, cowboy."

"Whoo-wee, you're pretty."

There was something about Ben being in the stands tonight that let Liv flirt a little. This time she enjoyed being safe, because it meant something else entirely. She was safe to flirt, *a little*, because at the end of the night, she knew which cowboy she'd be going home with.

Thoughts of Ben whirled around in her head, until she saw Jolene glaring at her from the fence. If Jolene had her way, Ben would be on the next bus out of town. She'd made that clear this morning when Liv showed up a half hour late.

"You think we agree to train just anybody, Miss Olivia?"

Well, she was paying them, but no, that wouldn't be enough to get them to do it.

"No, ma'am, I don't, and I'm very sorry I was late."

"If you aren't gonna take this seriously, there's no point in my even bein' here. I should get in the truck and head home. I got a family, too."

"Please don't leave, Jolene. I won't be late again. Ever."

"You see that you don't 'cause, tomorrow morning, you're as much as forty-five seconds late, I'm in the truck and gone. Got it?"

"I got it." Liv walked to where Mary Beth stood holding Micah. "She doesn't mean it."

"It's better if I believe she does." Liv shook her head. "She reminds me of somebody."

"Who's that, honey?"

"Colonel Stanford Gould—my father."

Liv was up next. The ground was a little softer tonight. It had rained earlier, not enough to make a big difference, but so far every rider had knocked over a barrel, resulting in a five-second penalty. Two riders remained after Liv, so if she left all three barrels standing, she had a very good chance to stay in the money.

She got the signal and Micah flew. He went left, circled around, headed right, and hugged the circle in the opposite direction. There was only one barrel left in the clover pattern. He was flying fast but hugging the barrels tight. They headed for home and finished with a time of sixteen point three. She beat last night's time by five-tenths of a second.

Liv rubbed Micah's neck. He loved to roll in the dirt, and tonight she'd let him.

She led him to the barn and saw a man standing with his shoulder up against the door. His cowboy hat sat low over his eyes, and his jeans hung low on his hips, the way they always did. His shirt hitched up enough that her eye caught his skin. The man was hot, no other way to describe him.

"Damn you're pretty," he said as she got closer. "You got any plans tonight, darlin', 'cause I sure want to be the man keepin' company with you."

She shook her head and smiled. "Sorry, cowboy, but my dance card is already full this evenin'. Maybe another time."

"Then, sugar, I'm gonna make sure you never make it to the dance." Ben took Micah's reins from her hand and pulled her in close. His thigh inched between hers and spread them apart, and he bent his head to kiss her without knocking her hat off. Liv reached up and threw it off anyway. She wanted to kiss him so hard she took his breath away. Never before had she wished somebody else could take care of Micah.

"Wait," she said. "Where are we going?"

"Back to the hotel."

"But what about Renie, and Paige, and Mark?"

"Sorry, sugar, but it's just you and me tonight."

He watched the heat rise to her cheeks.

"Liv, I need this. I need you to tell me this means something to you." He watched as her breath caught.

"It does, Ben."

"Tell me you belong to me, your body and your soul."

Her eyes widened, and her breathing became uneven.

"Tell me," he said again, as his fingers encircled her wrist.

"I belong to you, Ben," she breathed.

When they pulled up to the hotel, Ben came around and opened her door.

"When we get in the room, I want you to take off your clothes and wait for me on the bed."

She bit her lip, hesitating only for a moment.

Ben stood and watched her do what he asked. He didn't move. His mouth watered, longing for a taste of her. His arms ached, wanting to pull her into him and let her comfort his insecurities.

Liv stood next to the bed, her clothes at her feet. Her body trembled as she pulled the comforter back, then the sheets. When she lay down on the bed and reached for the sheet, he was on her, his hand on her wrist, stopping her.

"Watch me," he said as he pulled his shirt over his head. Her eyes moved over his body, the same way they had earlier that morning.

He reached behind her head and put one pillow on top of the other. "I want you to be able to see what I'm doing to you."

He stood before her, naked. His hands moved along her legs, up her thighs and her waist, until she arched instinctively.

"Ben—"

"Shh. Be still."

He wanted her to give herself over to him, even as hard as he knew it would be for her to do it. He wanted her to let him take control the same way he'd let her this morning, without her realizing he did.

Every second had been pure torture for him. He'd wanted nothing more than to grab her and throw her under him, but he hadn't. He let her eyes, her hands, and her lips linger on his body, unhurried, at her pace. Now he needed the same thing from her.

"Put your hands at your sides, Liv, and don't move them."

He needed to prove to her that he was the man to take care of her, love her enough to make it all about her, satisfy the need he saw in her eyes. He was long gone for this woman.

He hoped she hadn't gone to sleep, that he hadn't worn her out. "Liv?"

"Hmm?"

"Is there anyone else?"

"Ben—"

She sounded exasperated, and he couldn't let her dissuade him. "Tell me I'm the only one."

"You're the only one."

"Say it again."

"Stop it, Ben."

"I need to know."

Liv sat up and pulled the sheet over her. "What's going on?"

"I want to know."

"I answered you, but you haven't answered me."

"Why didn't you ask me to come, Liv? Why did Paige have to do it? Didn't you want me here?"

"Because *we* promised not to do this. Not just me, both of us. You promised not to ask me to give up my dream for you, and I did the same. That's why, Ben. I didn't think it was fair to ask something of you that I couldn't give you in return."

"Is this enough for you?"

"What do you mean?"

"Seeing each other once every three or four months?"

She got up and grabbed her clothes.

"What are you doing?"

"I'm getting dressed."

"Why?"

She turned and glared at him, dropping her clothes back on the floor.

"You tell me why, Ben. Why do you keep asking if you're the only one for me? *Jesus!* Isn't it enough that you're the only man I've been with in *twenty years*? You need constant reassurance that, as soon as we're apart, I didn't fall in bed with someone else? Why, Ben? Is that what you did?"

"I just want to know why it's so easy for you. It's killing me not to be with you, yet you seem fine."

"Fine? I seem fine. Really?"

When he nodded, she picked her clothes back up, but he yanked them away.

"Don't hide from me, Liv. You either run, or you hide, and tonight I'm not going to let you do either. Talk to me, tell me how you feel."

She reached out and grabbed the sheet, yanking it hard. It came off the bed, and she wrapped it around her.

"You always do this."

"What do I do, Liv? Is it so bad that I want to know you better?"

"It isn't that you want to know me better; it's that whatever you want, you have to have *right now*. You push too hard. You decided you wanted to know more about me, so you followed me around and asked me questions, endlessly. You wouldn't stop, Ben. You forced it. Let's go back further. You came to my house. You showed up there. You didn't even call. You came. And you didn't ask. You just stayed.

"You insisted I tell you about my life, whether I was ready to or not. Then, worse, you made me, forced me, to listen to yours. I wasn't ready for that.

"I asked you to give me time to follow my dreams. One rodeo, Ben. That's all I've done. Competed in one rodeo. Is that all I get before you swoop in…" Her eyes filled with tears.

Ben watched her pace back and forth next to the bed, trying to hold the sheet up as she did, but it would slip, and she would trip on it. And every time she did, she'd glare at him, as though it was his fault.

And he, asshole that he was, thought it was the cutest, sweetest, craziest thing he'd ever seen. She tried to be mad at him, but she sucked at it. It was harder than hell for him to fight the smile trying to escape his lips. She was adorable when she tried to be mad.

When she growled at him, he couldn't help it…he laughed, and she stopped moving. She stood next to the bed, holding the sheet up with one hand, glaring at him.

"I'm sorry," he said, but he couldn't stop laughing.

"No, you're not. You're not sorry at all. You think this is funny."

"Liv. Olivia. Olivia Fairchild. It isn't funny."

"Then why are you still laughing? You can't stop, can you?"

He couldn't. He tried to, but he couldn't. Maybe if he didn't look at her. But where else could he look? He grabbed her around the waist and pulled her on top of him.

She smiled, not mad anymore. He hoped what he was about to do wouldn't make her mad again.

"Liv."

"Ben." Her eyes softened, her lips still smiling. She was being silly now, but he had to do it anyway.

"I love you."

18

Ben held his breath. Her expression didn't change, and she didn't say anything. Nothing. Had she heard him?

Finally, she moved. Her hand came up, and her fingers stroked his cheek. Then she licked her lips. Twice. She put her hand on the back of his neck and pulled herself up, so her lips were closer to his.

She kissed him, softly at first. Lips brushing lips. Then she went deeper. Her hand pulled at him; her fingers dug into his skin.

"Liv—"

"Shh." She unwrapped herself from the sheet and threw it to the side. Her hands pushed at his shoulders, forcing him to lie on his back.

"Skin on skin," she murmured as she climbed on top of him and rested her body against his.

In the night, they turned, still holding each other, face to face. Ben opened his eyes. Liv looked peaceful, and breathtaking. He traced the curve of her jaw, once again moved by how deeply she affected him.

He glanced at the clock; it was a little after seven. If he woke her now, they'd have time to have breakfast together before she had to be at the barn. It would be a normal, everyday kind of thing, and it would be about her.

He'd listened last night. He pushed too hard. She said it to him that day in Vegas. When he'd asked if it was too much, she answered too soon.

"Hey, cowgirl, time to wake up." He kissed her eyelids, then moved down to the tip of her nose, then each soft cheek. "Wake up, baby."

"Hmm, what time is it?"

"Early enough for you to have breakfast and still be on time."

"Good," she groaned, and when she stretched, the sheet fell away from her body. "I'm starving."

Ben needed to get out of bed now, right now, while they still had time to have breakfast. They hadn't had dinner last night, and he had to make sure she ate this morning. If he got lost in her body again, they wouldn't have time.

"Come on," he said, pulling her arm. "I'll start the shower for you."

She pulled him toward her. "No, come back. We have time."

It would be so easy to climb back in bed and take what he needed from her, but she needed nourishment more than she needed him.

He let go of her arm, bent down, and put her over his shoulder. "Shower, baby, let's go."

"Nooo. What are you doing? Ben, stop!" Her fists pounded at his back.

Ben reached in and turned the shower on. Ice cold water. Perfect. He climbed in and set her on her feet. Liv screamed when the frigid water hit her back, and started pummeling him. And laughing.

It was going to be a good day.

"Pancakes. Wait. And sausage. Or bacon. Just bring both. And eggs, scrambled. Oh, and toast. Don't forget toast."

The waitress stood with one hand on her hip, waiting for Liv to finish. "Anything else? Hash browns?"

"Oh yes, hash browns, that sounds good. Thanks." Liv turned to Ben. "What are you having?"

Before he answered, she started talking to the waitress again. "Oh, and coffee. And juice. Um, do you have tomato juice?"

"Yep, got it. Coffee and tomato juice." She continued to look at Liv, expectantly.

"That's it for me. What are you having, Ben? Come on, order. We need to be quick, so I'm not late."

"I'll have what she's having."

That got a laugh out of the waitress, who seemed as amused by Liv as he was.

Liv read the program for the rodeo she picked up on their way into the diner.

"Whatcha' lookin' for?"

"Nothin'," she answered absentmindedly, as she hurriedly flipped through pages. She stopped, set the booklet down, and folded her hands on top of it.

"I'm sorry. That was rude."

"It's okay. You can read if you want to."

"It's not very polite," she murmured.

"I don't mind." Ben took her hands in his. "Relax. I can be with you without having your undivided attention."

She raised her eyebrow. "Can you?"

"I can do whatever it takes, baby."

"Whatever." She grinned and rolled her eyes at him, and then went back to reading her program.

"There you are." Renie plopped down on the bench seat, beside her mother. "Check your messages much?"

"Huh? What are you talking about?"

"Where's your phone, Mom?"

Liv reached into her back pocket and pulled it out. "Sorry, I don't remember turning it off."

"No kidding. I've been trying to get in touch with you since last night."

Liv squinted at Ben.

"What?"

"Did *you* turn my phone off last night?"

"No idea what you're talking about."

"What if something had happened to Micah?" Her tone changed.

"Everyone knows where we're staying, Liv. They would've come and knocked on the door."

"My daughter tried to reach me. What about that?"

"If it had been an emergency, I would have done what Ben said. Don't be upset," Renie answered for Ben.

The waitress, plus a helper from the kitchen, set plates of food down on the table.

"Who else is having breakfast with you two?"

"You are," Liv answered, her mouth terse as she spoke.

Yep, he screwed up.

Liv was distracted the rest of the morning. She knew it and so did Jolene.

"Get him out of here. Send him home."

"What are you talking about?"

"Ben. Send him home."

"I can't do that, Jolene. It's one more race."

"I don't like having him here. You aren't focused."

"That isn't fair."

"It's a simple rule, Liv, and one that'll make you win more often."

What was Jolene talking about? Was she suggesting that Liv not allow Ben to come to the rodeos she competed in? That sounded ludicrous.

"Mark my words."

"Jolene, come on, what would Larry have said if you told him not to come and watch you."

"He never did."

"He never came and watched you? Seriously?"

"I wanted to win more than you do."

Liv still thought Jolene unreasonable, but that night, when she knocked over not one but two barrels and rode herself out of the money, she started to think Jolene might be right.

"I don't care if you didn't place; we're going out and celebrating."

"Dottie, I appreciate it, but I'm not up for it."

"Buck up, buttercup. Since I've known you, there's never been a day that I haven't been proud of you. Don't make the first time it happens be tonight."

Liv felt five years old, between Ben turning her phone off last night and Jolene telling her that she shouldn't let Ben watch her ride. Now Dottie told her she was behaving badly. Liv wanted to load Micah into her trailer and drive home. And not to Texas, to Colorado.

"Don't do it," Paige said.

"I didn't see you standing there." Liv ran her hand through her hair and bit her lower lip. "Don't do what?"

"Leave."

"What the heck, Paige?"

"Tell me that wasn't what you were thinking about."

"Doesn't mean I'd do it. Hey, where is Ben?" She realized she hadn't seen him.

"He's with Mark. Thought he'd give you space."

Liv told Paige what Jolene said, about Ben not being there when she rode.

"Sounds like a load of crap to me."

Liv laughed. "Yeah, well, there's that. But also, I was distracted today. I was mad at him."

"So learn how to be mad at him and still stay focused. Practice that, instead of keeping him away."

Ben was nursing his second coke when Liv walked into the bar, her entourage in tow. Jolene walked by and glared at him.

"She doesn't like the balls," Mark snickered. "If she liked 'em better, she might not be such a bitch."

"I heard that," said Dottie, tweaking Mark's cheek. "We're gettin' a table. You fellas gonna join us?"

Mark stood to follow, but Ben stayed seated.

"What are you doing? Come on, we're gonna get something to eat."

"Give me a minute."

He watched as everyone else walked into the other room. Everyone but Liv, who walked toward him.

"You hidin' from me, cowboy?"

"Am I in trouble?"

"Nah, you're not. But here's the thing; is this about you, Ben? Or is it about me? You're not used to things being about somebody other than you. You might want to consider that."

She turned on the heel of her fancy cowboy boots and walked off in the direction of the table. When she got two feet away from him, she turned and looked back over her shoulder. It was the first time he'd ever seen her look back. He got off the bar stool and followed.

Before they got to the table, Ben put his hand on Liv's waist, and she stopped walking.

"This is what I'm talking about. This is my time, Ben. I've never had that, never let myself. Before I can give myself to anyone, I have to fill myself up. Do you understand?"

He was working on it, he just needed to try a little harder, not for just a day, but every day.

Liv almost wished she'd left yesterday. She wouldn't have to say goodbye to Ben now if she had.

She had the trailer hooked up to the truck and was ready to get on the road. She decided to go home for a couple of days, regroup, and then get herself back out there. It was a seven-hour drive, but instead of driving, she wanted to sleep. Thank goodness she'd have Renie with her to keep her awake.

Ben insisted she let him load the last of her stuff into the back of her truck while she said goodbye to everybody else.

"Ready?"

That wasn't what she expected. She'd expected at least a little drama from him. If she was learning anything, it was he was unpredictable.

He walked to her passenger door and held it open, as if he expected something from her.

"What?"

"Are you ready to go?"

"Yeah, I guess I am. Does Renie want to drive?"

"I'm gonna drive the first leg so you can rest."

"What are you talking about?"

"I'll drive for a couple hours, or I can drive the whole way if you want me to."

"Who's driving your truck?"

"Bill."

"Ben—" She sighed heavily and closed her eyes. "Oh, hell with it. Never mind. Let's go. Where is Renie anyway?"

"She's riding with Billy. We're caravanning, baby. At least until Walsenburg. This'll be fun."

It occurred to Liv that perhaps she had as many control issues as Ben. After all, she was furious that all of this had been decided without a single one of them asking her opinion.

"Hard, isn't it?"

"What?" she barked at him.

"Lettin' go."

"Shut up."

Ben put his arm around her waist and swung her up into the truck. "Use the time to figure out which events you're gonna enter between now and Las Vegas."

"As if I had a prayer of making it this year. Get real."

"Gotta dream, baby."

Liv hadn't gotten a penny of the purse in Woodward, not that she'd expected to. She'd be lucky if she earned enough to get her membership card before December.

"What do you want to listen to on our ride, baby?"

"Who's my favorite band?"

"CB Rice."

"Um, no. Isn't that weird, to listen to your own music? What do you do, sing along?"

Ben laughed. "Kidding, Liv. So, who?"

"Let's listen to a country station for a bit."

Ben rolled his eyes.

"I saw that."

Liv mapped out the events she'd compete in for the rest of the season. There were a couple of events in Colorado in August, and one in Idaho. In September, she'd be in Albuquerque and Salt Lake City.

"Is that it for September? If it is, you could come see me for a couple days."

"Well, there's another event, in Kansas City, but it's cards only."

"You're speakin' a foreign language now, sweetheart."

"I'll be on a permit until I win a cumulative total of one thousand dollars. Then I'll get my membership card."

"Yeah? I'm sure you'll win that much before Kansas City. Aren't you?"

Liv turned her face toward the window, and Ben put his hand on hers. "Scoot over here, closer to me. That's what bench seats are for."

She did, and he put his hand on her thigh. "You can do it. I believe in you. You gotta believe in yourself if you wanna fill yourself up."

"Okay, I hear you." Liv stared out the window, quiet for a few minutes. "In October I'll be in Tulsa, and then the second half of the month, there are two events in Texas. One is top thirty only, in Waco. And then Rock Springs is top twelve in the Mountain State Circuit."

"There you go. See? You believe in yourself."

"What's your schedule?"

Ben's eyes got wide, and he stared at her with his mouth open. "What? You haven't been on our website? You haven't memorized our schedule?"

She couldn't remember the last time she had.

"Pull it up on your phone."

Ben would be in the Midwest, and then on the East Coast until the middle of September, and he didn't have more than one day off at a time between now and then. The second half of September, he had three days off, before they went to Texas and back to Denver. After that, he left right away for the West Coast, where they'd be until the end of October. Beyond that, there wasn't anything scheduled yet.

"I guess I'll see you in November." She looked out the window again.

"Where are you?"

"We don't have to figure this out right now."

Ben took a couple of deep breaths, trying not to let her see him do it. He needed to learn to let go. He didn't need to know right this minute when the next time he'd see Liv would be. It would be hard, but if he wanted this thing to work between them, he had to get used to them being apart more than together. At least for the time being.

"I think I will try to sleep for a little while, if you don't mind."

"No, go ahead." He needed time to think anyway.

A COWBOY FALLS

They'd been lovers for almost five months. When they were together, it was so intense, it threatened to rob him of his sanity. Ben wondered why his lust for her hadn't cooled, because they'd been apart more than together. It hadn't diminished at all. Not even close.

Every time Ben thought he had a handle on wanting to pull the truck over and bend her over the tailgate, she'd make a soft, sexy noise. Or she'd turn, trying to get more comfortable, and the buttons on her shirt would strain enough that he got a glimpse of her skin. He got to the point where he thought he'd be better off if he didn't look at her. It was only an hour into the drive. Five more until they hit Walsenburg, where he'd get in his truck and drive west, and she'd head north.

This morning was the last time he'd be with her for…he didn't know how long. Skin on skin, that's what he thought about now. He needed her again.

Ben's hands gripped the steering wheel tighter. He took off his hat and started fiddling with the air conditioner. Man, it had gotten hot in here all of a sudden.

"Ben?" The way she said his name, the perfect little lilt in her voice, made him crazy.

"Need a break, baby? I can stop at the next exit."

"Okay." There it was again, that melodic voice that made his jeans more uncomfortable with every word she spoke. How in the hell would he be able to say goodbye to her in a couple of hours? He needed her underneath him. He wondered what she'd say if he said so.

"What're you thinkin' about, Ben?"

Oh, God, his mouth went dry. Bone dry. "When you say my name that way…it burns me up."

Liv knew what Ben meant. She hadn't slept, but instead imagined him stopping the truck and taking her up against her pickup—fast and hard.

The expression on his face was…dangerous. "Tell me what you want."

"I can't wait." Her body was on fire.

"Lick your lips, the way you did when I told you I loved you."

Her tongue ran over her top lip, twice, as she had then.

"Do it again."

She did, and the sound that came from deep in his throat made her eyes close.

"Stay here." Ben had driven into a service station and parked. Bill pulled Ben's truck behind them. Paige and Mark drove in behind him in their car.

"I have to talk to Bill," Ben opened the door of the truck.

"Why? Ben, what are you doing?"

Liv tried to see where he went, but the trailer blocked her view. She started to jump out and remembered he told her to stay put, and right this minute, she'd do whatever Ben told her to do. That was how badly she wanted him. If he came back and told her to take off her clothes in broad daylight, she doubted she'd be able to deny him.

Ben got back in the truck and slammed his door closed.

"What's going on?"

"They're goin' on ahead."

"Ben—"

"Not now, Liv. Listen to me. Please. And I'm begging you, please don't fight me on this."

She nodded.

"We'll meet them back at your place. I told them I wasn't sure when we'd be there."

Ben's eyes were fiery; there was no sign of his sweet smile. In its place, he was almost scowling.

She launched herself at him, throwing herself across his lap. Her mouth crushed down on his as her hands fisted in his shirt.

"I want you right now, Liv."

She didn't answer, but she hoped he had a plan. Her need for him bordered on primal. She wanted to be taken by this man—in every way he wanted to take her.

He scrubbed his hand over his face. "God, I can't even think."

Liv pointed across the road, to a chain hotel.

"You make me crazy. What I want to do to you."

"Anything you want, Ben…hurry."

"Wait here," he said for the second time.

Ben walked up to the desk and tossed his credit card on the counter. "Need a room."

"Sure. Only one night for you?"

"Yep, that works."

"Would you prefer a king-size bed or two queens?"

What was that? What was she doing with her eyes? Oh no, was she flirting with him? He didn't have time for this.

"Whichever one would be ready first."

"Either one." Ben saw it again, the eye thing. He recognized it, but it was the last thing he wanted to see right now.

"I'll take the king. Listen, I'm in a hurry here."

The girl all but jammed his credit card through the machine. Yep, he recognized that look too. He didn't care how pissed off she got, as long as she hurried.

"Around the back, number one twelve."

The door had almost closed behind him before he remembered to say thanks.

Ben opened the door to the room and let Liv go in before him. Once inside, he plastered his body to hers. One of his hands slipped into her hair, threading his fingers through it and pulling her head to one side, so he had full access to her throat. His lips followed the curve of it up to her ear. "Driving me crazy."

He stepped back, grabbed her hand, and led her with him to the bed.

Liv fisted her hands in his shirt, ripped it open and ran her fingers over his chest. He crushed his mouth into hers.

"I can't stop, Liv. I can't even slow down."

"Don't. God, don't slow down."

"Remember you said that."

His hands pulled off her shirt. Then her bra, jeans, and panties.

In an instant, he was inside her. His lips moved to her neck and lit it on fire. The calloused fingers of his strong hands rubbed across her wrists. He went still, his eyes boring into hers—his look so intense her eyes closed.

"Open them, baby. Look at me."

When she did, he started moving again, slowly. "I love you, Liv."

"Ben, I—" she closed her eyes, unable to bring herself to say the words he wanted to hear.

"Your skin on mine, where it's meant to be. This is where we're meant to be, Liv. You and me, together forever."

Ben's truck was in her driveway when they got home six hours later.

"When do you have to leave?" Liv asked.

"I'm not leaving until tomorrow morning. I'm trying to get in touch with my dad. I'm hoping he can fly over and get me. I can get the truck when we're back for the next show in Denver. If you don't mind me leaving it here."

"You can park your car in my garage anytime you want to."

"You've been spending too much time with Mark. And, by the way, you don't have a garage, baby."

"Minor detail. By the way, if you're hungry, I don't have much food in the house."

Liv had enough food in her freezer to feed every one of the hands who worked the Patterson Ranch. He'd never seen so much food in one person's house. "I think we'll be able to find something."

She unlocked the back of the trailer and chattered to Micah all the while. "You must be so tired of being on the road, boy. Mama got a little distracted on the way home. I'm sorry for that. I mean, I'm sorry for you, not so much for me."

Was she not the purest thing that ever lived? Ben would miss her so much. Laughing with her. Talking with her. Sitting in silence with her. Touching her. It hadn't been six hours since he touched her, all of her, and he craved her all over again.

"Hey, are you sure you aren't gonna need your truck? I mean, it's sweet and all of you to stay with me tonight, but when will you be back here again?"

"I'll be on tour, no need for the truck."

Tour. God. How in the hell was he going to get through it without her with him?

19

Liv dropped Ben off at the airport in Centennial but stayed in the car. They'd stayed up all night, talking, having sex, talking more. She was tired, but she wouldn't have traded the time with him for anything in the world.

"This is one of the hardest things I've ever done," he said to her before he got out of the car. "Every bit of me wants to ask you to go with me."

"I'm not full yet, Ben."

"I get it, Liv. I really do."

Part of what they talked about last night was how important barrel racing was to her. For the first time in her life, she was doing something for herself, and she had to do it. If she didn't, she wasn't sure what would become of her. It wasn't as though they hadn't talked about it before, but it was something Liv believed they needed to continue reminding each other of. Not just her dreams, but his too. She didn't expect him to give her space alone; she had to do the same for him. That's why she hadn't asked him to come to Woodward. It wasn't that she didn't want or need him there. She had.

All of it had resonated with Ben. He'd been there, more than once, he'd told her, when he knew that if he didn't do something, he'd be lost. True with his music, and his sobriety, once he'd decided to own it.

"I get it," he'd said. "It was also the way I felt the week I showed up at your place unannounced. And again when I threw a bag in my truck and drove to Oklahoma, not understanding why, but knowing I had to do it anyway." He'd told her he was powerless not to do either of those things.

"Olivia Fairchild, I'm gonna miss you like crazy."

"Me, too."

"I like knowing you will. Anything else you need to say to me before I go, get on a plane, and fly west?"

"I don't want to let go of this, Ben."

Liv cried the entire way home. She pulled off the highway in Castle Rock because she was sobbing. But it was good crying, not *end of the world* sobbing. It was *I'll miss him so much.*

Jolene was due to arrive at her place in the morning to coach her, but only for a couple of days. The next two events were in Colorado, then she'd head up to Idaho. She'd do these events on her own, and that's the way she wanted it.

When she pulled into the driveway and saw Ben's truck, she thought she might start crying again, but she didn't. Seeing it there soothed her. She went in the house, climbed into bed and fell asleep, clothes and all.

When Liv went to change clothes the next morning, she found another shirt of Ben's hanging on the knob of her closet door. She loved that he did that, and wondered what he took of hers this time.

She went out to get Micah ready and take care of the rest of the horses when Jolene pulled in. She parked next to Ben's truck and pointed at it.

"He's here?"

"No. He's not. His truck is here. Okay?"

Jolene grumbled. "Good" was the only word Liv could understand.

Jolene stayed for the planned two days, and then told Liv she was ready. They'd see what her times were at the next three events, and Jolene would review the videos she arranged to have taken of Liv's rides. Then they'd get together to work out whatever kinks crept up.

The first event was three nights at the Douglas County Fairgrounds in Castle Rock. Since it was only a forty-five-minute drive from the ranch, she didn't bother getting an overnight stall for Micah.

She did well all three nights, ended up in the top two, and won seven hundred and fifty dollars.

In Pueblo, she placed second at the State Fair rodeo, which meant she had enough winnings to get her full membership in the Women's Professional Rodeo Association. Next up was Idaho.

The tour bus pulled out of Chicago, headed for the show in Cleveland the next night.

"Go to sleep," Jimmy said to Ben, "and try not to be as much of an asshole tomorrow."

Ben wanted to tell Jimmy to go fuck himself, but his friend was right; he was an asshole. They'd been on the road three weeks, and every part of his body ached for Liv.

After Cleveland, they had one night off, and then they'd play four nights in a row, ending in Philadelphia.

As much as Ben hated being away from Liv and his boys, he loved touring and interacting with the audiences every night. These were by far the biggest venues and biggest crowds CB Rice had ever seen. On stage, he was fine. The rest of the time, he was miserable.

It was Sunday night, which meant Liv would be finishing up at the Magic Valley Stampede in Filer, Idaho. It would be her first event as a full-member rider. She'd been worried about making enough to qualify in two months, yet she did it in two events. He was so proud of her he thought his heart would burst.

He checked his phone for the hundredth time, wishing he'd hear from her, but still nothing.

At two in the morning, something jarred him awake, and he checked his phone. There were no calls from Liv, but there was one from Renie. It had come in around midnight, followed by a text from her, asking him to call her as soon as he got the message, no matter what time it was. *Fuck.*

"Ben?"

"Yeah, Renie—"

"There's been an accident."

Every muscle in Ben's body seized, and all the air left his lungs. He felt like he was about to have a heart attack. "Tell me."

"She's in a coma."

Ben's cry woke everyone on the bus. Jimmy slept in the bunk closest to Ben. "What's going on?"

"Oh no, *Jesus*. What are they saying?" Pause. "Okay, I'm on my way. I'll get there as fast as I can."

"What is it? Come on, Ben, tell me what it is, so I can help you."

"It's Liv. An accident."

"On it."

"Call my dad."

They were still three hours outside of Cleveland. By the time the bus got there, Ben's dad would be waiting with the plane. From Cleveland, it would take another six hours to get Ben to Twin Falls, Idaho.

Ben talked to Renie again, and then to Paige. Jimmy got on the phone with Frank, the band's manager, and asked him to cancel the Cleveland show.

At one in the afternoon, Ben walked into St. Luke's Hospital in Idaho's Magic Valley. Mark was waiting for him inside the front entrance, his eyes bloodshot, and his hands in his pockets.

No, no, no. Ben went dizzy and leaned against his father. "Tell me," he managed to say.

"She's critical."

Liv was in the intensive care unit, and Renie was with her when he walked in. There were tubes and machines hooked up to her everywhere. Ben put his head in his hands and cried.

"Stop that," Paige barked at him, then softened her tone. "She's going to get through this."

Ben's arms ached with the need to hold her. Renie's head came up when she saw him, and she came out.

"Go ahead and go in," she murmured. "I'll tell you more after you've seen her."

Ben put one foot in front of the other. He saw himself moving forward, but the walk to her bedside was the longest of his life.

She had a metal device on her head, with screws going into her skull. Her face had scrapes and cuts on the side of it, and a machine did her breathing for her. Ben kissed her forehead, sat down, and started to talk.

He talked, and talked, and talked. He told her every detail about the show the night before, in Chicago. He told her which songs had been crowd favorites and which ones he'd chosen to do for encores. He asked her about her race, and about what happened. He had the same conversation he would've had if they had talked last night. Except she couldn't answer.

Ben told her he wanted to play "Fall for Me" last night, but had decided that the first time he played her song, he wanted her in the audience, so he hadn't. And then he broke down.

Paige came in and put her arms around his shoulder. "Come with me, Ben." She ushered him out of the room, and Mark stepped forward, put his hand on Ben's arm, and walked him away from the ICU.

Ben sat, head in his hands, and cried. He'd found her, his reason for living. What would he do if he lost her now?

"She's gonna be okay." That simple statement from Mark brought him back. Ben turned to him.

"No one else is letting go of Liv. If you are, then you shouldn't be here."

"What do you mean?"

"When you're with her, you need to tell her you believe she's going to be okay. She lived. She's gonna be okay."

Mark was right. He'd only been thinking of himself. Liv herself would say, "This is about me, not about you."

"Paige can tell you what the doctors said, if you're ready."

Ben nodded.

Paige explained that the doctors had two treatment options. Liv could stay in traction for twelve weeks, to see if her neck injury healed on its own. Or, they could try surgery. With surgery, the risk was significant, with a chance Liv wouldn't survive it.

They wouldn't do anything, however, until they determined the reason for her coma. Nothing on the MRI indicated why she wasn't conscious.

"They want us to keep talking to her, just like you were, Ben," Paige said. "She may be able to hear us. Before you go back in, I want to talk to you about the tour," said Paige.

"What about it?"

"You need to get back to it."

"You've gotta be kidding."

"If there is a change in her condition, we'll get in touch with you. But Ben, you've got sold out shows, a band, and a crew depending on you."

He couldn't even consider leaving. If the doctors didn't know why she wasn't conscious, that meant that she might wake up at any time. He would be here when she did.

His father called Ben's cell and told him he'd found them a place to stay for the night, not far from the hospital, and he'd rented a car. "I'm on my way now," he told Ben before they ended the call.

Ben went back in to see Liv, while Mark waited for Ben's father.

"How is she?" Ben's father asked Mark.

"No change."

"How's my boy?"

"In bad shape. Paige has been talking to him about going back to the tour. How many concerts have they canceled so far?"

"Just tonight's. They didn't have a show scheduled tomorrow night."

"Something happened at the arena, right after Liv's accident. A close family friend was there. He was competing in another event and saw what happened. He waited with Liv while the medical team called for an ambulance. She was conscious."

"And?"

"She told Billy not to let Ben come if he tried."

"Why not?"

"She said that she and Ben had promised one another, but that was all. Has something happened between them in the last couple of weeks?"

"I don't know."

"Paige is convinced Liv can hear us; that's why it's so important we keep talking to her, but not say anything that might upset her."

"So she wants Ben to leave?"

"Yes. She does."

Billy Patterson came off the elevator with Dottie and his dad.

"Where's our girl?" Dottie asked Mark.

"I'll take you to her. Give me just a minute. Have you met Bud? This is Ben's father."

After they were introduced, Mark asked Bud if he minded waiting while he took Bill and Dottie back.

"Don't worry about me. I'll wait here, but before you go, can I talk to you for just a minute?" Bud went to the window, and Mark followed.

"Do you want me to talk to Ben?"

"Paige will, but she wants your help convincing him. We'll keep in contact with him and let him know if there's any change, but she thinks he should leave."

"I know my son. It won't be easy to talk him into leaving."

Mark nodded. "I completely understand."

Paige and Renie came out, and Dottie and Bill went back in their place. Ben came out a few minutes later.

"Hey, Dad."

"Hello, son," Bud answered.

"What the hell is *he* doing here? She doesn't want him here," Billy shouted.

"*Billy!*" Paige put her hand on his arm. "Please take Renie downstairs and get her something to eat, and bring me back a cup of coffee."

Billy pointed at Ben. "You be gone when I get back."

Mark stepped in front of him and turned him in the direction of the elevator. "Not now," Mark said to him.

A COWBOY FALLS

Ben turned to Paige. "What the hell was that about? And what is *Junior* doing here?"

Bud put his hand on his son's arm. "Ben, please sit. Paige needs to talk to you."

Ben did as his dad asked, as though he was on autopilot. Paige sat on the other side of him, leaned forward, and put her hands on his.

"You need to go back out on tour."

"I already told you I wouldn't leave."

"Son, there's something Paige needs to tell you." Bud looked at her. "Go ahead, Paige."

"Liv told Billy that you promised each other. I'm guessing you know what she meant by that."

Ben nodded.

"You know in your heart that Liv wouldn't want you to miss this opportunity. This is your tour. Your shot. Your year. We will be here with her, and so will Renie. We'll contact you the minute there's a change."

"No, Paige. I'm not leaving. The tour doesn't matter. Nothing matters but Liv."

Ben's father shook his head.

A nurse came out to the ICU waiting area and told them that Liv couldn't have any more visitors today. They'd already exceeded the number permitted.

Bud talked Ben into going to the hotel.

"Before you say anything, I'm not going back on tour, Dad. Don't try to talk me into it."

"It's your decision."

"But you think I should?"

"I didn't say that."

"What would you do, if it was Mom?"

"I *always* do what your mother wants." Bud laughed and so did Ben, almost.

"I can't leave her."

"What can you do to help her?"

He wanted to be there when she woke up. Until she did, he would hold her hand and talk to her, and sing to her. Anything to help her.

"What if she knows you're here?"

"Then it'll be one more reason for her to wake up."

Jimmy called and told him they'd posted on the website and social media that the concert in Cleveland had been canceled due to a family emergency. Once they had, the response from the fans had been overwhelming. Posts of support came from everywhere.

"Support for what?"

"For Liv."

"How does anyone know about her?"

A COWBOY FALLS

"You live in a fishbowl, Ben. We're on a national tour, and it's sold out. The fans' response to the new album has been phenomenal."

Jimmy was right. At the beginning of the tour, they were booking smaller venues, and they'd sell out in minutes. The tour promoters pushed for bigger venues, and they sold out too. Ben had a hard time wrapping his head around it. All the years they'd dreamed of success and suddenly, inexplicably, it was happening.

A few months ago, they'd played the Paramount in Denver, and now they sold out Red Rocks—where they'd been an opening band a year ago, and where he first met Liv.

There was a knock on the door, and his dad walked over to it. When he saw Paige, Ben told Jimmy he'd call him back.

"What does Liv want?"

"Let up, Paige."

"What would you want, if it were you? Would you want her to give up her dream? Would you tell her to sit by your side, and let her dream dissolve into nothing? Would you let her do that, Ben?"

No, he wouldn't. Ben got up from the bed and walked to the window. A few minutes later, he heard the hotel room door close. When he turned around again, his dad was sitting in the chair, his fingers steepled in front of his mouth and nose.

"Come to any decisions?" he asked.

"Yeah," he said with reservation. "I'll fly into Hartford tomorrow night. I'd like to use the plane, Dad. If there's a change in her condition, I want to be able to get back as fast as possible."

"We'll go together, Ben. I'll stay with you on tour for the time being."

Ben knew his father's biggest concern, and he was glad he didn't say it. Yeah, he wanted a drink more than anything. And not just one, he wanted a whole bottle.

The next morning, Ben visited the hospital, and told Liv he was going back on tour. He was doing it for her, because he loved her. He hoped Paige was right, and Liv heard him.

20

The following night, they were in Hartford, Connecticut. Ben walked out on stage, and was met by chants.

"*Liv, Liv, Liv,*" the audience shouted.

He pulled a stool to the front of the stage, sat down, and did what came naturally to him. He told them about her. Ten thousand people went silent and listened.

"I told Liv that I wouldn't play this song until she was here with me, to hear it live for the first time, but I feel her here, through you."

Ben started to play, just him, the rest of the band stayed silent along with the audience.

Sweet beauty on steps, waiting, like me
Sun masked by clouds, so free
Beautiful, if only you were able to move,
To go, to ride, to smile, to fly, to kiss, to fall.
I know how deep your smile, if only you could fall
I know how wild your passion, if only you
    would fall
I know how deep your longing, if only you
    could fall.
I know your fear, I know your tears

But that smile, so sweet, that longing so deep
Your eyes burn into my heart, my love, my joy, my fall.
You know my longing deep, you know my love, so hard
You know my longing deep, you know my passion, so wild
You know my fall.
To see you here then, in the midst of your fall
To know your joy, so deep, to know your passion, complete
To know your longing, my all, and then, my sweet, you fall.

When Ben woke up the next morning, Jimmy told him a fan had posted "Fall for Me" on YouTube. It had three million views. Overnight.

The doctors recommended Liv be moved to a hospital in Denver, which had a more advanced treatment center. It would also make things easier on Renie, who, like Paige and Mark, had been staying at a nearby hotel.

"Don't ask me to do this," Paige said to Liv when she refused to let her contact Ben.

"I don't want him here."

"I made a promise, Liv. I can't keep lying to him."

"Then leave, and don't come back. I won't ever forgive you if you tell him."

"Liv…"

"I don't want him here."

Liv spent hours replaying the accident over in her head. Micah hesitated, a split second, then went right. They were tight to the barrel, and they were going to knock it over. Then Micah went down. Her head was too close to the ground; she knew she was going to hit head first. She'd heard the snap, and now, she had no feeling in her legs.

Billy assured her that Micah had been checked out and suffered no injury in the accident. He promised her he'd make sure her horse was exercised daily, and ready to get back at it as soon as she was.

Renie, Paige, Mark, and Billy were the only people she permitted to visit. She even refused to see Dottie and Bill.

Paige told her that Ben had come to Idaho the day after her accident, and that she had convinced him to go back on tour. "Now I regret my decision, Liv. I promised him I would tell him if your condition changed. I promised."

"I don't care, Paige. He and I made a promise to each other first, and that's all that matters."

Renie had begged her to let them call Ben, but Liv refused her, too.

"I know you don't understand, but Ben and I promised each other that we wouldn't let the other give up on their dream. I can't let him give up, Renie. You know as well as I do that, if he knew I was out of the coma, he'd cancel the rest of the tour."

"He'd want to, Mom. He'd want to be here with you, helping you."

"Do what? You and the nurses can push me around in the wheelchair just fine."

"That's not the point. He loves you."

"The person Ben fell in love with doesn't exist anymore."

When Renie tried to discuss Ben further, Liv closed her eyes and asked her to leave.

Philadelphia, Toronto, Saratoga Springs, Virginia Beach, and now Raleigh. Every night, the same thing happened. The crowd chanted Liv's name, and Ben opened the show by telling a story about her. He didn't plan what he'd say ahead of time. Sometimes he told a new story, sometimes it was one he'd already told. Then he'd play "Fall for Me."

There was so much demand for the song, the band recorded a live version and put it on digital music outlets. Not only had the song moved into the number one spot in a few days, their new album was currently number seven, and the song wasn't even on it.

The band had been gaining mass market popularity before Liv's accident, and since, fan support had grown exponentially. The worst pain he'd ever known fueled the success of his life's dream. The irony ate him alive.

He called Paige at least once every day. Nothing to report, she'd tell him.

Liv was being moved to a rehab facility outside of Colorado Springs. She still didn't have any feeling below the waist, and the doctors were recommending surgery. Liv was in favor of it, even with the risk. She could end up as a paraplegic, or it might kill her.

They agreed to wait three more weeks, to let her body heal more.

"Let me tell him something, anything."

"No."

"I have to tell him you're being moved."

"No, Paige."

"He's capable of calling the hospital, Liv. They may not tell him your condition, but they'll sure as hell tell him you're no longer there. You know him; he'll be here as fast as that little plane will fly him."

"Tell him they're moving me. But that's all."

"What will happen when the tour ends?"

"I have six weeks before I need to worry about that."

CB Rice was bigger than they'd ever dreamed possible. The record label wanted them to start the European leg of their tour in January. Ben told them he couldn't agree to it yet.

They'd be off from the middle of November until the end of December, and once he saw his boys, he'd spend the rest of the time with Liv. He'd spend every minute of it with her, until she came out of the coma, and then he'd spend every minute after she did with her, too. He'd even bring his boys over from Crested Butte to stay with him.

Liv checked the social media feed for the second time this morning and saw they'd posted photos from the concert last night. Then she went on YouTube to watch and listen to the story he told about her, as she had every morning for the last five weeks.

Tomorrow was her surgery. It had been delayed two additional weeks, but now, the doctors believed her body could withstand it.

During the seven-hour operation, surgeons would take one of the discs from Liv's back and fuse it where the damage occurred. Then they'd mend the broken bone with surgical cement and use titanium screws and plates to fix her neck.

The next afternoon, Renie and Paige held hands and Mark stood behind them, his hands on their shoulders when the doctors came out to tell them how the surgery went.

"Everything went well. Now we have to wait and see. We won't know anything until she wakes. She'll be under sedation for a few more hours, and then moved to a room, where you'll be able to see her."

Jimmy saw it first and prayed Ben would stay distracted until he could confirm if it was true or just a cruel attempt by the press to make a buck.

The post read, "CB Rice Cashes in Big with Fake Coma Story." It went on to say that CB Rice's recent meteoric rise to fame was due in large part to the fans' near hysteria over Ben Rice's girlfriend's accident and subsequent coma.

According to reports, the woman in question had been out of her coma for weeks. She'd come out of it not long after the first concert Ben told his naive fans the tragic story of the alleged love of his life.

Jimmy looked at Ben's face. He'd seen it.

"What the fuck is this?"

Ben, Bud, and Jimmy were trying to reach Paige, Renie, Mark, or the hospital. None were answering, and the hospital wouldn't even confirm that they had a patient by the name of Olivia Fairchild.

Paige and Renie were talking with Liv when Mark saw the story on CNN.

"You better turn on the news," he said when he walked in the room.

"Oh, my God." Liv's head fell back on the pillow.

Paige looked at her phone. "Shit. Seven missed calls. All from Ben." She raised her eyebrows at Liv. "What now?"

"Get me on a goddamn plane."

They were in LA, and it would take two hours to fly to Denver if Ben took a commercial flight.

Three hours later, Ben stormed into the hospital... and Mark was waiting for him. Again.

"Tell me," Ben managed to say. "No, wait. I'd rather hear this from Liv, since she's awake." The bitterness dripped from his tongue like poison sludge.

Mark took him up to Liv's room, where Paige and Renie sat with her.

"Hello, Liv," Ben sneered. "Ladies, I need to talk to Liv alone."

Renie stopped in front of him, tears in her eyes. "I'm sorry," she said. "It wasn't ever about you, Ben. My mom needed to come first."

Ben didn't think anything could get him to take his eyes off Liv, but that had.

He closed his eyes. That's the way it was, wasn't it? It wasn't about him, or what an absolute fucking idiot he was. It wasn't about him unintentionally duping millions of people, who now thought he was the scum of the earth for lying to them.

It wasn't about the pain he carried in his heart, his head, throughout his body for the last two months. Or him thinking he wouldn't have the chance to tell the incredible woman in front of him how much he wanted to spend the rest of his life with her.

No, this was never about him.

Paige and Renie left, but Ben didn't move. Liv was right in front of him, and her eyes were open. He'd dreamed about it, prayed for it to happen, but he couldn't move.

"Why?" he asked. "And don't say this wasn't about me. Don't."

"It was all about you," she answered.

"All about me?" Ben scrubbed his hand over his face. "I guess you didn't think about the other people in my life who would be affected by this. Do you have any idea what this will do to the band? Forget about me; think about the band, and the crew, all the people we employ. We're done, Liv. People think we've been conning them. So, you wanna tell me how this was all about me?"

He was angry, hurt, and confused, but when he saw her tears, it all went away. None of it mattered. The need to touch her overwhelmed him.

He stalked toward the bed and leaned down, close to her. "I don't want to physically hurt you, but I'm going to kiss you, and I'm going to kiss you hard. So if there's a part of you I can't touch, tell me now."

Liv shook her head and wiped at her tears.

When Ben's lips met hers, his mouth devoured hers and dared hers to respond. His hand came up and stroked her face. He tasted the saltiness of her tears as they ran down her face and into their mouths. He heard her cries, but he chose to ignore them. He needed to take this from her and let everything else be damned. She pulled at him, trying to bring his body closer to hers.

"Don't make me hurt you, Liv," he said as he pulled back from her. "It isn't your body I want to hurt, just your heart." His eyes were dark, not from hunger, but from rage. "Are you even going to try to explain?"

"I never meant to hurt you. I wanted to protect you. We *promised*."

He backed away from her. "Protect me? Is that what you said? You wanted to *protect* me? From what? Peace? Sanity? Do you have any idea how these last few weeks have been for me?"

He stood up and walked toward the window. "I called every day. Every. Single. Fucking. Day. I'd ask how you were. And every single day, Paige lied to me."

"It wasn't her fault. I made her do it, *to protect you.*"

"Look at me. Can you see me? I'm not a man who has been protected. I'm a man who has had his insides chewed up every day for the last two months. My body has been racked with pain. Every single fucking day." His eyes welled with tears. "I would've crawled into that body, taken the coma on myself, and set you free. I didn't care about me, only you."

Her leg moved, a reflex, and it startled her. It had been so long since she felt anything below her waist. She gasped.

"What?" Ben asked.

"My leg moved."

Since Ben hadn't known she'd come out of the coma, he also hadn't known she was paralyzed. He didn't know that she had surgery and that they'd been waiting to see whether it was successful.

The nurse came in then to check her vitals. "Any sensation yet?"

Liv looked at Ben, and then at the nurse. "My legs."

The nurse's eyes opened wide, and she pulled the sheet back. She started tapping different areas. "Can you feel this? What about this?" Liv kept nodding. She felt it all.

"Oh, Liv, this is wonderful! Let me call the doctor. I'll be right back."

Ben watched the scene play out in front of him. He didn't know what it meant, but he started to put it together. He didn't speak. He stood and stared at her.

She looked uncomfortable, yet elated.

The nurse came back. "I paged him and he's on his way. Oh, honey, I am so happy for you. This soon after the surgery." She turned to Ben. "It's wonderful news, isn't it?"

Ben nodded his head.

The nurse continued to check Liv's extremities, making notes.

"It's been a long, hard road for our girl here, but what a miracle. Liv, by tomorrow, you may be walking. Short distances and with a walker, but walking."

The doctor came in before the nurse finished. He appeared as excited by Liv's ability to move her legs as the nurse had been.

"We'll take it slow. Don't get any ideas about getting up for a drink of water in the middle of the night. Tomorrow morning we'll see if we can get you on your feet. Do not, I repeat, do not try to do it tonight."

The doctor turned to Ben. "No one more stubborn than our girl here. Don't let her try to get out of bed."

Liv smiled but hadn't said anything since the nurse asked her if she had any sensation. Not a single word.

The doctor leaned down and kissed the top of Liv's head, then stood back. "I've become fond of many of my patients through the years, Olivia, but I can tell you, few have come to mean as much to me as you do. If there was anyone I would've wished this for, it's you."

The doctor said goodnight and left, and the nurse said she'd be back in a while to check on her again, but to ring if she needed anything. She asked Liv if she wanted something to eat, but she only shook her head.

"What will you do?" Liv asked Ben once they left.
"Tell the truth."
"Well," she said, as if she expected him to leave.
"Scoot over," he said, kicking off his shoes. He lay down next to her and put his arm around her waist.

"You have a lot to tell me. Start at the beginning. Tell me about the accident."

"Ben, we can't do this."

"We can, and we're gonna. You kept me away for weeks. I'm not going anywhere tonight." He saw Liv was struggling to keep her eyes open. "We can talk tomorrow. Sleep. I'll still be here when you wake up."

Liv's eyes closed, and within seconds, her breathing evened out.

There was a war of emotions taking place in Ben's head. Anger, hurt, confusion, and love waged a battle in his heart.

Why had Liv done this? None of it made sense to him. Why would she let him go on believing she was in a coma? If it was because she thought he'd leave the tour, she would've been partially right. He would've come to see her. But knowing she was awake would've fueled his desire to make music. He would've rejoiced.

It was clear that up until tonight, Liv hadn't had feeling in her legs. Which meant she was paralyzed, and she'd tried to protect him from it. It was like a bad remake of a movie that had been done ten times too many.

Ben wondered if he'd ever get through to her. *She* mattered. Not what she did or achieved. Just her. She was enough.

That was the point, though, wasn't it? He'd *never* get through to her. In the last year, he'd begged her to let him be a part of her life, but she held him at arm's length.

Was it that simple? Liv meant more to him than he did to her. Even ten minutes ago, she said it again. "Ben, we can't do this."

He wanted to touch her for just a little while longer. Maybe his arms would memorize how it felt to have her wrapped in them. His chest would remember how it felt to have her head resting softly on it. Maybe his heart would remember how to rejoice in the fact that she walked this earth, rather than mourn that he couldn't watch her as she did.

Hard as it was, he had to force himself to do it. He eased her head down on the pillow, got up, and walked out of Liv's life.

21

The fallout with CB Rice's fans had been less than anyone initially expected. Since they had a number of shows still booked, Ben did what he did best. He came out at the start of every show and told the truth.

He told people he never meant to deceive anyone, and until the story broke in the press, he believed Liv was still in a coma. He told them about her paralysis, and that Liv was so strong, so independent, so brave, that she'd wanted to protect him from it. He went on to say she'd had a successful surgery, and everyone believed she'd be walking, and back to her old self, in no time.

Each night the crowd roared when he said it. He didn't tell them that he and Liv were no longer together, but then, they never really had been anyway.

For the first time in almost three months, Liv was home. She hated not having her independence, and while her recovery went faster than anyone anticipated, not being back in her routine made her wretched to be around. She'd be the first to admit it.

Renie took it in stride. She wouldn't go back to school until January, and in the meantime, she'd be home with her mom, helping with her continued recovery.

"Would you like to ride today?" Renie asked.

"No, it's too soon," she murmured. "I'll walk to the barn; that'll be enough for today."

Liv wasn't sure she'd have the courage to walk into the barn when they pulled into the driveway. She needed to see Micah, as much as the thought of it terrified her. She missed her boy, but worried how he might react to her.

She didn't see Micah when she walked in, but by the time she got to the stall, his nose peeked out. She stood and let him nuzzle her. His hind leg bent, and his breathing evened out. He almost purred.

Liv stood and loved him until one of her legs gave out. She grabbed the top of the stall's half door, and Renie ran over to her with a stool for her to sit on.

Renie tried to hide her tears, but Liv saw them. "Will you be okay for a few minutes, Mom?"

"Sure, honey, go ahead. I'll catch up with my boy."

Liv managed to hold in her sobs until she heard the back door of the house close.

"Oh, Micah, what have I done?" she sobbed.

***

When she woke up in the hospital and Ben was gone, she'd thought maybe she dreamed everything from the night before. She moved one of her legs to be sure that part wasn't a dream. It hadn't been.

The nurse came in with breakfast and told her she'd be going to rehab in two hours. And then she was gone, leaving Liv alone. The ache of what that meant spread through her chest.

He didn't stay, even though he said he would, and Liv had to face the fact that he wouldn't be coming back.

She spent the following two weeks trying to get her legs to work properly, and doing her best to kick everyone close to her out of her life. Even Paige reached the point where she'd had enough.

"I'll be your friend until the day I die, and I love you, but I won't be your punching bag. You know where to find me when you want to," she said before she stormed out.

Mark still came to visit every day. He didn't talk much; he rarely even said hello. He arrived when she began rehab and left when she finished. In between, he helped.

Renie also came every day, in the afternoon. They'd spent so many afternoons in silence, that Renie started bringing a book with her. Liv would stare out the window, lost in thoughts she had no desire to discuss.

"Depression is normal," Liv heard the doctor tell Renie. "Her body has been through a significant series of traumas. She needs to heal. She'll come around. I've offered to prescribe something for it, but your mother refuses it."

Billy came with Renie as often as he could. He was in the top five nationally for saddle broncs, and slated to go to the finals in December. He'd tell her about the barrel racing standings, and who was winning in each region.

At first it bothered her, but then she realized Billy talked to her as though she was on the injured list, not the retired list.

"I'll help you. Anything you need. I'll be there for you, Livvie. Soon as you're ready, we can get back out on the road together."

"I appreciate that, Billy. We'll see, okay?"

***

Thanksgiving morning, eight days after she came home, Liv decided it was time to ride. Renie suggested her mom ride Pooh, but Liv was determined to ride Micah. Her leg muscles were stronger than they'd ever been. She'd never exercised before; she'd rode and worked. Now she had a strength-building regimen she followed every day.

The day dawned a perfect bluebird Colorado morning. Pooh wouldn't be able to keep up with Micah, so Renie rode one of the boarded horses.

"Where do you want to ride today, Mom?"

"I'm gonna let Micah run."

"To the meadow?"

Liv nodded.

"You're sure?"

"Never more sure."

As soon as they came over the hill, the prairie stretched out in front of them, and Micah took off like a rocket. Liv hadn't felt this alive in months. There was no hesitation between her and her horse. It was as though they rode this way every day.

Ben walked out on the back porch with a cup of coffee in hand. In an hour, he'd leave to pick up the boys and bring them back for Thanksgiving dinner with his family.

He looked out at the valley and up at Mount Crested Butte. The sky was blue, the sun was shining, and he was spending the day with family. He should be happy, but nothing could have been further from how he felt.

He went to The Goat the night before, wanting a distraction, and he found one. Pretty little thing, and sweet. Her name was Melinda, or Melissa…or Melanie. He couldn't remember, so he called her Mel. She danced up a storm, like a firecracker. He had fun with her, the most fun he'd had in a long time.

"Let's get out of here," she said, pulling him by the hand. He grabbed his coat off the rack and followed her to the parking lot. When they got around the corner, she was on him so fast, Ben didn't see it coming.

He picked her up and held her against him, and she wrapped her legs around his waist.

"Wait," he said, unwrapping her body from his and setting her back on the ground.

"What?" she answered, breathless. "What's wrong?"

"As much as I want to get close to you tonight, pretty girl, I can't do this." He was about to say it was him, not her, and he decided against it. Better to just walk away.

"Come here, girl, and give me a big ol' hug," said Dottie when Liv walked in the back door.

"Hey, Dottie."

"God, I missed seeing that shade of pink in your cheeks. How are you feeling? Billy said he saw you and Renie out ridin' a bit ago. He told me it was like watchin' a beautiful wind blow."

"I can't describe it. If felt right."

"You goin' back out, then?"

"Soon as I can. Not much left this year."

"Nothing stoppin' you from training. Get yourself down to Texas in January and get busy."

"Am I crazy, Dottie? Do you think I should just give up?"

"I've told you before; there hasn't been a day, since I've known you, that I haven't been proud of you, Liv. Don't make it today. You're no quitter, but what do the doctors say?"

"That I'm fit to ride, or do whatever else I want to do. My injury is healed, and that part of my spine is in better shape than the rest of me."

"Any pain?"

"Not much."

"What does that mean?"

"My pain has nothing to do with my injury, Dottie."

"You wanna talk about it?"

"Not today."

Renie walked in with Billy behind her, carrying pies. "Where are these supposed to go, Miss Dottie?" Renie asked.

"Down to the bunkhouse. We've got a crew with us this year. We'll eat in the main dining hall down there."

"Hey, Livvie, you comin'?" Billy asked.

"I'll be right there."

"You're missin' him, aren't you?" Dottie asked after Billy and Renie left.

"More than anything."

"Then do something about it, Olivia."

"What, Dottie? I don't know what to do."

"Of course you do, sweetheart."

Bill finished carving the last turkey when the door to the dining hall opened and Paige and Mark came in with their youngest daughter. Renie and Blythe hadn't seen each other in months, and it had been weeks since Liv had seen Paige, who walked up and put her arms around Liv.

"I figured Thanksgiving was as good a day as any for us to make up."

"There isn't any making up to do." Liv hugged her back. "I'm sorry, Paige. I hope you can forgive me."

"I forgave you before I walked out that day. You needed space, but I kept tabs. If you needed me, Mark would have said so, and I would have come."

"Mark is such a good man."

"The best. No one else would've put up with you and me combined all these years."

The dining hall soon filled with ranch hands and wranglers.

"Gotta love cowboys," Liv heard Renie say.

"Yep, you do," said Billy. "How about you and Blythe sit with me today, Renie?"

"You're not flirtin' with my daughter, are you, Billy Patterson?" Liv asked.

"Is this really the first time you noticed it?" Paige asked Liv.

"What are you talking about?"

"Never mind." Paige winked at Dottie. "Must be my imagination."

"Whatcha' doing, Dad?" Luke asked.

"Hey, buddy. Nothin' much. What are you up to?"

"I been watchin' you."

"Oh, yeah? And what have you seen?"

"You're sad."

He hugged his son to him.

"It's easy to see when someone is sad if you love 'em, Daddy."

"How'd you get so smart, partner?"

"I don't know, but if you're sad, you should do somethin' about it." Luke looked at his feet. "That's what you'd tell me."

"What if I don't know what to do about it?"

"Come on, Daddy, you know what to do."

"I do?"

"Sure. You gotta go see the girl."

Thanksgiving dinner came to an end, and Paige and Mark went home. Renie and Blythe went into town to meet up with friends home for the holiday, and Liv sat out on the porch of the bunkhouse, looking at the stars, not ready to go home yet.

"Mind if I sit here with you for a minute?" Billy asked.

"Of course I don't mind." She scooted over, and he sat on the bench next to her.

"Did you have a nice Thanksgiving?" he asked.

"I did. How about you?"

"I did. I'm glad you and Renie were here with us this year. That's what I'm most thankful for."

"You're such a good friend to me, Billy, and to Renie, too. What would we have done without you these last few weeks?"

"Livvie, I'm tellin' you, you ought to consider hookin' up with a bronc rider. You might like it."

If Billy Patterson wasn't so much younger, there might have been a day she would've considered it. It made her think of Ben, and how she thought he was younger too. But he wasn't.

"I want you and Renie to go to Las Vegas with me in a couple weeks. My mom and dad are going too."

"We'd love to go. Thanks for inviting us."

There wasn't a serious competitive cowgirl, or cowboy for that matter, worth her or his weight in salt who didn't try to attend the finals every year.

Billy Patterson was ranked second in the world going into National Finals Rodeo, or NFR, the highest he'd ever gotten. Liv missed Jolene and Mary Beth, who would be there too.

"I booked us rooms at Bellagio, hope that's okay."

As long as they weren't staying at Mandalay Bay, Liv didn't care where they stayed.

The NFR consisted of ten rounds on ten consecutive days. Cowboys and barrel racers earned money by placing first through sixth in any round, and picked up more money by placing first through eighth in the average—cumulative times or points earned during the ten rounds.

At the end, there would be two champions in each event. One was the average winner, who won the NFR by having the best cumulative time or score in his or her event over the ten rounds. The other was the *world* champion, the person who finished the year with the most money, including what he or she earned at the

NFR. For each event, the average winner and world champion might be the same person.

Once Billy got to Las Vegas, he rode better than ever, consistently placing first or second in every round. Before and after each ride, he'd find them in the crowd and wave. She and Renie were the recipients of several dirty looks from girls in the stands whenever he raised his hat and smiled in their direction.

Ben sat in The Goat, nursing a coke, a little out of it. There wasn't enough snow to ski, the boys were with Christine, and he was bored. Worn out from the tour and the emotional roller coaster with Liv, he didn't want to play, or write songs, or do much of anything.

When he looked at the big screen TV on the other side of the bar, the last thing he expected to see was Liv, but there she was, with *Junior,* bigger than life. The news ticker across the bottom of the screen read, "Billy Patterson, NFR's Saddle Bronc Champion." Based on the smile on Billy's face, it was Liv he planned to celebrate with.

Ben felt as though someone sucker-punched him.

22

It snowed Christmas morning, and a beautiful white blanket covered the ground. Liv and Renie were joining the Pattersons later, and Billy promised to take them out on a sleigh ride after dinner.

"Let's go skiing tomorrow," Liv said to Renie when they finished opening presents.

"That sounds wonderful. Are you sure you're up to it?"

"Won't know for sure until I'm on the slope."

"Where, Mom?"

"Where else would we go, Renie? Crested Butte."

"Is there something you want to tell me?"

Liv hadn't heard a word from Ben since the night in the hospital. For a couple of weeks, she'd continued to check the social media feeds.

She saw photos of his boys, which he posted right after Thanksgiving, during an outing the three of them took together. They were beautiful boys.

Liv closed her eyes and imagined how their Christmas morning would be. In her daydream, Ben's boys were with him, at his parents' house. Will and Matt, and their wives, were there, too.

Whenever she thought about Ben, she could see him so clearly, as though she was with him. Like every other time, she didn't want to open her eyes and have him go away. He crept closer, so close she felt his breath, his arms, his kiss. The ache for him spread throughout her body.

"I have to see him, Renie. I have to try. I love him."

"Come in here and talk to me for a minute," Ginny said to Ben.

Ben smiled and gathered his mother into him for a hug. "Yeah, Mama?" Thank goodness he had his family around him today. They distracted him enough, that morning, that he only thought about Liv two or three hundred times.

"I'm worried about you, Ben. Is there anything you can do?"

"About?"

"Don't. You know what I mean. Let's not waste time playing games."

"It's over. There isn't anything to do about it. If you work that hard and it still doesn't come together, it's time to give up and move in another direction."

"She's the one for you."

"Thanks, Mom. It makes me so happy to hear you say that." Ben walked away from her.

"Do something about it, Ben. *Do something.*"

"*What? What the hell am I supposed to do? Jesus—*"

"What's going on in here?" Bud asked, coming in through the kitchen archway. "You're raising your voice to your mother on Christmas, Ben?"

"I'm sorry, Mama." He pulled her into another hug. "I'm sorry, Dad."

"It's okay, Bud. I started it. I'm pushing him to contact Liv, which means I'm pushing his buttons."

Bud shook his head and walked back out of the kitchen.

"We're both so worried about you," his mom continued.

"She's with somebody else."

"How do you know that?"

"I saw them together."

"Oh."

Even if she wasn't, Ben wasn't sure he had the balls to try again with her. She hurt him. Bad. He couldn't imagine opening himself up to her again.

She knew where to find him. If she wanted him, she could make the first move this time. Which, obviously, she hadn't. Again, he had his answer. He needed to keep reminding himself she meant more to him than he did to her.

"We're leaving in the morning," Liv told Dottie after dinner.

Renie and Billy were sitting in the family room, in front of a roaring fire.

"Who's leaving in the morning?" Billy asked Renie.

"We are. We're going skiing. Billy, do you ski? Why don't I know that about you?"

"Not my thing."

"Have you ever tried it?"

"Can't say as I have. Where you headed?"

"Crested Butte," Liv answered.

"That's where Ben lives."

"Yes, it is, Billy."

"You gonna see him?"

"I'm going to try."

Dottie put her hand on Liv's shoulder. "I'm proud of you, sweetheart. You gotta take the chance. The same way you have to race again."

Both things scared her, but Dottie was right. She had to take the chance. She'd never forgive herself if she didn't.

All these years she'd resented not chasing her dream, but her dream wasn't just to barrel race; her dream was to spend the rest of her life with the man she loved, and she could only do that if she told him so.

He saw Renie first. He was next in line for the lift and was focused on Jake and Luke, making sure they had their boards lined up and were paying attention. He looked up, and there she was, flying down the hill. She looked behind her, who was she looking for? Was Liv with her?

Seconds later, Ben saw her, the woman who held his heart. Liv was skiing, and it was a beautiful sight. She was laughing, talking to her daughter, and skiing toward the racks. They must be taking a break.

"Daddy!" Luke yelled.

Ben hadn't been paying attention, and they hadn't moved forward to get the next chair.

"Sorry," Ben murmured to the lift operator. They couldn't get out of line, so they moved up and took the next chair. Ben hoped he'd be able to find her when they came back down. If not, he'd camp out at the base of the mountain until he did.

Liv was in Crested Butte. That had to mean something, didn't it? She had to know there was a chance she'd run into him. He wondered when she had gotten here. Surely they would've spent Christmas at home.

And where was Junior? Was he here with them? Just because he'd only seen Renie and Liv didn't mean he wasn't a minute or two behind them.

"How did it feel?" Renie asked Liv after they'd gotten their hot chocolate.

"*Amazing!* I was so wrapped up in not being able to ride again, it didn't occur to me that I might not be able to ski."

"You look happy."

"I'm having such a good time with you, Renie. Thank you for coming with me."

"Are you going to call Ben? You're not avoiding it, are you?"

"No, I'm not avoiding it. I'm going to call him tonight. I wanted to have a day with you first."

"Okay, as long as you're not backing out. I'm gonna hit the ladies room, and then you wanna take another couple runs?"

"You bet. I'll meet you down by the skis."

Liv paid the bill, refastened her boots, and put on her helmet and gloves. She walked toward the door, looking down to make sure she didn't trip on anything, and bumped into someone.

"I'm sorry, I didn't…" Liv tilted her head and looked up at the man she'd bumped into.

"*Ben!* Oh my God." She gasped and started to fall backwards. He caught her and righted her on her feet. Liv couldn't take her eyes off him—here he was. She'd longed for this and dreaded it at the same time. Now what?

"Liv," he said softly, "there's a couple of people I want you to meet."

His boys, she'd recognize them anywhere. They were such beautiful boys, like their father.

"Olivia Fairchild, I'd like you to meet Jacob and Lucas Rice." Liv extended her hand, and both boys shook it. They were polite too, just like their dad.

"It's very nice to meet you both," said Liv.

"You too, ma'am," they said in unison.

"Ready, Mom?" Renie said adjusting her helmet and goggles. "*Oh!* Hi, Ben."

"Hi, Renie, it's nice to see you," Ben answered. "These are my boys, Jake and Luke. Boys, this is Liv's daughter, Renie.

Renie took her helmet back off and tossed her head around to fix her hair. "Helmet head," she said, and both boys laughed. "Bet you're in here for hot cocoa. Am I right?"

They nodded, and Renie motioned for them to follow her.

"Wait," said Ben, trying to hand Renie money.

"Don't worry, I got it."

He watched them walk away, and took a deep breath before he turned toward Liv.

"Hi," he said.

"Hi."

"I'm always bumpin' into you."

"I never watch where I'm going."

Ben touched the side of her face. "It's so good to see you."

Someone else bumped into Liv, and he realized they were standing in the doorway.

"Come with me," he said. "Let's get out of the way."

Liv took her helmet and gloves off and followed him. He motioned for her to take a seat on the couch next to the fireplace. Liv waited until he sat down, and then sat next to him.

"Good to see you're back out on the slopes."

"It's great to be back. I just told Renie, I hadn't thought about whether I'd be able to ski. Not until Christmas morning."

"Did you have a nice Christmas?"

"It was okay. How about you?"

"Not the best, but Christmas is always fun with the boys."

"So they were with you, then?"

"After about mid-morning. They're used to waking up with their mom, then coming to my place a couple hours later."

"Ben, I—"

"How long are you in town?"

"Until the second. Ben…"

Ben reached out and touched her face again. Her eyes closed, and she leaned her cheek into his hand.

"Is there anyone else with you?"

"No, we're alone. Why?"

"I wondered if you brought a new boyfriend along with you."

"Nope, no new boyfriend. What about you?"

"Nope, no new boyfriends for me either."

"Very funny."

"Ask."

"No."

"Why not?"

"I'm afraid to, Ben."

He reached out, cupped her neck with his hand, and pulled her closer to him. "There's nobody. *Nobody.*

Only you." His eyes were dark, angry, when his lips covered hers. His kiss was just as angry, just as dangerous.

Her cry was stifled by his mouth on hers.

He licked her lips with his tongue, bit her bottom lip, and crushed his mouth back into hers for more. There was nothing like kissing her. Nothing.

Whoever else was sitting near them, the rest of the people in the lodge, all disappeared. He couldn't hear anything other than her soft, sweet murmurs.

Liv pulled back from him. "Your boys," she said.

His boys. He'd forgotten about them. Not that he minded them seeing him with Liv, but she was right—he needed to take a step back, at least while they were in the lodge.

Ben stared into her eyes. Nothing was any different. The hurt, longing, anger, pain—none of it mattered. He loved every single thing about this woman, the good, the bad, all of it.

Renie returned with Ben's kids in tow. "They're ready to go back out. Do you want me to take them? I'm on skis, they're on boards, but they should be able to keep up." Renie turned and smiled at Luke and Jake, who were about to argue.

"What about you, Ben? Are you ready to get back out on the hill?"

No, he wasn't. He wasn't ready to do anything but get Liv alone and out of her clothes.

The five of them spent the afternoon together. Liv and Renie skied, Ben and the boys snowboarded. When they announced the lifts would be closing in fifteen minutes, Renie offered to take Jake and Luke up one more time if Ben and Liv wanted to relax for a few minutes.

"That was the best afternoon I've had in a very long time," Ben said. "I'm sure my boys would agree."

"Me, too." Liv didn't remember the last time she was this relaxed…and happy. She took off her helmet, gloves, and started to unfasten her boots.

"Here, let me help you with that," Ben offered. He knelt down and ran his hand up the inside of her leg.

"Uh, my boots are in the other direction, cowboy."

Ben leaned forward, his mouth next to her ear. "I cannot wait to be alone with you, Liv. Am I wrong about this? Please tell me you want this as much as I do."

"I do, Ben, but we need to talk first."

"Wait, what? You want to talk. I can't tell you how much that turns me on, baby." He nipped at her neck.

"I know. Who am I?"

"Will you and Renie have dinner with us tonight?"
"We'd love to."
"She's good with my boys. They love her. You'll be a distant second, I'm afraid. They're already smitten."
"I will not begrudge my daughter your boys' affection. I'm generous that way."

There were so many ways she was generous. She had no idea. He wasn't exaggerating when he said today was one of the best he'd had in as long as he remembered. The last time he was this happy was the day they drove back from Woodward, Oklahoma, before her accident.

"I want pizza," Ben heard Luke say when Renie came into the lodge, his boys in tow. Luke always wanted pizza; that didn't surprise him.

"I'm sick of pizza," argued Jake, standing up straighter than Ben had ever seen. "We should go to Uncle Matt's restaurant."

"What's there?" asked Renie.

"Sushi."

"A man after my heart. I love sushi."

Ben watched as her response took his son completely over the top. Renie Fairchild may very well be Jake Rice's first love.

He shook his head and smiled. Family and Liv. It's what he wanted more than anything. He wanted forever with her; it was what he'd always wanted. Did she want the same thing? Is that why she came to Crested Butte?

"Sushi, then?" Ben asked Liv.

Liv smiled. "Sounds great."

"Luke, you like sushi. Plus, Uncle Matt will make you anything you want."

"Pizza? Will he make me pizza? 'Cause that's what I want, Dad."

Ben ruffled Luke's hair. This was what happiness felt like. He loved it.

When they walked into the restaurant, Matt stood near the end of the sushi bar. When he spotted Liv, Ben thought his brother might have strained his neck, his head spun around so quickly.

"Well, hello. This is? Remind me your name again."

Ben almost choked. As if Matt didn't remember her name. What a crock.

"Liv…Olivia. And this is my daughter. Renie, this is Matt, Ben's brother."

Renie stepped up to shake his hand. "Pleasure," she said.

A COWBOY FALLS

"A table tonight, Ben? Something away from the noise of the sushi bar?"

"That sounds great," Ben answered, not bothering to look in Matt's direction. His eyes were focused on Liv's smile, and he intended to keep them there.

Matt led them to a table near the back, hidden away from the rest of the place. "You'll get fewer interruptions back here," he said as he placed menus in front of Liv and Renie.

"Daddy said you'd make me pizza," said Luke.

"You want pizza; you'll get pizza...how about squid pizza, or octopus, or tuna pizza, how's that sound?"

Luke started giggling and fell sideways, right into Liv. She reached around and hugged him closer to her, laughing with him. Suddenly Luke realized where he was—and there it was; Ben knew that look. His son had fallen in love with Liv, too.

Luke monopolized the conversation with Liv for the rest of the night, which was okay with Ben. He enjoyed sitting back and listening to the two of them. Luke was a huge rodeo fan, and Liv told him about going to the finals at the beginning of December. She talked about the cowboys and the bullfighters and the barrel racers.

"Do you really race around barrels?" he asked.

"I do, but I'll tell you a little secret if you promise not to let anyone else know, unless they're a real rodeo insider."

He nodded.

"We call it chasing the cans," Liv whispered in his ear.

"O-o-h...cool," said Luke, as though he'd learned the secret of the universe.

Ben reached his arm around her and pulled her back, closer to him. He leaned down so his mouth was close to her ear. "I love you so much, Olivia Fairchild."

She turned to him and smiled before she brushed her lips across his. A shudder of pleasure ran through his body.

After dinner, they walked down Elk Avenue. The boys wanted frozen yogurt, and Renie made fun of them for wanting something cold when they were already freezing.

"She's very playful," Liv commented to Ben as they walked behind them. "It's too bad she never had any brothers or sisters."

"I'm sure Renie would say her childhood was perfect."

Liv shook her head and laughed. "I doubt that. No father in her life, no siblings. There are definitely times I regret my choices and what they meant for her."

"Your daughter is one of the most gracious, seemingly well-adjusted people I've ever had the pleasure to meet. You did a great job as her mother, Liv."

"Thank you. I appreciate you saying so."

"You have no idea. It always surprises me."

"What do you mean?"

"You have no idea how great you are."

"I'm a sure thing, cowboy. You don't have to pile on the charm."

Ben thought he might lose it right there, on the sidewalk in the middle of his hometown. Had he heard her right? Yesterday he would've predicted he'd never see her again, now it felt as though no time had passed since they were together. The hard times forgotten, for now, for tonight. Unless that was why she wanted to talk. He almost dreaded it. He didn't want to talk; he wanted to hold her close. *Skin on skin.*

"Will you stay at the house tonight?" he asked.

"I don't think you want to stay in the hotel room with Renie and me, do you?"

"Uh, no," he laughed.

"Well then, I guess, I better stay at your house." She said it softly, demurely, seductively. Very, very soon, Ben would have a difficult time walking.

"How about a horror movie marathon?" he heard Renie say to the boys.

"Yeah," said Jake.

"Nooo," said Luke. "Liv, I don't want to watch horror movies. Can we watch somethin' else?"

Oh no, Luke wasn't horning in on his time with Liv tonight. No way. There'd be plenty of time later for movie marathons with his boys. Tonight she was all his.

"Well," said Renie, "tonight we should watch what Luke wants to watch, and tomorrow night it'll be Jake's turn to pick. Does that sound fair?"

"Boys, a gentleman would let the lady choose."

"Um, okay. Renie, you can pick, but please, don't pick horror," said Luke.

"I want to watch Ghostbusters," she said.

"Ghostbusters? What's that?" asked both his boys.

"You haven't seen Ghostbusters? You're kidding. It's the funniest movie ever. Don't tell me you haven't seen Airplane either." Both boys shook their heads.

"Oh, this will be a very fun week. Renie's ride through the funniest movies ever made before you both were born. We'll have a blast."

"Are you gonna stay at my dad's house?" asked Jake.

Liv nodded.

"Yay!" Luke jumped up and down.

"Do you remember how to get there?" asked Ben.

Liv smiled. "I can probably find it."

"Tell you what, we'll follow you to your hotel. You can check out, and we'll help load your stuff into your car. Then you can follow us to the ranch."

"Perfect." Liv kissed his cheek.

Ben really, really hoped this wasn't a dream.

23

It was dark, so Renie wouldn't be able to appreciate the ranch for what it was until tomorrow. The boys fought over who got to carry the bags inside, and once they did, they had no idea where to put them.

"Where are you sleeping?" Jake asked Renie.

"I don't know; let's ask your dad. This is a very nice house, by the way."

"My mom used to live here too, but now she lives in a different house, and she has a different husband," Luke told her.

He was a wealth of uncomfortable information, thought Ben. "Okay, partner, let's get Renie settled in the guest room downstairs, and we'll let Liv stay in the one upstairs."

"Liv isn't gonna sleep in your room, Daddy?"

Luke again. Where did his kid get this stuff?

"We'll see about that later. Now, how about that movie? If you don't start watching it in…thirty seconds, you won't be able to watch it tonight, because it'll end later than your bedtime. Follow me, Renie. I'll show you where you can set up your movie marathon."

A COWBOY FALLS

Liv stood in the family room, looking out windows she never thought she would see again. She was here, with Ben, and Renie was with her. If anyone had told her last week that this would be happening, she would've bet a million dollars they were wrong. Yet here she was.

"Come on," Ben said, taking her hand. "They're settled in, and Renie promised she'd make sure she'd find whatever they needed on her own."

Ben led her into his bedroom and closed the door behind them. Somehow, suddenly, she was in his arms. She pressed herself into him so she felt his heart beating. The warmth of his body seeped through the clothes she longed to rip off him.

"You're shaking," he whispered. "It's okay, Liv. This is where you're meant to be. Kiss me; give it all to me, every bit of you."

"Ben, we have to talk."

"No, Liv, we don't. Not now. Now, I want you under me, naked. Then later, over me. And then, all around me. I love you so damn much I can't think about anything else."

"But—"

"Liv, I'll get down on my hands and knees and beg if I have to. Please, take off your clothes. Please, I can't stand it another second."

"Okay," she said, as if the battle was lost and she had no fight left in her. "But you first."

Ben's clothes were off as fast as he could tear them away from his body, and he was helping Liv get rid of hers.

"God, I need you so much."

"Ben…" There it was; the way she said his name, as if he wasn't on fire already.

"Ben, stop."

Something in the way she said it resonated with him, and he stopped.

"Tell me," he said, his breathing lumbered.

"I'm not on birth control anymore."

"Liv, I—" What? What could he say? That he didn't care? They would be spending the rest of their lives together, and if she had his baby, it would make him the happiest man on earth? She'd run out of the house naked to get away from him if he said any of that.

"Don't worry, sweet girl," he said instead, kissing down her neck. "I'll take care of you, you know that." His mouth worked its way lower, across her breasts, down to her stomach. He put his arms around her and pulled her close, laying his cheek against her, imagining how it would be to know she carried his child inside her.

He stood and lifted her onto the bed. "I need you, baby, all of you." He rolled onto his back, so she was on top of him. "Be still, this way, your skin on mine. Look at me, Liv." He put his hands on each side of her face, and sang to her.

Having had your joy, having had your desire, and then, baby, you fall.

"I dreamed of this," she said. "Fantasized about it, would be a better way to put it."

"Oh, yeah? When?"

"All the time."

"Tell me."

"Better to show you." Liv opened the drawer on the nightstand, but Ben held up his hand and showed her he already had what she was looking for.

"Put it on for me," he said.

Liv's cheeks turned pink, but she took the package from him.

"We could go without, if you wanted to," he ventured.

"Ben—I don't…"

Why had he opened his mouth? Now wasn't the time to have this conversation. "I'm sorry. Forget I said that. Keep doin' what you were doin', baby. Don't stop."

She rolled it on, then straddled him until he was buried deep inside her. She leaned back, but her hands rested on his chest. Ben held her still, then started to move beneath her. He leaned up, to get more of her against him as he drove himself into her. Her hands dug into his skin as his cupped her bottom.

"Liv, I can't wait. Waited so long for this. Oh, God, I love you."

His mouth moved over her lips, his teeth scraped hers, and he bit her swollen bottom lip.

He rolled her beneath him, the way he saw her in his fantasies, writhing under him. "Here," he said, "right here, Liv." He drove into her, relentlessly, pushing her, pushing himself, until they both came together.

Liv put her face against his sweaty neck and licked up under his ear. She breathed in deeply, as though she wanted to say something.

Ben stilled, waiting. But nothing. Her lips kissed from his ear to his jaw until her mouth found his. She kissed him hard, putting her arms around his shoulders to hold herself closer.

"Tell me," he said, easing her back down onto the pillow.

"Ben."

"Don't just say my name. Tell me. You know what I want to hear."

She closed her eyes and turned her head on the pillow, away from him. Here he went again, pushing her too hard. What was wrong with him? She was back in his arms; they were joined, two as one, but he still pushed her.

"Liv, open your eyes." He waited until she did. "I'm sorry. I won't push. I need you so much, but I'll only take what you'll give. I won't keep asking for more."

She nodded and reached up again to put her lips on his. "Ben…will you catch me if I fall?"

"You know I will, baby."

He eased off of her and went into the other room to get rid of the condom. He looked in the mirror and shook his head. Why was he so impatient with her? What was it he had to know right now? That she loved him? She did, but something stopped her from saying the words.

Ben got back in bed and pulled her closer to him, so her back was to his front.

"What did you want to talk about?"

"We should wait until tomorrow."

She was killing him. He wanted everything, her body, her love, and now her thoughts. This woman made him crazy with the desire to get inside her in every way possible. He could never be close enough to her and yet, the harder he tried to hold her close, the more she inched away.

"Okay, I'll talk." He felt her body tense. "I was so afraid I'd lost you forever. I never would've allowed myself to think about you being here, as you are right now."

"I know, Ben. I felt the same way."

"The universe is telling us something. We keep coming back to each other. Maybe we should try harder to stay together."

"It won't be easy."

"Why not?"

"I want to race again. Give it all I've got. It will take hard work and training. And travel."

"As long as we're both committed, we can make this work, Liv."

"What about you? You're going back out on tour."

"I am? Have you been on our website, darlin'? You watchin' my tour schedule?"

"I'm a stalker, remember?"

"We need to get you set up with your own barrel racing fan page, so I can watch you. See you in those tight jeans and cowgirl shirts. The way your body bends and moves when you're racin'. Jesus, that gets me hot."

A COWBOY FALLS

What had it been? Five minutes? And he wanted her again. He planned to wear her out tonight. She might not have enough strength left to ski tomorrow.

There was a good idea. Renie and the boys could go to the mountain, while he and Liv stayed here at the house. There were all kinds of places he imagined making love to Liv's sweet body.

"What are you thinking about, cowboy?"

"You. Naked. All over my house." She shuddered. Evidently, she liked that idea as much as he did.

Luke woke them the next morning. He climbed up on the bed and situated himself between his dad and Liv.

"What's up, partner?" Ben groaned, his voice still thick with sleep.

"What're we doin' today, Daddy?"

"What do you want to do?"

"Let's go snowmobiling around the ranch."

That wasn't a bad idea. They had several. He wondered if Renie would be interested in doing that. He could show her and Liv all the best views on the ranch.

"How's that sound, Liv?"

"Good to me. I don't know about you, little guy, but I'm starving. What do you say we get up and make a giant ranch breakfast?"

"You know how to make a ranch breakfast?"

"I do. I live on a ranch. Guess you didn't know that."

"You do?" Luke's voice caught. "Does Renie's daddy take care of it for you?"

"No, Renie's dad died many years ago. He was a pilot in the Air Force."

"Oh." Luke's voice shook a little. "Does that make you and Renie sad?"

"It used to, but we know he keeps us safe."

"Who takes care of your ranch for you?"

"I do. And we have hands. Do you have ranch hands that help your daddy and your grandparents?"

"We do," he answered, and then proceeded to tell her about the more colorful guys that worked their ranch.

Ben slipped out of bed to let the two of them talk. He pulled on sweats and a shirt, and went to the kitchen to start the coffee, and saw Renie standing by the window.

"It's breathtaking," she said, hearing him behind her.

"It isn't bad."

"How do you ever leave it?"

"I could say the same thing about your spread."

"It's my mom's spread, but you're right, it's awesome too." Renie walked to where he was in the kitchen.

"Somethin' on your mind, young lady?"

"Hoping you two figure it out this time," she sighed.

"Me, too." He laughed, pulling her into a hug.

"I like you, Ben, and you're good for her."

"What about the Patterson guy? What happened there?"

"Billy?" Renie blushed, and then laughed. "They're friends. That's all they've ever been."

"Are you sure?"

"Um, yeah," she laughed. "I'm positive."

"Is there more to this story?"

Renie smiled and shrugged her shoulders.

"I want bacon." Luke pulled Liv behind him. It occurred to Ben that he abandoned her under the blankets without any clothes, but here she was, wearing a big shirt of his and her long underwear from yesterday.

Ben raised his eyebrows as she walked into his arms for a hug.

"It wasn't easy. Thank goodness little boys have to go potty."

Ben threw his head back and laughed. "I wondered."

Liv started rummaging around Ben's cabinets.

"Whatcha' lookin' for, baby?"

"Finding my way around your kitchen."

"Make yourself at home," he winked. There was nothing he'd like more.

They spent the day exploring the ranch, and Ben took them by his parents' place mid-afternoon.

"Well, well, am I happy to see you." Bud came off the porch and swept Liv into a big hug. "I prayed hard for you, little lady."

Liv buried her face into his shoulder to hide her tears. A few simple words, coupled with his unmasked joy, made her cry.

Ginny came out of the door and gasped when she saw Liv standing next to Ben, his arm around her shoulders.

"Aren't you a sight for these old eyes? Come here, girl, and let me look at you."

Liv was touched by the warmth and love these two people, who barely knew her, expressed so openly. The same way Ben did. She envied the way they loved without hesitation. For the second time, Liv was moved to tears when Ginny put her arms around her.

"When did you get here?" Ginny asked.

"We got into town the day after Christmas."

Ginny raised her eyebrows at Ben, who laughed and pulled Liv back closer to him. His body craved hers.

Riding on the snowmobile, with her arms around his waist, her body pressed against his back, was heaven to him. Whenever she moved away, he wanted her back, closer, so his hands were on her, somewhere, anywhere.

He leaned down and whispered, "My mama gave me a little lecture on Christmas. Somethin' about getting off my butt and going after you. I bet she's givin' herself credit for you being here today."

"Ah." She turned back to Ginny and saw the happiness etched on her face.

"Let's have a big dinner here tonight. We'll get your brothers and their wives to come."

"I'd like to help," Liv offered.

"Me, too," added Renie.

"We'll take the snowmobiles back to the house, okay, boys?" Ben turned to Liv again, pulling her close. "I can't keep my hands off you. And you in the kitchen…I'm hot for you again already."

Liv laughed. "Is there anything that doesn't make you hot for me?"

"You in another man's arms didn't do it. I can tell you that." There he went, opening his mouth again. He needed to work on filtering.

"What are you talking about?"

"The rodeo finals, I was watchin' them, and there you were with *Junior*. Bigger than life on the screen in front of me."

"We were there, but it wasn't that way, Ben. I wasn't with him."

"Not somethin' I can let myself think about, Liv. I'm sorry I brought it up."

"I can't let myself think about you with anyone else either."

"Nobody, Liv. I told you that. There isn't anybody else for me. I would have become…what did you call it? A re-virgin if you hadn't come back to me."

Liv laughed. "Me, too."

"Come on, Daddy." Luke tugged on his coat sleeve. "Let's go ride again."

Ben looked at Jake, who hadn't said more than two words this morning. He was so wrapped up in Liv, he hadn't noticed.

"Sure thing, Luke. In a minute. Why don't you see if your grandma has any cookies you can snack on?" Ben pushed Luke in the direction of the house. "And don't forget to wash your hands. Oh, and bring me some."

Ben motioned with his head in Jake's direction, and Liv nodded.

"Come on, Renie, let's go help Ginny."

A COWBOY FALLS

Ben sat down on the porch steps, waiting to see what Jake would do now that they were alone. He turned and faced the mountains, his back to Ben.

"What's on your mind, Jake?"

"Nothin'."

"You've been awful quiet. Not that you're talkative to begin with, but this seems quieter than normal."

"It's nothin', Dad. I'm fine."

"Okay. Well, if you decide it's somethin', let me know."

"It's…"

"I'm listening."

"You really like her."

"I do."

Jake kicked at the snow with his boot.

"What's worrying you, man?"

Still nothing out of Jake. He waited for a while, but all Jake looked was uncomfortable.

"Okay, let's get your brother, take the sleds back to the house, and get the truck. We can talk later if you want."

Jake got on one of the snowmobiles and started it up without answering his dad.

Bud came out on the porch. "I'll ride one back with you. That way, if you want to go out again this week, they'll be up at your place."

"Thanks, Dad. Hey, somethin's bothering Jake. Any idea what it might be?"

"Nope. But I'll try to get him to talk to me about it later."

"Where's Luke?"

"He's stayin' here. You won't be able to get him away from those two pretty girls. Not sure which one he's more taken with, Liv or her daughter."

"They're easy to get taken with." Ben knew that first hand. "She okay? I mean, should I go in and see if she needs anything before we leave?"

Bud put his hand on Ben's shoulder. "She's fine. You can be out of touching range for another five minutes or so, don't ya think?"

"No. But I'll leave her be anyway. She and Mom getting along?"

"As though they've known each other for years. You know, she reminds me of your mama. She's got that way about her."

24

After dinner, Ben went into the kitchen in search of Liv and found her seated at the center island, deep in conversation with Allison and Maeve. Whatever they were talking about seemed serious. He wondered if he should try to back out of the room before they noticed him.

"Heya, Ben," said Maeve, stretching her hand in his direction.

"Am I interrupting?"

"No, Liv was telling us about the fall she took. Serious stuff. I can't believe she's skiing and riding the ranch on the back of a snowmobile only four months later. Isn't it unbelievable?" said Allison, Matt's wife.

"Unbelievable," he murmured.

He still felt it, the pain, the worry, the hurt. He tried to push the hurt down deeper. He didn't want to think about it; she was here now. He closed his eyes and tried to shake the ghosts away. When he opened them again, Liv was studying him. She'd been right yesterday. They did need to talk.

"Everything is cleaned up in here. Liv, you ready to head back to the house?"

"Sure." She hesitated before she stood up, then stretched a little.

"Are you going skiing again tomorrow?" Maeve asked.

"It's up to Ben."

"I guess we should; that's why you're here."

Liv's gaze settled on him, and she put her hand in his. "Let's go, Ben."

"Let me find the boys." He dropped her hand, trying hard to keep the hurt buried, but it wouldn't. It had risen to the surface, and he had no way of pushing it back down.

Ben carried Luke to the car—he'd passed out sitting next to Renie on the couch, while Jake sat on the other side of the room, sullen.

Bud and Ginny lingered on the porch saying goodnight to Liv. Ben came back up after he got Luke in the truck.

"Any luck with Jake?"

"Nope," answered Bud. "He was closed up tight. Not interested in talking about anything, not even baseball."

Jake wasn't the only one in a funk, Ben was too, and he couldn't shake it. He was coming down from the heady rush of being with Liv again, but the reality of their recent past was raising its ugly head.

"Are you okay?" Liv asked when Ben got in the truck.

"You said it yourself—we need to talk."

"Yes," she sighed. "We do."

Jake was sitting in the third row. Ben turned up the radio a little and motioned for Liv to lean closer to him.

"Something is going on with Jake. He gets more withdrawn with each passing minute."

Liv had noticed. Luke had become her shadow, but Jake kept his distance. Even Renie was unable to jostle him out of his sullenness.

She had no business trying, or even offering, but she was willing to see if he'd talk to her. She asked Ben if he'd mind.

"I don't think you'll get anywhere, but if you wanna try…"

Ben carried Luke in and put him in bed, and when Liv told her she wanted a minute with Jake, Renie went downstairs too. Jake was ready to follow Renie when Liv stopped him. "Got a minute?"

"Yeah?"

"Can you come sit with me?"

"I guess."

Liv walked to the chair next to the fireplace and motioned for Jake to sit across from her.

"I can tell you have a lot on your mind," she began.

"I guess."

"Does it have something to do with my being here? Would you rather I wasn't?" She kept her voice low and soft.

"No!" Jake's cheeks flushed.

"Sounds as though you might be more worried about my leaving."

Jake looked away from her and into the fire.

"Jake, I care about your dad."

He flinched, and his eyes met hers. "He told us about you."

She nodded.

"He wanted us to meet you. It was after he visited you while we were in Arizona with our mom and Joe."

Liv leaned forward, to hear him better. He turned back toward the fireplace, so she bent her head. "Keep talking."

"Luke and I were excited to meet you, 'cause my dad told us you meant a lot to him."

"I'm sorry I didn't get a chance to meet you that visit."

"My dad…he was so sad. He tried to cover it up, but he didn't fool us. He didn't want to talk that much, and my dad loves to talk." That got a little smile out of him. Liv smiled too.

"He does like to talk. Go on, Jake."

"Then you had your accident, and my dad was on tour, and then all that stuff happened when he thought you were in a coma, but you weren't."

Liv nodded and felt her own cheeks warm.

"He was so sad." Jake turned his head away from her, so she wouldn't see his tears.

"Your dad tried to hide it from you, didn't he?"

"Yeah, but I knew anyway."

"Your dad tried to hide his sadness from you to protect you from it. He was hurting, and he didn't want you to hurt too."

"Is that why you lied to him?"

"Yes, Jake, that's why I lied to him. I didn't want him to worry about me. I wanted him to enjoy the tour and be successful, and have all the things he's been working so hard to attain all these years."

"It didn't work."

"You're right, it didn't. What I did jeopardized it all. He hadn't lied to anyone, but people thought he did."

"When my dad does his talking thing, people don't stay mad at him."

"Your father is a very good man, and as soon as people get to know him, even a little, they see it. Even if it's only seeing him on stage. They know he wouldn't lie."

Jake nodded.

"You're afraid I'll hurt him again."

He nodded again. "You kinda do it a lot."

He sure got right to the heart of it. "I'm sorry for that, and I'm sorry for how it's affected you. I care about your dad very much."

Jake faced her.

"I don't want to ever hurt him again."

"That would be good, if you didn't."

Liv marveled at the depth of caring Ben's son possessed. He was so much like his father.

"Do you ride, Jake?"

"Horses? Yeah."

"I was hoping you and I could ride while I'm here. And someday soon, I'd like it if your dad brought you and Luke to my place. I board horses at my ranch. Did you know that?"

"No."

"Think you might like to take a ride with me."

"Yeah, it'd be okay."

"And come and visit?"

"Sure. I'd like that."

"How about coming to see me race? Would you like to do that, too?"

Jake sat up straighter. A smile started to form.

"That'd be cool, I guess."

"Cool, you guess? Sugar, there ain't nothin' cooler than a barrel-racin' cowgirl. The sooner you figure that out the better."

He smiled. He had his dad's smile. It lit up his whole face.

"Okay. It's cool."

"You got that right. And Jake?" She tilted her head again, hoping he would look her in the eye. "Thanks for talking to me."

"Sure. Anytime."

She said goodnight, and he went downstairs. Liv leaned her head back against the chair and closed her eyes.

Ben stood around the corner from Liv and Jake, listening to their conversation. She might as well have been talking to him. All of Jake's concerns were his, too. When would she decide she needed to leave again? And when she did, would he have any idea when he might see her next? And, how much a part of her life did she want him to be?

She'd answered all those questions while she talked to Jake. She made plans with his son. Plans for them to come and see her ranch, and plans for them to see her race. Those were significant plans. Coming to see her ranch meant she was willing to let his boys in, to get to know her better. He knew Liv well enough to know that she wouldn't take his sons' feelings lightly. She wouldn't lie to them, and she wouldn't let them think they mattered if they didn't.

"Hey," he said softly.

"Hi, Ben. Come sit with me." Liv stood and moved to the couch, holding out her hand for him to join her.

"How'd it go?"

"It went well. He cares about you. He wants to make sure I do, too."

"And?"

"You know I do."

"I overheard your conversation with him."

"I know."

That made him smile.

Liv leaned into him, resting her head on his shoulder, and put her arm around his waist. "You're too used to being in control of everything to not get involved."

"You think that was about control?"

"Of course it was. I was talking to your son. The one you're worried about. If things had started to go badly, you would've stepped in to make sure he was okay."

"I guess I would've."

"We have a lot to work on, Ben."

"If you're willing, so am I."

Liv stood and held her hand out to him. "Take me to bed, cowboy."

They went back to the ski area the next day. A long-time snowboarder, Jake wanted to ski instead, so Ben rented him ski equipment.

"He's got the best snowboarding stuff made, and today he wants to ski. What's that all about?"

Liv raised her eyebrows. "You should consider this a good thing. At least he's talking."

She was right. If Jake wanted to be closer to Liv or Renie all day, it was better than having him off sulking in a corner, or refusing to go along.

When Renie decided at the last minute to try snowboarding, Ben's groan was audible.

"Great. Now he'll want to go back to slidin' down the hill. I know the guys in the rental place; I'm hoping they'll give me my money back."

But Ben was wrong, Jake wanted to spend the day with Liv. The two of them went on several runs on their own and showed up twenty minutes late at their designated lunch stop.

Ben put his arm around his oldest son. "Tryin' to steal my girl, are ya?" He messed up his son's already mop-top hair.

"She enjoys my company," answered Jake, standing up taller and throwing his shoulders back.

"We're making dinner tonight," Liv and Jake announced when the group met back at the lodge at the end of the day.

"Who is?" asked Ben.

"Jake and I are."

"What are you making?"

"You'll see."

"Are you makin' pizza?" asked Luke.

Jake started to answer his little brother, but Liv stopped him by putting her finger in front of her lips. "Shh," she said.

Ben knew that, if heaven existed, today was a slice of it.

"Stop at the market on the way back to the house. Jake and I will run in and get what we need."

"But—"

"Ben, please, let us do this. Let go a little; it's only dinner."

Damn, she knew how to call him out on his shit. He'd always have control issues, because he knew control meant sobriety. That part he couldn't let go.

To let go with other people, that took trust. And with Liv, trust was harder. He had visible tread marks lingering on his heart, left by her. If he was honest about it, every morning when they woke up, he wondered if that day was the day she'd leave him again. He wasn't sure if he'd ever get over it.

Jake and Liv made paella, along with other Spanish food. Liv also made an individual pizza for Luke. The kitchen was spotless because Liv insisted she and Jake clean as they go, the exact opposite of Ben's approach.

Throughout dinner, Jake extolled the virtues of Liv's style of food preparation at the expense of his father's.

All Ben could think was how much he wanted this to be their lives, all the time. He wanted to spend every day with Liv—and Renie too, for that matter—and his boys. If this was his world, he would give up everything else in order to have it.

But it wasn't their world. Soon the boys would go back to their mom's, and then in January, Ben would be halfway across the world, on tour. Renie would be back at school, and Liv would be out doing the thing that almost killed her only a couple of months ago.

Control? *Shit*. He had none over that. He wanted to wrap her up and take her on tour with him, but then she'd be a thing, not a person, and her greatest fear, losing herself for him or anyone else, would become a reality. Ben needed to figure out how to respect her independence but not go insane with worry at the same time.

"Fret, fret, fret," she whispered in his ear.

"You caught me."

"Why the scowl?"

He hadn't realized he'd been scowling. "I don't want this to end."

"None of us do. But that's what makes it so special. Otherwise, diminishing returns, and nobody likes that."

"What?"

"The more you have of something, the less joy it brings you."

"I don't agree with that at all. I would be very happy to have your skin on mine all day, every day, for the rest of our lives, and I would never, I repeat *never*, experience less joy from it. My joy will only continue to grow."

"On the subject of skin on skin, what do you want to do for New Year's Eve?"

Ben's eyes roamed over the scene in front of him. "It may be what I want to do, but whether I get to or not, that's another story."

Liv smiled. "Blythe is flying into Gunnison tomorrow, and I've been meaning to talk to you about that. I'm glad you reminded me. She and Renie have been best friends since kindergarten, so the two of them are going to hang out and ski for a couple of days. Since we don't have the room at the hotel any longer—"

"Yes."

"You don't know what I'm asking yet."

"I don't? You aren't asking me if she can stay here?"

"No, as a matter of fact, I wasn't. I was going to ask you if you had any connections in town to help me get a room somewhere. I've called everyone, but they're full."

"I just said she can stay here, Liv," Ben snapped.

"I didn't want to impose, Ben," she murmured.

He wasn't sure why, but that made him angry. Something twisted inside of him. "Liv, for God's sake. What are you, a guest here? Is that how you see yourself?"

She stood and walked toward the stairs.

"What are you doing now? Leaving?"

She turned back, her eyes met his, and he watched them fill with tears. She kept her hand on the stair rail as she slowly turned and sat on one of the steps.

Ben ran his hand over his head and walked back and forth in the kitchen, then hit the counter with his hand. "Shit, I'm sorry. I don't know why I said that."

He sat down next to her.

"You said it because we're pretending. We're pretending that we know each other. We're pretending that this is fun, and perfect, and everything we want it to be, but the truth is, we're all walking on eggshells. Even Luke."

She was right. The first thing Luke did every morning was come and crawl in bed with them. It was as though he was checking to make sure Liv was still there.

"The only person who has expressed and dealt with their uneasiness is Jake. I'm including myself in this, Ben. I haven't done it either."

Ben put his head in his hands. "You hurt me, Liv."

"I know."

"Did I hurt you?"

"No, you didn't. You only scare me."

"I scare you. As in you're afraid of me?"

"I'm afraid of letting myself depend on you. I don't know how. I'm used to being on my own, not relying on anyone else."

"You rely on Paige and Mark. You rely on Dottie and Bill, too." He didn't say Billy. He hoped she didn't rely on him. "And Renie."

"With the exception of my daughter, I keep very strict boundaries with everyone you mentioned, even Paige. Do you know the last time I talked to her?"

"No."

"Neither do I. It was sometime before Christmas. But the thing is, it doesn't matter. We'll talk when we want to, but we don't have to."

"Are you suggesting that's how you want it to be with us?"

"Not at all, but it's the way I am, Ben. You need more."

"Please tell me we're not going back to that again."

"But it's true. You need more from me than I know how to give."

"So we're at an impasse. I love you, and I want you in my life. But according to you, I need you too much. Before you say it, I know you're right. I do need you, all the time. I want you all the time too." Ben tilted her chin. "Is that so bad?"

"Ben, listen to me. *You need more than I know how to give.* It's not that I can't, or don't want to, I don't know how to."

"What does that mean?"

"It means that I'm willing to learn. Why do you think I came to Crested Butte?"

"To ski?"

"No, Ben. I came to Crested Butte because I love you, and I need you in my life. It isn't just barrel racing, it's you too. You're part of the dream, Ben. *You.*"

"You love me?"

"You know I do, Ben. Like I've never loved anyone before."

"Then why is this so hard?"

"I've been telling you we need to talk. We haven't yet."

"Okay, let's talk. What do you—"

"I can't talk until you stop, cowboy."

Ben made a motion that he was zipping his lips and held his hands out for her to continue.

"I have a plan."

Ben nodded.

"When you leave for Europe, you'll fly out of Denver, right?"

He nodded again.

"We'll fly to Denver together, that way I'll be with you as long as possible before you leave for Europe."

When Ben didn't say anything, she continued.

"While you're on tour, I'll be training. But, Ben, if I don't believe it's working, I'll quit."

Liv felt Ben's body tense.

"I have to try, but if something isn't right, I'll know. If it is right, and I believe Micah and I can compete, that's what we'll do. By the time you get back from Europe in March, I'll know."

Liv stopped talking and turned to him.

"Can I talk now?"

"Mmm hmm."

He let out a huge sigh. "Wow. That was hard."

"I bet. Imagine how hard it was for me? I actually had to make plans from now until March."

"What about going to Monument, and leaving from there?"

"What about your boys?"

"Yeah, that would be hard. If you're sure—"

"Shh." Liv put her fingers on his lips again. "Since I'm staying, do you mind if I start the laundry? I need to wash a few clothes."

"No, not at all, go ahead," Ben answered, as though he was in a *Twilight Zone* episode.

When Liv left the room, he leaned forward, put his elbows on his knees, and his head in his hands.

Liv came back in and sat down next to him. She tucked her legs under her and leaned into him. "Ben?"

"Yeah?" He kept his elbows on his knees.

"I've never done this. I barely remember the few months I lived with Scott. I was a kid. A nineteen-year-old kid. Renie is three years older than I was when Scott was killed. Work with me, okay?"

He leaned back, put his arm around her, and pulled her closer to him. "I was either on the road or drunk the whole time I was married to Christine. I didn't know what I was doing then any more than I do now."

"We're gonna be okay, Ben."

"You really love me?"

"More than anything."

"Tell me."

"I love you, Ben. More than I've ever loved anyone."

"Say it again."

25

"These have been the best two weeks of my life."

"Mine too."

"Is Paige picking you up?"

"Or Mark. I should see if they're here."

"Not yet."

Ben got a text from Jimmy saying he needed to get through customs or he'd miss the flight.

"I gotta go, baby. I'm gonna miss you so much." Ben pulled Liv in close. "I hate saying goodbye to you." He put his hands on either side of her face. "Thank you for coming back to me, thank you for giving us a chance. I love you so much."

Liv reached up and pulled him closer. Her lips brushed across his, and she kissed her way across his cheek, to the spot below his ear. "I love you too, Ben. So much," she whispered.

***

"He did it to you," said Paige on the ride home.

"He came to visit. This is different."

Paige shrugged her shoulders. "Not that different. By the time you get back from Texas and put everything in motion, he'll be on his way home. Just do it, Liv."

"Okay. I'll talk to Billy tomorrow."

* * *

"You can do this," said Jolene in a comforting tone Liv hadn't realized the woman possessed.

Liv and Micah had been working hard for three weeks—riding hard, riding fast, but the one thing Liv couldn't bring herself to do was take him around the barrels.

"Start slow. Ride around the barrel, don't try to hug it, just ride around it."

In took three more days before Liv completed the entire cloverleaf pattern, and even then it was barely at a trot.

A few days later, Liv was starting to pick up speed. She knew Micah was itching to do it right, but each time she pulled him back.

"Let him go this time, all out," Jolene yelled from the fence.

"How's she doin'?" asked Mary Beth, standing near her.

Jolene showed her Liv's last time. Thirty-four seconds.

"This ain't a race timer, but it's close enough. She's ready, but she's sure not gonna be happy with these times."

"Does she know you're timin' her yet?"

"Nope."

"Keep at her. Get mean."

"What're you talkin' about?"

"She likes it when you're mean, you remind her of her father."

"I am *never* mean."

"Jolene, I love you dearly, but you are *always* mean. You're coddling her. Stop it. Push her, make her do it. You've eased her in enough. I've been watchin' Micah. He's fine. He's ready and waitin' for her."

"I don't know."

"Do it, Jolene. She'll be okay. Stop protecting her."

"That's it for today," Jolene shouted to Liv, who waved and rode Micah in the direction of the barn.

Jolene walked away in the opposite direction, but Mary Beth knew she'd been listening. She couldn't wait to see what was going to happen tomorrow.

She made a couple of calls on her way home that night. "Yep, you might wanna try to get down here tomorrow morning," she told each person she called.

"We're running the timer today," Jolene said when Liv walked into the barn.

"Good morning to you, too. What did you say?"

"You heard me. I've had enough sittin' around watchin' you stroll around the barrels. We're either gonna start runnin' times or you might as well go back to Monument."

"But—"

"Those are the only two options I'm willin' to put out there, Olivia. Which is it gonna be?"

Liv turned and stomped out of the barn.

A few minutes later Liv stomped back in. "Are we gonna do this or not?"

"Sure, um, you wanna get Micah saddled up?"

"Yep." She stomped to Micah's stall and led him out.

"Can I ask you a question?"

"Sure."

"Where'd you go?"

"To change my shirt." If she and Micah were doing this today she wanted Ben wrapped around her, so she went back to the hotel and put on one of the shirts he'd left on the doorknob of her closet, but that was none of Jolene's business.

Over and over Jolene made her do it. Her first times were in the high twenties.

"Get the lead out, girl."

Sixth time out, she came in at twenty seconds.

"What're you doin' out there? Is that Micah or Pooh you're ridin'?"

Mary Beth was sitting on the fence at the opposite end of the arena and wasn't certain, but she swore Liv flipped Jolene off.

She turned around and waved at Renie, Paige, and Mark, who were sitting in a truck, taping Liv's practice, and Mark gave her a thumbs up.

The next day, when she came in just above seventeen seconds, Liv jumped off Micah, threw her arms around Jolene, and kissed her. Mary Beth hoped Mark had a zoom lens strong enough to pick up the tears on Jolene's cheeks.

Mark uploaded the video and hit send on the email.

"Ready?" Renie said, and the three of them got out of the truck.

Liv heard yelling and turned to see her daughter and her two best friends jumping up and down, waving their hands, and running toward her.

"What the—"

"Mary Beth," said Jolene. "They've been here since yesterday." Jolene doubted Liv even heard her; she was halfway to them already.

"Did you see me?" Liv kept repeating.

"We did," answered Paige. "Mark even recorded it."

"How was it, Mom?"

"So amazing…even better than skiing," she laughed.

Ben had been sitting by the computer waiting for Mark's email. The last couple of weeks, he'd only gotten what Jolene sent him, which were bits and pieces of Liv's day.

He hit the play button and watched her fly around the barrels, as if she'd been born to do it. In the video, Mark panned over to the timer Renie held in her hand. *Seventeen point three.*

Ben was alone in his hotel room, but he jumped up and down and danced around anyway. One more week, he'd be home, and he and Liv would celebrate together.

Epilogue

Ben was in the stands in the second week of December, when Olivia Rice came in fourth place in Barrel Racing at the National Finals Rodeo. He knew next year his wife would win; he felt it in his bones.

The CB Rice concert, taking place later that night at the Mandalay Bay complex, was sold out, as every other show on their tour had been.

They met backstage right before he went on. "I can't wait to get you home, baby."

"We're not getting out of bed until Christmas," Liv answered.

"The only thing is…"

"What? What could there possibly be, Ben?"

"I miss your kitchen."

"Then we'll remodel ours."

"I doubt Billy Patterson appreciates what he got when he bought your place. Do you think he even knows how to cook?"

"Doubt it, but I'm sure he'll find a pretty little cowgirl to do it for him."

About the Author

USA Today and Amazon Top 15 Bestselling Author Heather Slade writes shamelessly sexy, edge-of-your seat romantic suspense.

She gave herself the gift of writing a book for her own birthday one year. Forty-plus books later (and counting), she's having the time of her life.

The women Slade writes are self-confident, strong, with wills of their own, and hearts as big as the Colorado sky. The men are sublimely sexy, seductive alphas who rise to the challenge of capturing the sweet soul of a woman whose heart they'll hold in the palm of their hand forever. Add in a couple of neck-snapping twists and turns, a page-turning mystery, and a swoon-worthy HEA, and you'll be holding one of her books in your hands.

She loves to hear from my readers. You can contact her at heather@heatherslade.com

To keep up with her latest news and releases, please visit her website at www.heatherslade.com to sign up for her newsletter.

MORE FROM AUTHOR HEATHER SLADE

BUTLER RANCH
Kade's Worth
Brodie
Maddox
Naughton
Mercer
Kade
Christmas at Butler Ranch

WICKED WINEMAKERS' BALL
Coming soon:
Brix
Ridge
Press

K19 SECURITY SOLUTIONS
Razor
Gunner
Mistletoe
Mantis
Dutch
Striker
Monk
Halo
Tackle
Onyx

K19 SHADOW OPERATIONS
Code Name: Ranger
Coming soon:
Code Name: Diesel
Code Name: Wasp
Code Name: Cowboy

THE ROYAL AGENTS OF MI6
The Duke and the Assassin
The Lord and the Spy
The Commoner and the Correspondent
The Rancher and the Lady

THE INVINCIBLES
Decked
Undercover Agent
Edged
Grinded
Riled
Handled
Smoked
Bucked
Irished
Sainted
Coming soon:
Hammered
Ripped

COWBOYS OF CRESTED BUTTE
A Cowboy Falls
A Cowboy's Dance
A Cowboy's Kiss
A Cowboy Stays
A Cowboy Wins

Made in the USA
Monee, IL
18 January 2024

52017500R00213